Wavesong

A Joint Task Force 13 Legacy Novel

By Michael Gants

Three Ravens Publishing
Chickamauga GA USA

Table of Contents

To my loving wife
Without you, this would never have been possible.

and

To Richard Timothy "Uncle Timmy" Bolgeo
A man who believed in writers becoming authors, and
heartily encouraged them to do so.

Prologue

The Barents Sea, Northeast of Bear Island
26 January 1961
2333 CEST/2233 Zulu
S-80 (Soviet Project 613 unit) (NATO Whiskey Class)

Sergi Palpovich was the first to hear the singing. He glanced around the galley. No one was speaking, let alone singing. The other cooks were bent to task, scrubbing out the remains from dinner while bracing themselves against the sink as the submarine slammed back and forth on the storm-tossed waves. There were no radios in this part of the ship, which meant that he could not be hearing some type of broadcast. He was not even sure he was hearing anything real since the diesel engines just aft of the galley were running at top speed as the ship snorkeled in the storm.

He hoped he was not hearing things again. His mother had warned him to be normal and not mention things he heard on the wind. Even if he were right, and the milk next door would be sour due to a cow illness or that planting the south field would yield the best crop. He shook his head. These were not things right-thinking Soviet men contemplated. They listened to the State and to the science.

Yet, right at the edge of his hearing came a song. Pulling him; beckoning him towards it with whispered strands of sound to join in the symphony.

Dropping the scrub brush, Sergi stumbled to the bulkhead on the other side of the mess deck and pressed his ear to the freezing hull. The faint sound intensified once he was in contact with the metal. It was unlike anything he had heard before. This music had none of the harsh crashes of sound the national marches had, nor the soft tones of the waltzes his grandmother had played for him. It did not even sound anything like the "rock and roll" he had surreptitiously overheard one time coming from the officer's club on the base back home. This was more. Beyond comparison. It was everything music should be. Rich. Soft. Alluring.

Sergi pushed himself reluctantly away from the hull, absently rubbing life back into his cold-numbed ear. He worked his way towards the command deck. The constant tossing of the ship made his progress slow. His continual smashing into protruding valves and piping bruised him, but he was ignorant of the pain throughout the song. Climbing up the five steps into the command deck was almost impossible as the tiny vessel staggered under the relentless pounding of the Barents Sea.

Crew members turned from their stations as Sergi pushed past, confused as to why a cook was in the control space. Without a word, he grabbed the headset off the sonar operator's head. The surprised operator tried to stop him but missed his grab as the ship slid to port in the waves. Sergi pressed the headset to his ears. The sound was better, but still off. Unconscious hands twirled dials and flicked switches. He had no clue how the sonar system worked, though those watching could not have said so. In this moment, he understood everything.

Now the music was clear. Inside the headset, the caress of the song stroked Sergi, lifting him from the dreary, day after day, mundane life he experienced in the Navy. He had to share this music with everybody. He…

Strong hands ripped the headset off and pulled him away from the station.

"No!" he screamed. "Listen! We all must listen!"

Four men pressed the struggling little cook to the deck.

"What's he babbling about?" one person asked.

"Watch out for that swing." Another man ducked to avoid the cook's flailing arms.

"Listen to what?" another of the command crew questioned.

A sharp jab stung Sergi's left bicep. He turned his head and found himself staring at a bloody needle in the hand of the ship's surgeon. A drop of clear fluid broke free from the end of the needle and splashed onto the deck.

"The muuthicccc…" he slurred out as the morphine took effect.

"Take him and tie him to his hammock. I will deal with him later. Are any of you injured?" There was a round of negative headshakes. The surgeon waved the men to carry Sergi's limp body out of the command deck.

The captain and the zampolit both stumbled into the command room, drawn from their sleep by the commotion. They watched as the surgeon followed the men out of the room. "It gets to some men," the zampolit breathed out. "The nearness of the walls."

"My men are made of sterner material, Comrade. I suspect that it is a sickness of some kind." The captain looked around. With the zampolit in the room, each watchstander had returned to his duties, observant and focused as all good Soviet sailors must be. The only concession to the storm were splayed legs and hands gripping surfaces to maintain their positions. Then the captain noticed the slack-jawed look on the sonar operator's face.

"Michman Ondropav, what is your problem?" The captain snapped a finger under the operator's eyes. There was no reply or response. The captain leaned close and caught a faint noise emanating from the sonar technician's headset. He plucked the headset off. The sonar michman paid no attention. The captain slipped the headset over his own ears.

Joy. Beauty. The health of a thousand years.

As in a dream, the captain switched on the sonar speakers so that everyone could hear the perfect sounds arising from the ocean around them. Dazedly he ordered the helm to come south to one-nine-two degrees and maintain that heading.

A smile of satisfaction slid across the zampolit's face. This was not just the right thing to do; it was the *proper* direction to go.

Two nautical miles away, the creature sang its wavesong. The prey would come.

The stormy sea had slowed the boat. It continued along, snorkeling in the freezing air. Though the temperature had dropped considerably both inside and outside the boat, no orders were given to change any of the ship's settings. Stringers of frozen rain stretched from the scope; frozen teeth created by the howling gale. White patches of ice formed on the hull, some holding on, others breaking free as waves impacted them. Along the flapper valve on the diesel intake, ice began to form and freeze, streaks of black crystals worming down toward the spinning engines.

Fifteen minutes later, *S-80* neared the source of the music. The captain and the zampolit stood side-by-side, eyes half-lidded, listening to the song as it played through every speaker on the boat. The music was loud enough that all the crew could now hear it through the hull.

It called to them all. Rapture and beauty. No one paid attention as the first tentacle wrapped around the hull of the submarine and pulled. The stern of *S-80* dropped, and men slipped as the deck jerked beneath them.

For some, the change in deck position caused falls and injuries. Senior Matrose Raag slammed his head into the deck when he fell, causing a mild concussion and momentarily deafening his ears, breaking the spell of the wavesong. He fought to stand as the boat tilted further under his feet due to an unseen second tentacle wrapped around the rudder, pulling the submarine deeper.

An unusually high wave battered the conning tower and splashed into the diesel ventilation suction. Sensors noted the water, and a signal was sent to shut the flapper valve. Pneumatics strained, but the ice held the valve open, allowing more waves to follow the first, and frigid seawater poured into the engines. The sudden influx of liquid quenched the diesels, stopping the twin screws and removing all motive power from the ship. Without the engines operating, there was no way to escape the clutches of the creature as it continued dragging the ship into the depths.

Raag shook his head, trying to determine what was going on. Dizziness and nausea fought to double him over. He grabbed a handrail and retched. No matter where he looked in the fifth compartment, the sailors all appeared half-asleep. Their actions were the same whether they were still standing or slithering across the deck. None of them seemed to notice that anything was wrong.

There was the sound of tearing metal, and a maintenance panel for the number four engine blew off, crushing a sailor's face and shoving him across the compartment. The doomed man fell into the churning water. Crimson blood mixed with the ivory foam rushing in. The sight focused Raag's mind.

The shut-off valve thought Raag, *I must get to the shut-off valve.* Dizziness hammered at his will to stay standing.

Hand over hand he pulled himself up the canted rail until the array of valve handwheels stood before him. *The control panel. I can shut it off from here, at the control panel. Right?*

Deep in his mind he knew that one of these valves would stop the onrush. His feet became numb as the freezing waters of the Barents Sea swirled around him. He grabbed one handwheel and then thought better of it.

Maybe the blue handle. No, it would be the color of…of what? He could not think through the fuzziness and the pain. *That one, the one with the green handle.*

Raag ducked as a second maintenance panel, this time off the number one engine housing, exploded free, flinging a flat metal plate across the room. It ricocheted off the valve panel with a monstrous *CLANG* and embedded itself in the soft insulation surrounding one of the seawater intake pipes. Raag righted himself and groaned. The plate had smashed several handwheels, including the one he needed to turn, and bent the valve stem over at least fifteen degrees. Nothing he could do would make the valve turn.

The ship passed forty-five degrees and began slipping beneath the waves. Raag shouldered his way past the dazed men and reached the front of the fifth compartment. Water was cascading from the forward sections of the submarine. No one was going to survive that. He had to save what he could. Whomever he could. With a cry of anguish, he slammed the door shut and spun the center wheel, locking the metal bars into the grooves of the watertight bulkhead.

Elsewhere, screaming began as the creature somehow tore a gaping hole in the starboard side of the third compartment. The inrush of water made the ship heavier, but the creature rode the sinking vessel down. A tentacle slithered through the new hole and grasped prey. A sailor screamed in agony as the appendage wrapped about his torso and spines as big around as pencils pierced his body. He cried for the pain to stop, for the music to take him away from this.

Then the music changed. It segued into something different, something primal and ancient. No longer soothing and comforting, this music channeled the cry of the predator, the victory of pursuer over prey, a dirge of the dead.

This song awoke men instead of lulling them to safety. They awoke in horror from their stupor, the horror of knowing inescapable death as the ship was dragged to the bottom of the Barents Sea, away from the prying eyes of the sun.

Chapter One

Naval Surface Weapons Station, White Oak, Maryland
16 November 1986
1914 EST/0014 Zulu
Bldg. 207 "Underwater Ionization Field"

I can stop this. Just turn around and walk away. I'll go in tomorrow and tell the chief…or maybe I'll tell the CO what has happened. Just walk away.

His feet continued towards the door, slowing to a near crawl as he turned over the possibilities in his mind.

Then I'll never see Her *again. Never feel* Her *again.*

One small part of Howard's mind nervously wondered again how he had allowed himself to fall this far. It drifted backward in time, back to his younger days. When he joined the Navy, he'd been proud. Proud of his country, proud of what he could do, proud to serve. He discovered that he had an unknown knack for electronics, especially magnetic field theory. High school hadn't offered anything of the like, but his knack and interest propelled him forward. Within a few years, he was a petty officer 2nd class and attached to one of the most interesting research groups the Navy had to offer.

Then something had changed. He'd gone with a group of his buddies to a big casino and wound up at the bar after getting separated from them. That is where *She* had found him. The *Woman*.

Capital letters and no name. That was the only way he dared think about her. *She* had been everything he thought he was looking for in a female. Sexy. Gorgeous and more than willing to let him look at her. Sultry in ways he didn't know how to describe. *She* had introduced him to the magic of cards and gambling. How to make the money grow with the toss of a die or the spin of the wheel. *She* had suggested that the Navy wasn't his only path for life, that there were easier paths. Paths that could include *Her.* *She* had shown him a whole new way of living. He'd listened to the stories and trusted her, and things had gone horribly wrong.

In reflection, it was clear that she'd coaxed him to gamble more often and with riskier stakes, pushing him deeper in debt. When the debt was getting too high to hide from the bank and the Navy, she had introduced him to a "gentleman" who guaranteed loan money to help Howard get back on his feet. Fearful of the growing debt, Howard took the loan. The "gentleman" had promised easy terms for repayment.

The loan hadn't solved anything. Howard was addicted to both *Her* and the gambling. Within months, he was even deeper in debt than ever before, with no way to pay the loan off and the "gentleman" knew it. Then came the first request.

A simple job to help pay down the debt. Just a small bit of information about a specific frequency used by an old model torpedo. Wasn't that worth a couple of bucks or an extra month to get caught up? Nothing dangerous. Those Mark 37 Mod 3 torpedoes had been in service since the late 1960s. Howard convinced himself that the information wasn't *really* that secret anymore, so it wasn't really stealing. It wasn't really… treason.

Howard shied away from the thought of treason. He paused, taking a deep breath before continuing to the main entrance of Building 207.

Unfortunately, getting the information that first time had only proven he could be bought. Now they had him. Blackmail joined the debt. If he talked, everything would come out. The debts, the gambling…the *treason*. The deal was simple: *She* would make a request—he would provide the information.

Now they wanted more. Not just pictures or typed words. Actual hardware. Real honest-to-goodness technology. The target: the completed computer guidance core of the new Mark 48 ADvanced CAPability (ADCAP)torpedo.

Thankfully, Sunday night was the emptiest time of the week on the base. People didn't work overtime on Sundays. No one was in the building this time, nor did Howard expect anyone to come in. He pushed open the door, feigning a confidence that he didn't feel.

The front room was empty and dark. Howard breathed a sigh of relief. He locked the main door and left the lights off, making certain that he would be undisturbed. Since this portion of the building had outside windows, he waited to turn on his flashlight until he was in the testing bays. They had no windows that could betray his presence.

He fumbled for the switch on the flashlight, his palms slick with nervous sweat. It turned on and he panned the light around. The testing room was orderly, everything locked in the cages near the back of the bay. Howard shakily pulled a key from his pocket. It was a copy he had made of the storage cage's key. It slipped out of his slick hand and jangled on the floor. His heart raced at the loud tinny sound. Silence descended again. He waited for his heartbeat to slow, then stooped and picked up the key. He grabbed the security lock and slid the key in. Half a turn and the lock clicked open, the metallic sound echoing in the empty bay.

Gingerly, Howard removed the key and lock, ensuring he placed the lock on the open door so that he knew exactly where to find it.

I still haven't done anything. I'm allowed to be here. Just lock the cage and throw away the key. That's what is going to happen to you, traitor: a locked cage and thrown away keys.

The cage was claustrophobic, barely large enough for a person to turn around in. Boxes of varying sizes packed the shelves. Hands shaking, Howard swept the light in an arc until he found the four containers with the code for the ADCAP guidance package.

Still time. Still time to not take this, not do this. Make things right.

He hefted one of the containers and took it out into the main testing bay.

Then you will never be with Her *again, never feel* Her *mouth on yours, wake with* Her *wrapped around you.*

Howard set the box on a testing table, opened his jacket, and removed the folded gym bag from inside. The bag was warm and moist to his touch, sweat-stained where it had touched his body. He unzipped the bag and laid it open, hoping it would be large enough to hold the guidance package.

I could just stop. Put it back. Be done and leave. Just stop.

He paused, sighing.

The time to stop this was gone long ago.

Next came the hardest part, opening the box. He waited for a moment until his hands stopped trembling. It had to look as though the container had never been touched. The razor blade of the box cutter split the tape, and the top popped open like a clown from a jack-in-the-box. Howard hopped back, nearly dropping the knife, and stifled a shout of surprise. He breathed, trying to get his heart rate back under control again. Air blew loudly in and out through his nose. He pulled the guidance computer out. A glittering collection of bronze and copper revealed itself as the dim beam of the flashlight filtered through the bubble wrap and tape. Cautiously he lifted it into the gym bag and zipped the bag shut. Snug but it fit. That completed task one. He took a deep breath and moved to the next part of the plan.

Howard swiftly exited the test lab and half-walked, half-ran to the maintenance section, the flashlight beam bouncing wildly across the linoleum floor. Diesel oil fumes and cleaning solutions stung his nose as he pushed through the swinging door of the maintenance bay. The room was full of tools and machinery used to cut and bend metal. The light passed over them, creating shadows of midnight creatures that danced on the walls. Huddled in a lonely barrel were several scrap pieces of bronze and steel. Howard looked over the pieces, gauging which ones would fit back into the container. He found three that together, he hoped, would be approximately the same weight as the original guidance package.

Flashlight in mouth, he returned to the test bay and filled the box with the scraps, then positioned it behind two of the other guidance packages.

No one should see anything out of the ordinary. The package shouldn't even be checked until the inventory next Wednesday. By then, She *and I will be on a beach somewhere that doesn't have an extradition treaty with the United States.* A darker thought flickered on the heels of the first. *Because I am a traitor.*

He shook his head to clear the thoughts away and locked the cage. With a dry mouth, Howard took a final look around, ensuring that nothing was conspicuously out of place. He hefted the gym bag onto his shoulder, shut off and pocketed the flashlight, then retraced his steps to the front of the building.

The wind was cold but invigorating. Howard could see his breath as he crossed the empty parking lot to his used Chevy sedan. He carefully tucked the gym bag beneath a blanket in the back and climbed into the driver's seat. Shoving the clutch to the floor and twisting the key, he listened to the engine stutter, working to turn over. This was normal for the beater.

A new car to go with the new me, Howard thought as he twisted the key a second time. *Something sporty. Like a Supra.*

After three tries, the engine finally caught with a cough of smoke and squealing belts. He backed out and flipped on his lights. He breathed a sigh of relief and for the first time that evening began to relax. He had done it. No one had seen him. The hardest part was over.

Naval Surface Weapons Station, White Oak, Maryland
16 November 1986
2023 EST/0132 Zulu
Naval Surface Weapons Station Front Gate

"There he is," Agent Reynolds murmured gleefully. "Our little mouse took the bait and is taking the cheese back home,"

Agent Hillson glared across the car at Reynolds. "Really? Every time we are on one of these things, you spout that same stupid line. Find a new one." He grimaced and turned on the car's engine.

The two men watched from a parking lot across the way as Petty Officer Howard turned his car onto New

Hampshire Avenue. Once he was a quarter mile or so away, Agent Hillson turned to follow him.

"If he follows his routine, he will jump onto I-495 and follow that up to Baltimore. The question is, where is the drop going to take place? He hasn't deviated much from his routine except to go bowling last week with the other guys from the lab. I doubt that he made any sort of contact there."

Reynolds nodded in agreement. "Especially since NIS had someone there watching him the whole time."

"You figure a dead drop then?"

"Sounds reasonable. Makes it less likely for Howard to be able to squeal about who he gave the item to if he never sees the man's face."

"Or woman," countered Hillson.

"Or woman," agreed Reynolds.

As they tailed Howard's car discreetly, the two lapsed into the comfortable silence that partners developed. Traffic on the beltway was constant but less dense than it would have been earlier in the day. It was easier to keep a close eye on Howard's Chevy while staying far enough back to minimize the chance of anyone noticing the tail.

Twenty-eight minutes after leaving the base, Howard took his expected exit off the freeway and drove into the older outskirts of Baltimore. Here some gentrification was going on, slowly pushing the crack dealers and homeless away. Still, not the best part of the city, but rental rates were low and security not so bad. Brownstones loomed out of the darkness like ancient forts, overlooking tiny lawns where skeletal trees stood watch over scatterings of dead leaves in the mid-autumn evening.

Home sweet home…What a dump, Howard thought as he pulled around a brownstone and into the small parking lot nestled behind and between two of the buildings. Several other cars, similar in age and condition to his, filled the lot. *Well, things will be different now.*

Yeah, came a darker thought, *your next place could only have four light gray walls and a toilet that everyone can see.*

He glanced around nervously as he got out, though nothing out of the ordinary caught his attention. Cars continued slowly along the street; the traffic normal for Sunday evening hours. His heart rate rose as he opened the back door, lifted the blanket, and retrieved the red and white gym bag. He hefted it carefully onto his shoulder and kicked the door shut with his foot. Another glance around showed he was the only person out here. Howard headed to the front of the building, his ears straining to catch anything out of the ordinary.

Hillson gently coasted the car to a stop across the street in front of the brownstone. The tinted windows of the dark blue sedan prevented anyone from easily noticing the pair inside.

"There he goes. Right on time." Reynolds noted as he jotted down the time in his notebook. "Looks like he went to the gym tonight and brought home something heavy. I mean, based on how the bag is dragging over his shoulder."

Hillson grunted. "Possibly the package, since we know he hasn't been to the gym today, let alone tonight."

Reynolds shrugged. "Very likely the package. Now we wait. See if he sets a signal or calls someone." Reynolds gestured to the radio phone tap unit in the car.

Six minutes later, the tap squealed. Hillson hit the record button on the tape and picked up the headphones, pressing his right hand against them and adjusting the volume with his left. He listened intently to everything Howard was saying. As soon as Hillson removed the headphones and stopped the tape, Reynolds quirked an eyebrow.

"The usual for a weekend night: Golden City II Chinese delivery. He ordered egg drop soup, beef lo mein, pork fried rice, and a side of crab rangoon. Similar order to what he had last week and," Hillson paused and flipped through the binder of phone printouts, "uh, three weeks ago. The restaurant checked out clean. It's a family-run business with no ties to any group or individuals we're interested in. There's low to no chance that was the signal." Reynolds marked down the time in the notebook, and Hillson turned back to watch the front of the building.

"I hate stakeouts like this. Nothing to do but drink stale coffee and watch some idiot who thinks he's better than the law mess around. I would rather just charge in and grab the little treasonous bastard. Deal with him the right way." Reynolds waved towards the building.

"Right now, he's probably watching some episode of *Murder, She Wrote* or *Family Ties* while we sit here in the cold watching his apartment. He should be the one freezing. Holding cells are nice and cold this time of year."

Hillson tuned out Reynolds's bitching. Nothing he was saying was original or exciting. During their five years as partners in the Naval Investigative Service (NIS), Hillson had determined that Jason Reynolds would never be happy as long as service members continued to commit crimes. He seemed of the opinion that the men, and women when he remembered them, who raised their right hand were somehow better than everybody else in the nation. That somehow agreeing to put their life on the line meant that they were angels of some sort.

Roger Hillson mentally shook his head. He had never viewed the world so narrowly. In fact, he was personally convinced that anyone, given the right set of circumstances, would commit a crime with little to no thought. Human nature, that's what it was. Service people, especially sailors, came from all walks of life. Many of those paths were less than stellar: broken homes, divorces, abuse, gang activity…the list went on. Most of those people were escaping from horrible lives and then someone dangles a seemingly better plan—more money, a better place to live, drugs—anything really, in front of them. Of course they were going to jump for it. Patriotism had nothing on a full stomach and a good roof over your head. Maybe he could get Reynolds to read Maslow's *Hierarchy of Needs* and see how it played into crimes.

His mulling was interrupted by Reynolds speaking suddenly. "Heads up. Food delivery's here."

Both men lifted binoculars and watched as a white Toyota Supra pulled up to the curb. A short person, impossible to tell sex from the way they were dressed, hopped out of the car and popped the rear hatch. They pulled out several white sacks and headed up to the building's entrance. Moments later they saw Howard open the door, take the sacks, and pay the delivery person. The brownstone's door closed, and the delivery person turned for the first time towards the two agents. She looked to be an indeterminate age, somewhere between sixteen and thirty-five. She hurried back to the car and drove off.

"Not our meetup person."

Hillson lowered his binoculars and agreed. Silently the two went back to observing the brownstone. They took turns, one watching the street and one covering the house for changes.

Sometime later Reynolds murmured, "Hello…there we are."

"What do you see Jason?" Hillson asked as he continued to watch an older man walking his dog a half block away.

"Kid just opened his blinds all the way, then shut them, then opened them a quarter way back up. I would say that is the signal that the pickup is ready."

"Might be," Hillson partially agreed, "but it could be a signal that it's not safe. We'll wait a bit more before we head in. With luck we'll capture the courier as well."

"That would be the best-case solution. Worst case is that we wait too long. Lose the chance to stop any of this exchange."

Reynolds rubbed a hand through his thinning brown hair. "Alright…We wait."

Less than half an hour had passed before a blonde man of slight build buzzed into the brownstone. He wore a red Member's Only jacket, faded blue jeans, and white sneakers.

Reynolds reached for the door handle. "That, I suspect, is our courier. No one looking like that has ever been recorded coming into the house."

Hillson paused, placing a hand on Reynold's shoulder. "Wait. Could be a new boyfriend or someone lost." The young man entered the house while they talked.

"No, this feels right. We're going." Reynolds popped open his door, waiting just long enough to ensure that Hillson was right behind. The two men unsnapped their holsters as they ran to the brownstone. Reynolds tapped the override code that NIS had received from the apartment manager, and the two were through the door.

The entry hall was quiet and empty. A quick check by Hillson ensured no one was coming up from the basement. The two raced up the stairwell to the third floor.

A single bulb in the center of the small hall poorly lit the top floor. The dim light reflected off the tarnished 303 on the door, a tiny bit of sparkle in an otherwise drab space. At the opposite end of the hall and staircase was a hinged door, a laundry chute Hillson assumed. Reynolds stood to one side, gun pointed at the floor, and Hillson knocked on the door.

"Petty Officer Second Class Howard Giles. We are representatives of the Naval Investigative Service. Open the door."

There was a scrambling sound inside the room.

Hillson took half a step back and slammed his booted foot into the door near the knob. His heart raced. The frame splintered, and the door flew inward on its hinges, hitting the interior wall with a crash. Intent on overwhelming the suspect, the two agents charged in as fast as they could. Reynolds woofed as the red and white gym bag slammed into him, sending him sprawling. Hillson grabbed for Howard but was shoved aside by Reynolds's body and tumbled to the floor. The two men scrambled to get untangled and up as Howard sprinted out.

"Stop!" shouted Hillson as Howard fled into the hall. At the end, he dumped the gym bag into the chute and then ran down the stairs.

Hillson got his feet under him and followed, trying to keep on top of the faster young man. It was evident in seconds that Howard would get away. *Not today you punk.* Unconsciously shaking his head in disbelief, Hillson climbed onto the railing and leapt down onto Howard's back half a flight below. The two men tumbled into the wall, bounced away, and hit the railing, driving breath out of them both. Hillson recovered first and grabbed Howard's left arm, twisting it painfully behind the petty officer and slapped a handcuff around his wrist.

"Stop struggling or this is going to hurt worse." The younger man continued to struggle and Hillson pushed him against the wall. "Stop. You're done." Howard relaxed a bit, whether from understanding or simply the fact that he was gasping for breath. Hillson fought the right arm around and cuffed the wrists together. The sound of footsteps drew Hillson's attention as Reynolds clambered down the stairs. "The laundry chute…He threw the bag down the laundry chute!"

Reynolds nodded and ran to the wooden door. He flicked on a flashlight and pulled the hinged hatch open. The light did not fully penetrate the multistory drop to the basement. "Looks like it went all the way down!"

"Shit! Go after it. I'll cover the rights with this piece of trash." Hillson turned the bound petty officer, so they were facing. He pulled a well-used card from his inner jacket pocket and began reading it aloud. "You have the right to remain silent. Anything you say can and will be used against you in a court of law."

Reynolds ignored the too-familiar words as he pushed past the men, running down the stairs for the bottom floor landing. The stairs leading to the basement were not directly connected to the staircase leading to the other floors. Nobody else was on the flight as he rounded the banister and tore down the final flight of stairs, puffing slightly. The basement's lights were on, and an old Kenmore dryer rattled on one side of the room. The washing machine stood empty; the lid propped open with a wooden dowel. Under the laundry chute sat a pitiful wire rolling cart with an off-white canvas insert. Reynolds peered over the edge of the cart and pawed through the dirty blankets and trash that half-filled the basket. The gym bag was not in the mess.

The basement was not fully underground, and one of the vent windows sagged open with a broken hinge arm. Reynolds shone his flashlight through the opening and could just make out a pair of white sneakers climbing into a car.

"Dammit." Reynolds turned and ran back up the stairs. Agent Hillson had finally read Howard's rights to him and was leaning against the wall holding the young man. He started as Reynolds crested the basement stairs.

"Guy's got the bag. He's in the parking lot. Going after him," Reynolds huffed as he tore the front door open and jumped down the three steps out front. His right foot slipped on a patch of windblown leaves, turning his ankle painfully. Grunting in pain, he half ran, half hobbled around the corner of the brownstone towards the parking lot. A tan sedan was pulling out of a space as Reynolds made it to the lot.

He lifted his pistol and shouted for the man to stop. Either the man did not hear, or he ignored the shout. He squealed the tires, leaving dark black prints on the asphalt, and raced onto the street. He was around the next corner before Reynolds could catch up to the turn.

Dammit. Reynolds almost shot at the car before he realized that he would more than likely miss, and there were civilians around that might catch a stray bullet. Verifying first that the safety was on, Reynolds holstered his pistol. Then he leaned against the wall, head down, trying to recapture everything he had seen. His ever-present notebook was out, and he filled a partial page with what he had seen. Flipping it shut, he pushed himself up with a soft grunt and limped back towards the car, meeting Hillson and the handcuffed Howard as they cleared the brownstone.

Hillson cocked an eyebrow.

"He got away. I got a look at the car he was driving though. I'll call in a BOLO to Baltimore City, Maryland state police, and highway patrol. Got the full license plate so we should be able to find it." Both men knew that the chances of catching the perpetrator with the vehicle were slim. However, evidence could and would be gained from the vehicle.

Careful not to put too much pressure on his twisted ankle, Reynolds slid into the passenger seat while Hillson worked Howard into the back seat of the car. He opened the notebook and keyed the radio. "Control, Agent Reynolds."

"Reynolds, control. Go."

"Did not acquire the package. One person in custody. Request a BOLO through Baltimore local and Maryland state and highway patrol for car of following description: Late model Ford Taurus, tan color, plate Maryland Juliet Kilo Tango Five Five Niner. Driver is a male, mid to late twenties, one hundred thirty pounds, five eleven, blonde hair, wearing red Member's Only jacket, faded blue jeans, and white sneakers. May or may not be carrying a red and white gym bag. Unknown if suspect is armed. Proceed with caution. Inform NIS upon sighting." Reynolds unkeyed the microphone.

"BOLO request in process. Understand that one suspect in custody. Control out."

"Reynolds out." He replaced the microphone in its holder.

Hillson started the car. "We'll get it back, no thanks to this asshole." He nodded his head towards the back seat where Howard sat staring out the window, only now realizing how bad his life had become.

No one spoke during the trip back to the Bethesda field office. Hillson pulled the car into the well-lit garage and up to a trio of Master at Arms standing by the prison transfer door. He unlocked the doors and put the vehicle into neutral. The first Master at Arms opened the right rear door, and a second helped Howard out of the car, making sure that he did not hit his head on the way out. The final Master at Arms brought a clipboard to the driver's window. He handed the clipboard, associated papers, and a pen to the agent. Hillson grunted a thanks and scribbled his name, date, and time for the prisoner transfer. He verified that the car doors were shut and then drove the car to the agent's parking section.

Three hours later, the Baltimore police found the Ford sedan in a mall parking lot. The car had been taken from a rental lot earlier that evening, and the plates had been stolen from a tan Ford Taurus in Boonsboro. The car was clean, even of any prints, but the Baltimore Crime Scene Investigation unit was continuing to work the sedan. No one really expected any breakthroughs though.

Special Agents Hillson and Reynolds sat at their respective desks, sipping stale black coffee from the vending machine. Hillson sighed deeply. "I was hoping to stop this from continuing. Damn Soviets seem to be pushing harder and harder every year."

Reynolds nodded and cocked a thumb over his shoulder at the picture of President Reagan on the wall. "Don't have much of a choice, do they. We keep pressing hard with the

Star Wars project and aircraft carriers. They think they have to try anything to get ahead of us."

"Yep. He won't be able to fly it out of the country though. Every airport from Maine to the Gulf Coast is locked down. No way they get it out that way." Hillson frowned. "What if they just sit on it?"

"Then they are even further behind than when they started. No, I just wish we had the kind of control over the sea lanes and seaports as we do over the airports. It will be easier to slip out of the country that way. No, I suspect that one way or another," Reynolds continued, "that gym bag and the guidance package are heading out to sea. Soon, if my gut is correct."

New York Waterway, Edgewater, New Jersey
17 November 1986
0711 EST/1211 Zulu
Deep Sea Fishing Boat *Takin' Chances*

The cold steel yellow light of a northern morning was just creeping across the sky, outlining the New York City high-rises. Each building a black, hidden world, unseeable in the faint light of the incipient sunrise. A slight, blonde man walked carefully down the pier, a pair of deep-sea fishing rods and reels gripped tightly in his left hand and a green canvas seabag slung over his shoulder held in place with his right. Breath fogged the air faintly as he passed.

He scanned the boat's names during his passage, squinting at the various fun titles bestowed on the ships by their owners. *Two Forever*, *Reel Affair*, *Off Duty*, even a not-so-playful *Bite Me* with a huge fishhook looming under the words. Towards the far end of the rightmost pier, he finally spotted the *Takin' Chances*. He reached the edge of the dock and leaned over.

"Ahoy on board."

There was a sound of someone moving around below deck. Seconds later, a squat, brown-haired man appeared at the wood and glass door at the rear of the vessel. "Ahoy yourself."

"Are you the owner of this fishing boat?"

"Yes. Name's Harold Eaton. This is my boat."

"My name is Jim O'Neil. I'm looking to charter a ride to the east."

Harold's face did not budge. "Well Mr. O'Neil, I can charter if you have the money. Cold cash is necessary on such a morning as this."

"A red morning it is, and I take warning for that."

Harold grunted at the countersign. He reached out a hand and beckoned the blonde man aboard. As Jim stepped onto the boat, William steadied him and took the fishing poles.

"I'll get these set near the sockets. You can stow your gear in the number two cabin. Second door on port."

Jim smiled and thanked Harold, then silently took the duffel into the dark interior of the ship. Harold placed the two rods in a floor locker on the port side of the boat then carefully untied the mooring lines aft and forward. With the boat bobbing free, he climbed into the upper driving position and started the engine. Cautiously he backed the ship clear of the dock and turned out of the slip.

Harold contacted harbor control, relaying his intention to leave the marina and head out to sea for a day of fishing.

The harbormaster acknowledged the information and wished Harold a safe and profitable journey.

"Thank you harbor control. I certainly hope it is profitable. *Takin' Chances* out." Harold placed the radio microphone back in its cradle and watched intently for other traffic as he guided the forty-two-foot boat through the piers. Once clear of the end of the docks, he advanced the throttle a notch and steered for the harbor breakwater.

As soon as the boat cleared the No Wake Zone, Harold advanced the throttle to full. The boat leapt forward, quickly accelerating to a top speed of twenty-seven knots. Few personal craft were out this early on a Monday morning, but there was plenty of commercial traffic. Harold kept a weather eye on the mid-sized freighters as he steered for the deeper water of the Atlantic.

Jim climbed up into the upper deck. Harold glanced over his shoulder at his only passenger. He steered well clear of an auto carrier looming to starboard.

"We should get to the rendezvous point in about thirty hours. No sign of anyone trailing us by boat or by air. Looks like you got away clean."

Jim just smiled and looked at the horizon.

Chapter Two

JTF 13 Training Facility, Jacksonville, North Carolina
17 November 1986
1242 EST/1742 Zulu
Ocean Training Facility

Sun-warmed water sparkled in the afternoon light, and a faint breeze brought the scent of marshland with it. Four marines, their M16A2s at the ready, scanned the water and the reeds along the river's edge, watching for any motion. Each marine monitored his section of the zone. Sergeant John "Mores" Morehouse scanned the horizon, his rifle tucked into his shoulder and ready to fire. Corporal Riley glanced occasionally into the area patrolled by one of his teammates.

None of the four noted the faint ripples in the water ahead of them, just where the waterway entered the larger estuary. They proceeded, unaware, as the ripples became V's indicating something moving just below the surface.

In an explosion of dirty water, the white-striped, black creature leapt out of the water two feet from Sergeant Morehouse, drenching the marine with brackish water. He stumbled backward, shocked by the sight of the giant creature but caught his footing before he could fall into the river water.

"Shit!" Morehouse whipped his rifle down and right towards the creature, finger already tensing on the trigger. He had been pointing his rifle at an empty spot some one hundred and fifty feet away, above the water and outward. There was no way to intercept the monster before the huge mouth could attach itself to his chest. He took a deep breath and prepared for the impact.

"FREEZE!"

Everybody froze at the command, even the creature. It stopped in midair, liquid dripping back into the river, loud in the sudden silence. A thin, square metal tube ran from the creature's back to a fixture hidden under the murky water.

"Just where exactly do you think that you are pointing that rifle, sergeant? What is the threat vector?" yelled Master Gunnery Sergeant Peck as he slapped the offending rifle barrel down to the water. "Unfreeze." A captain watched silently while a lieutenant wrote up findings as they occurred. Standing where they were, the participants in the exercise could not see them.

"Outward Gunny!" yelled Sergeant Morehouse and almost swung the M16 back across the water, watching for the threat to appear.

"Outward? Dammit, Mores, the threat is underwater. The damn devil rays do not just attack by flying at your face. Scan the damn water, watch for the surface indicators. Indicators like the little V's that y'all ignored so nicely. Then unload on the thing as it approaches. Warn the rest of your team. Most of all, everybody keep to your damn sector. Riley, let Mores worry about the front and Johansson worry about the left flank. You keep your eyes and your rifle pointed toward the right flank of the river. And Hubbard, you have to check the entirety of the back trail." Gunny threw his hands up and waded out of the simulated river basin in the middle of the building. He waved to the control room set above everything.

"Give me a reset. I want them to attack like what we saw on the video from Jamaica. Can we pull that off?"

"Semper Fi, Gunny," came the reply from the unseen marine running the target range. The fake devil ray slipped back down with a faint hiss of hydraulics and disappeared under the waves.

"Once more you morons. Keep the rifles pointed right, and keep your eyes on the threat vector. The damn supernaturals will not, I repeat, will not give you a second chance. Once they sight you, they will attack. If you do not respond in the proper manner, which is to fill their sorry carcasses full of as much ammunition as possible, they will tear your throat out. Or drag you away to kill you later, the whole time you're screaming for help and in pain. Or implant you with their young like something out of *Alien*. Am I making myself clear to you, you snot-nosed, deaf-eared, limp-wristed wastes of my time?"

"YES GUNNERY SERGEANT!"

"Fine…Let me see you prove it."

With a sniff, the master gunnery sergeant stepped back into the reeds on the side of the fake river and up onto the observation platform. He waved his hand at the control room. They waited.

Four minutes later a pair of faint V's showed in the river's slow-moving current, moving parallel to the four marines. Riley spotted the pair first and called out "Two left. Engaging."

The rounds from the M16 kicked up water in the path of the V's, shattering the calm surface into a frothing mess. The white froth gained a tint of a pale lavender as the bullets found the 'flesh' of the fake devil rays. The first one floated, dead.

Three more Vs appeared, one to the front and two on the right.

"Right engaging…one tango down."

Morehouse stated, "Engaging front," and stroked the trigger. Three rounds snapped out of the rifle muzzle in a burst. The water frothed with the high-velocity impacts, though no blood appeared. He fired a second burst, then scanned for the creature.

"Front missed. Left and right, watch for it to come around."

"Second tango left down."

The four men waited, shifting slightly in the sluggish current of the river. Minutes passed. Morehouse stated, "Scanning behind." He turned in time to catch sight of a single V racing towards the group. In a stroke of unfortunate timing, Corporal Hubbard's scan had him looking in the wrong direction, left rear instead of right rear.

"Threat behind. Engaging." Sighting down the barrel, Morehouse stroked the trigger twice. Six rounds slammed into the beast just as it exploded from the water. Hubbard snapped his rifle to the right and sent two additional rounds into the creature as it passed him. Morehouse, realizing how close to the creature he was, braced for the impact.

Nothing happened.

A buzzer went off.

The target froze, water sliding off the back of the metal and vinyl mock-up.

"Debrief in ten," stated Gunny and watched as the rifle team exited the room.

"Devil rays are primarily aquatic, and it is believed that as young they initially feed on fish and small crustaceans. As they grow, they will engage in eating prey that might be near the water's edge, like raccoon, opossum, or fox."

Captain Dupree tapped the pull-down screen with his wooden pointer for emphasis as he spoke. "That means that they are harder to see and much harder to track during an engagement than terrestrial threats like lycanthropes or chupacabra. Plus, they are pack hunters. Like wolves, they will circle on you. I think all of you are more cognizant of that after the display out there." Several of the marines nodded.

"Recently they have become a problem in the Caribbean, primarily in Jamaica. No one is sure where the first nest came from, but we have three confirmed sightings and one confirmed attack. One of the sightings and the attack was caught on video."

The captain turned on the large TV in the corner and shut off the lights. An obviously home-shot VHS video came up. A woman with light brown hair in a swimsuit, just slightly too tight for her, laughed and played in the sand. The marines hooted.

"Quiet down," growled Gunny.

The video showed an obviously deserted section of beach with pristine khaki white sand and tropical trees beyond the young woman. The timestamp from the recorder showed that the filming had occurred slightly after seven-thirty p.m.

"The video was shot near the Milk River in Jamaica," stated Dupree. The woman said something about putting down the camera and going swimming, pointing an arm towards the cerulean ocean. A man laughed in the background and replied about staying on the sand. Suddenly the image pitched crazily, and a man screamed. The camera fell to the ground, and the picture rolled, producing an uncomfortable Dutch tilt of the woman and a man racing away. Several devil rays were visible leaping out of the water's edge and attacking the couple. The devil rays pursued the pair of humans out of frame.

Captain Dupree stopped the video and flipped the lights back on. "Neither civilian was seriously hurt thankfully. The State Department is in charge of that side of the situation and is responsible for debriefing the two civilians. However, as you can see in the video, there was no provocation against the devil rays. They simply attacked and in numbers. This shift in behavior takes them out of the 'we will eventually deal with them' category into a defined mission. Tasking is Priority Metal, Amber Bronze. Briefing to follow this after-action hot wash. Gunny?"

"As usual with our hot washes," Master Gunnery Sergeant Peck started, "I want to look over what went right as well as what went wrong. We'll start with coverage and zones of responsibility. Riley, what part of 'left' is so hard for you to comprehend?"

CIA Headquarters, Langley, Virginia
17 November 1986
0748 EST/1248 Zulu
Secure Briefing Room Bravo

"We believe that the Mark 48 ADCAP experimental guidance package, code name Paladin, is no longer in Baltimore. There is a high percentage chance that, by now, the item is on its way to the Soviet Union by ship. Local law enforcement was able to successfully lock down all local airports in the five surrounding states."

A blurry black and white photo of a fishing trawler flashed onto the screen from the overhead projector.

"A Soviet AGI trawler, the *Zhiqulesk*, is currently about one hundred and fifteen nautical miles outside of New York City. We have an asset on board, code name Flute. The asset signaled that the vessel was to receive a package 'soon' and then return at best speed to its home base." Agent Keith Butler looked up from his notes. A faint haze of cigarette smoke hung in the air.

"Investigative Division places the chance at greater than fifty-eight percent Paladin will be the package. Once Paladin is aboard, our asset will signal us again."

One of the men at the table looked up at that. "Is it your plan to allow the Soviets to keep Paladin?" He wrote a note on the yellow tablet before him.

"No. The plan is to track Paladin. Once Flute verifies that Paladin is indeed onboard, Flute will activate a low-frequency sonar transmitter, which is already in place and has not been activated as of this briefing. At that point, the plan is to use a Naval underwater asset to track the vessel and, at the proper time, recover both Flute and Paladin."

One of the other men at the table laughed incredulously. In his deep Texas accent, he commented, "So, let me get this straight. Y'all are plannin' on usin' a nuclear submarine, your so nicely named 'Naval underwater asset', to track and overtake a Soviet AGI trawler, a tattletale, while it is on its way into Soviet waters?" Pointing around the room with a smoldering cigar, he continued, "All the while, the ability of us, and by us I do mean the United States as well as the CIA, to deny involvement will be practically nil. Tattletales are specifically designed to record information about our submarines and other underwater Naval equipment."

"Which is exactly why the Soviets would never expect us to trail them this way." Butler took a quick calming breath and continued as he changed out slides, "The current plan is to use a SEAL team out of Little Creek, Virginia. They will link with the USS *Sea Devil* out from Charleston. We have assigned her the code name Efficiency" The slide showed a dotted black line from the Virginia coast meeting with a solid black line that started in southern South Carolina. "Once the team is on board, the submarine will track the *Zhiqulesk* to north of Bear Island in the Barents Sea. Flute will then be signaled that the extraction plan is a go." A new line was uncovered showing a combined black solid and dotted line transiting to an area in the Barents Sea. Another slide was laid on top, this one a close-up of the map showing a circle several miles across north of Bear Island and south of the island of Svalbard.

Agent Butler paused to let the men in the room take in what he had stated. He placed another photo up, this time an underwater color photo of divers exiting a submarine through a top hatch. "Flute will remove Paladin from its stowage location and jump overboard with it. The SEAL team will recover both Paladin and Flute from underwater. This will likely lead the crew of the *Zhiqulesk* to believe that their crew member committed suicide and drowned. There will be no need for the SEAL team or Efficiency to surface. The trawler's crew will never see anything, let alone suspect that this was a recovery operation by the United States. Efficiency will then return by a southern route to Charleston Naval Base. Upon arrival, the ship will moor. That evening, under the cover of darkness, the SEAL team, Flute, and Paladin will all be transferred from the submarine. The SEALs will return overland to Little Creek Naval Station. Flute and Paladin will be dealt with through our channels, with Flute being debriefed here at Langley." Butler shut off the projector and turned up the room lights. "Questions?"

The man who had first questioned having the Soviets keep Paladin stubbed his cigarette out in an ashtray and raised a hand. Keith nodded to him. "Why not just have Flute destroy Paladin and dump it overboard? It seems like this plan requires way too many moving parts and a fair amount of interaction with non-Agency personnel. Statistically, each additional piece means that the chance of discovery, either during or after the event, goes up by a considerable margin."

And you hate the idea of anyone else but your boys in Operations getting the credit, Keith thought through a poker face. He nodded and answered the question. "There are several issues with performing the mission that way. One, Flute is not a trained technician. Thus, Flute doesn't have a way, short of physically destroying Paladin, to render the computer useless to the Soviets.

"Second, just dumping the unit overboard also doesn't guarantee that the Soviets won't find and recover the computer. Third, and most importantly in the eyes of the Station Chief and myself, the chance of recovering Flute rapidly drops to zero if the plan is to have Flute simply destroy Paladin. There is no way that Flute can dispose of Paladin without blowing their cover. Contrary to what the *New York Times* and *The Washington Post* like to put out in their opinion pieces, it has never been CIA policy to leave assets in the cold nor to sacrifice them. Flute went in knowing that we will do everything we can to bring them home." Agent Butler stared around the table. "Alive.

"As for the second part of your question, there are a lot of parts without a need to know. The advantage we have working with a SEAL team is that it's a normal operation for submarines like Efficiency. The sailors on the ship will have no reason to question the presence of the team. For recovering Flute, the captain will be briefed to use the cover story of a sailor lost at sea. Submarines also perform Search and Rescue operations, especially if they are the closest to the scene. The SEAL team and the commanding officer of Efficiency will be the only personnel read in. This reduces the overall chance of leaks to seven people: the captain and the six SEAL members. All of whom have the proper level of security access, and training to be exposed to this information."

"What about the tracker? How will it be disposed of? Will it be left aboard the *Zhiqulesk* after the recovery, or are the SEALs going to somehow manage to get it too?"

"3M Corporation discovered an interesting adhesive that de-bonds under certain electrical conditions," Butler segued. "They were working on a new underwater adhesive when this particular mixture's properties became apparent. The company could not see any use in normal conditions for the adhesive and offered it to the government at a low cost. We agreed to their terms, and various programs use it for tracking situations of this nature. The transmitter is designed to self-remove from the hull of the *Zhiqulesk*," Butler continued, emphasizing the name of the trawler a little, "three days after it is activated. From there it will sink to the bottom of the ocean. The unit itself is about the size of a package of cigarettes and mottled gray in color. Even if the Soviets had a good notion of where to look, finding it on the ocean floor will be almost impossible." He could see that answer would not quite satisfy the questioner so he added, "Additionally, the same surge that de-bonds the adhesive will also short out all of the transmitter's circuitry. That way if it is recovered somehow, the transmitter will already have been rendered useless. It will be nothing but a mass of fried computer chips in a depth-crushed case."

There was patient silence in the room as everyone waited for additional inquiries. No one raised any further concerns.

"I'll keep each of you apprised of any changes to the plan. We will reconvene for situation updates tomorrow here at the same time as today. Good day, gentlemen."

Keith watched as the three other men gathered their notes and quietly exited the conference room, leaving him alone with the slides, projector, and the scent of stale smoke.

Charleston Naval Base, Charleston, South Carolina
18 November 1986
0730 EST/1230 Zulu
Squadron 4 Commander's Office

Commander William Owens politely knocked on the edge of the doorframe. Rear Admiral Reager, Commander Submarine Squadron 4 (COMSUBRON 4), waved him in. The admiral was currently on the phone and motioned for William to close the door and grab some coffee. William quietly shut the door and then availed himself to a mug of coffee from the carafe on the far wall. He sent a questioning look and gestured at a cup for the admiral. The admiral shook his head negatively and continued with the phone conversation.

William picked up one of the cups adorned with the squadron emblem, a blue circle with a silhouette of an attack sub on a black line splitting the bottom half into two quarters. On the left was the palm tree and the crescent moon of South Carolina's flag, the right a red fox. Below these were a small white banner declaring "Swamp Fox". It tickled the commander that the squadron got its name from one of the most famous rebels of the Revolutionary War. *Francis Marion*, Commander Owens thought, *would have been a serious sub-driver, right at home skulking about underwater hunting the enemy without letting the enemy know he was there.*

He shook off the thought and poured a cup of the dark roast. The aroma of the blend followed him as he crossed to the desk. William sat down in one of the two chairs facing Admiral Reager. He glanced around the room while the admiral finished his phone call. Nothing had changed since his last visit. Oil paintings of submarines and tenders dominated the left side of COMSUBRON 4's office, while a massive mahogany bookshelf filled with various reference works loomed up on the right side of the room. A model of the USS *Cavalla*, Admiral Reager's last command, sat in a proud position on the beige metal desk, half buried under the clutter of loose papers. Behind the admiral, a floor-to-ceiling window dominated the wall.

The window looked over the Cooper River where William could see the tender USS *Frank Cable*, three destroyers, a pair of *James Madison* class SSBNs, a smattering of frigates, and six *Sturgeon* class SSNs in port. A bustle of activity on the Oscar pier caught his eye where a crane was loading materials onto one of the destroyers. Further downriver, just at the edge of sight, peeking out of the cold November fog, were the Old and New Cooper River Bridges. A frigate was steaming away from the base, beginning to near the New Cooper River Bridge as he watched.

Commander Owens returned his attention to the inside of the room as he heard the phone receiver click back into place. He took a small sip of his cooling coffee and waited, savoring the full-bodied flavor. He was certain the squadron commander had a good reason for requesting him here.

"William, glad you could make it in so short a time," Admiral Reager beamed broadly. "I know that you're still working on fixing the hydraulics issue with the IMA."

"We are sir." William nodded his head and returned the smile. "However, when the squadron commander requests my presence, it seems like a good idea to leave the XO in charge and head over. I take it something has changed for the boat. I haven't heard of any growing problems, but then again, if this is serious, you'd hear before me." William leaned forward in the seat. "And if it had been something with one of my sailors, the COB would have informed me before I headed this way."

Admiral Reager laughed at that. "Yes, I do believe that if this had anything to do with your crew, Master Chief Sterns would be the first to know. Before me, I would suspect. That chief has his ear closer to the ground than anyone else I know." He leaned forward and clasped his hands together on the desk, his demeanor becoming more serious. "Everything I am about to tell you is your eyes only, Top Secret—Codeword Railroad. This job is a snap-kick. High priority and your boat is my best choice from a readiness standpoint, stores load out, and the fact that you are one of my best, probably the best, commander. The Secretary of the Navy, with the approval of the Joint Chiefs, has requested a submarine to track down a Soviet AIG carrying sensitive US military equipment. Not sure what it is, but they have designated SEAL Team Four to rendezvous with you off the coast of Norfolk."

Admiral Reager pushed a folder containing a couple of sheets of paper across the desk, its cover bearing a large red and white stripe across it and the words TOP SECRET and RAILROAD. Commander Owens picked them up and quickly scanned the contents.

"From there, you will then proceed to track the vessel using a locator sonar transmitter that is already established. I need you to depart within twelve hours. I realize this means that your crew will be missing a few people who are on leave. I'll scrounge up replacements if required. Your cover story is a readiness sortie drill for an inbound nuclear strike. You'll have cover orders to that effect. I am also going to sortie the *USS Seahorse* at the same time. She actually will be performing the drill."

"Bit of a haul…*Sea Devil* can do it though. Why not one of the boats out of Groton?" William asked. "Not trying to get out of anything, just curious."

"Didn't figure you were. Two reasons. One, this is a better position to link up with the SEAL team. Two, a boat leaving Groton suddenly is a more likely suspect for the North Atlantic. We keep the other side thinking that boats out of here primarily cover the mid and South Atlantic. This minimizes the chance they will look here for anything that we are sending to track them."

"A double-blind." William nodded in agreement with the plan. "Watch the right hand, ignore the left." He read the two sheets inside the folder more carefully. "Bit thin on the particulars."

"The SEALs will have the primary job. You just need to get them there and then get everyone back home." The admiral extended his hand and took the file folder back.

"I'll send the FLASH orders for the drill in the next ten minutes. That gives you time to get back to the ship."

William stood up, careful to avoid knocking the cooling coffee to the floor. "We will get this done sir. Request to return to my boat and get everything prepared?"

Admiral Reager stood and extended his hand. "I will send a few items over, plus some additional stores. Most of the new stores will come with the SEAL team. Fair seas and following winds Commander. Now get out of here."

Commander Owens shook the proffered hand. "Thank you. We will do the squadron proud."

"I am sure you and your crew will, Commander."

Commander Owens hurried out of the building and towards the distant piers. The COMSUBRON 4 watched from the window and whispered, "I'm sure you will make us all proud."

Roosevelt Roads Naval Air Station, Puerto Rico
18 November 1986
1041 EST/1541 Zulu
MH-53 Pave Low III on approach

Sergeant Morehouse gripped the cargo strap tightly as the Pave Low III banked hard to port on approach to the island. He hated flying in the choppers. It always felt like they were trying to tear themselves apart while in the air. The rising sun broke over the ocean and streamed through the side windows, momentarily blinding him.

Corporal Riley stuck his nose to the window and stared out. The deep emerald greens of the jungle were richer than anything he had seen back in the States. This time of year, all the trees had changed color and dropped their leaves in Northern Idaho. Sometimes, the first snows of the year had fallen. Here, it was seventy-three degrees and green. He whooped as the chopper hit a patch of rough air and bounced.

Despite the rattling and engine noise, Morehouse could still hear Riley enjoying himself. "Can it, Riley. Some of us want to be airsick in peace."

Riley laughed harder. "You knew you would be flying around when you joined the Marines, didn't cha?"

"No…I thought marines rode around in jeeps and armored vehicles. Not choppers."

"Or ships. Don't forget the wonderful vessels the Navy so kindly allows us to ride upon." Corporal "Clink" Gustav punched the sergeant in the shoulder. "Bet you get seasick too."

Morehouse shook his head. "Not that I know of. Airsick, yes. Ships don't seem to bother me. What really sucks about this is we are going to have about enough time to stretch our legs here and get the kinks out before we are back on this bird and headed to Jamaica. That's another two and a half hours of flight time. Make sure you pit stop and grab some pogey bait. I don't think they are going to give us an in-flight meal today."

The intercom crackled. "All crew. Two minutes until landing. Brace for landing."

The eight marines stopped talking and checked the gear. None of it had shifted during the rough flight from Mayport Naval Station. They grabbed cargo net rigging and leaned towards the center of the compartment.

Moments later the Sea Dragon settled on its large wheels with a thump and the starboard cargo door was slid open by a Naval air rating.

The large, tanned petty officer wore a flight helmet and dungarees. He leaned in and spoke in a loud raspy voice. "Keep your heads down and cross to the far side of the pad. Do not stand up until after you are clear of the red line. Heads down until the red line." He pointed as he spoke towards the hangars farther away on the tarmac.

A chorus of "Ayes" followed the instructions. "Sergeant Morehouse, you and your team will meet with Captain Tanner in the hangar for final brief. Remember, heads down till past the red line."

The petty officer stepped aside and tapped each marine on the back of the head as they chicken walked out of the helicopter. Rotor wash from the five huge blades threw tiny dust devils up and forced the six men down as they made their way across the tarmac.

Sergeant Morehouse felt the reduction in the downwash just before he passed the red line. As soon as he was over, he straightened and verified the rest of the team was careful as they too entered the safe area. The air was warm and filled with the scent of tropical green. Several of the men paused and took deep breaths, enjoying the bit of fresh air.

Once everyone assembled, the squad settled their packs and locked their rifles in carry position. Morehouse led them in a quick time march to the hangar indicated by the petty officer. The large rolling aircraft doors remained shut, but the smaller personnel door opened at a touch. The team entered and paused, letting their sun-blinded eyes adjust to the gloom inside the cool hangar. A lone marine in undress khakis stood near eight chairs and a flip pad. Twin bars glinted in the overhead lights.

"Captain Tanner?" The officer nodded and the sergeant saluted. "Sergeant Morehouse and team of seven reporting as ordered sir." He held the salute until Captain Tanner returned it.

The captain looked over the team quickly and pointed towards a pair of doors as he spoke. "Go ahead and drop your rucks. Heads are over there, and there is water and snacks in the room beside them. Do your business and then get back out here. This will be the final brief for Operation Decision."

"Thank you, sir." Morehouse turned to his men. "Five minutes. And if you wiggle it more than twice, you're playing with it." The men all slid their rucksacks down, placing them in a neat pile behind the chairs. Then en masse, seven marines headed for the two doors. Morehouse followed, ensuring everyone took time to stop in the head. Sometimes marines had not learned that any chance to empty one's bladder was not a chance to be passed up. Morehouse was not worried about his guys, but verifying they stopped in and did their business was a habit he had formed years earlier. Food and sleep were nice, but nothing beat an empty bladder when something from the ninth circle of Hell tried to climb out and eat your face.

Chapter Three

Roosevelt Roads Naval Air Station, Puerto Rico
18 November 1986
1102 EST/1602 Zulu
Primary Aircraft Hangar

The men were all back sitting and ready for the brief before the five minutes were up. Every one of them pulled a small weatherproof notepad out of their gear and all were ready and attentive.

"Operation Decision is classified as a tasking priority of Metal, level Amber Bronze. One squad of two rifle teams is considered sufficient to kill the devil rays and destroy the nest site." Captain Tanner flipped up the chart. Bright red TOP SECRET—CODEWORD RAINBOW stamps adorned the top and bottom of each sheet. "The teams will insert at the airstrip here. The airstrip is at a small regional airport that the State Department is controlling during the time that we are in country. Final load-out of material at the site is in progress now. Those additional materials are loaded into a pair of HUMVEEs, which have been tasked for the teams. The load-out includes a set of overland maps that will be with the vehicles. The maps are pre-marked with the exact locations of the attacks and possible zones for nests. Everything will be ready when you arrive at the airstrip."

"Rifle Team Alpha under Sergeant Morehouse will conduct the sweep from two miles east of the latest attack westward. Rifle Team Bravo, under Sergeant Wade, will take the area from two miles west of the attack area and proceed east. Corporal Grizzle, how far inland have devil rays been sighted?"

"Sir, devil rays have been sighted in flight as far as three miles inland from a beach." The large marine, nicknamed Bear for both his name and deep voice, continued. "They have also been sighted in brackish water up to ten miles upriver from a coastal area. Sir."

"Correct. Devil rays, like other normal sea creatures, do not survive well or for long periods in fresh or even brackish water. Preferred hunting times and methods…Corporal Hanzo?"

"Sir," began the whip-thin man, "the devil ray is an ambush hunter, preferring to hunt during dawn and dusk, though occasional attacks have occurred in both full daylight and full dark. They lay in the shallows and leap to take out smaller creatures. A young devil ray may feed on ducks, opossums, mice, and other small creatures. Evidence suggests that adults have taken down and eaten full-grown deer. Underwater, they are slower than much of their prey and instead rely on a type of suction to draw their prey to them. Coloration of black and white banding allows them to hide in most sand-covered shorelines. Sir."

"You missed that for hunting on land against larger creatures they tend to swarm in packs of no less than three."

"Yes sir," stated the chagrined corporal.

Captain Tanner flipped the map over, and a black and white line drawing of a devil ray followed. "Primary organs for hunting are the eyes when going after land-born prey. This set of sensors," Tanner used his wooden pointer to tap a set of black dots on the ventral side of the drawing as he spoke, "is used to sense electrical disturbances, much like a shark. Because of this, each team member will carry a cattle prod with them. The research group postulates that a large discharge of electricity near the creatures will disrupt their ability to track prey in water. Of course, that seems to disrupt most creatures." The marines chuckled at the mild humor.

"The mouth is one of the biggest differences that these supernaturals have from terrestrial rays. Most rays have a set of flat crushing plates that allow them to eat clams and other shellfish. Devil rays instead have an elastic mouth that can stretch nearly to each wing joint and jaw structures filled with inward-pointing teeth. They attach and chew like a lamprey, sawing the teeth in a semi-circular motion."

A hand shot up. "Yes, corporal?"

"Sir, do we know how these things ended up in Jamaica?"

"Current best guess is a voodoo ritual for river guardians went wrong…or right depending on who set up the ritual. JTF 13 Research and the Arcane Research Group of the State Department are looking into that. More than likely, we will never find out what caused them to end up in Jamaica. How or why they ended up there isn't your job. Your job is to make sure that they die there."

A good-natured chuckle ran through the group.

"Back to business. Historically, this particular supernatural threat has shown no particular defense against any form of small arms or rifles. Explosives are useful for destroying nests since the egg sacks seem to be unnaturally hardened against the elements. Fire is almost useless against both the egg cases and the rays themselves. Even magnesium incendiary rounds quench soon after striking the flesh. No one has briefed me on why this happens. Sea monsters, what can I say?" Captain Tanner shrugged comically.

"The nesting sites will be easier to find at night since the egg cases fluoresce in the blue-green spectrum. Thankfully, like the few oviparous terrestrial rays, the egg's nests are not guarded. Familial care ends with the laying of the eggs. These nests are normally found past the breakwater, and more often in a depression surrounded by sea grasses or seaweed. No one has ever discovered a nest in water deeper than fifty feet. This could be due to sunlight requirements. Currently, belief is that the eggs and young of the devil ray have no natural predators. That makes it your job to ensure the nest is fully eradicated or the problem will return in a month or two after we leave. Several sets of scuba gear are part of the load in Jamaica."

"Finally, stay away from the creature's mouth. It combines the worst nastiness of sharks and lampreys. This group of devil rays also seems to have a mild poison, a first for this type of supernatural. State thinks that's why the attacked couple was overcome by them so quickly. Unfortunately, Medical is not sure if it is delivered through bites as a venom, poison in the saliva, or is a surface poison in the mucus covering of the rays."

Tanner flipped the chart to the final page. "As usual, nothing on this mission will be discussed outside of JTF 13 personnel or groups. All material recovered will be turned over to JTF 13 Research or the ARG of the State Department as determined at end of mission. No trophies. I hear even a hint of something like that and the person will find out whether the CIA really does have a drug that removes memories. Am I clear, Marines?"

The group chorused in one voice. "Clear sir!"

"Wheels up in ten. Semper Fi!"

"Oorah!" the men shouted back. They grabbed their rucks and rifles and headed out onto the tarmac once more.

A palpable sense of menace radiated from the helicopter. The MH-53 squatted like an assassin beetle, the refueling drogue out front ready to inject its next victim. The rotor blades were still, drooping slightly like spider legs waiting to grab their next victim. John Morehouse shook off the feeling and quickly found the marine loadmaster for the Pave Low.

"Pardon me, Staff. Are the cargo packets on board?"

The marine staff sergeant looked up as Morehouse approached. "Yep. The batteries are stored in the red-banded boxes. Everything else is in the normal containers." He handed Morehouse the load list who carefully studied it. Everything they had requested was in the load out. Morehouse initialed in the indicated spot for taking control of the gear.

"Excellent. Appreciate the assistance, staff sergeant."

"Semper fi. Hate to think what the drug cartel has done to rate cattle prods," the loadmaster half-joked.

"Nah, those are for the mules. Guess we are going to be riding in on some mountain trail, and the mules they got us are even more stubborn than a new recruit on First Night."

The staff sergeant laughed at that. "Recruits. Can't live with them, and we are forbidden from beating sense into them anymore."

Morehouse nodded and waved as he ducked under the tail and walked back to the marines waiting just outside the red lines.

"Mount up."

He tapped each of the seven men on the back as they entered the cargo compartment. Following the last of his team members, Morehouse followed and strapped down once more. A quick check verified the headset was plugged in.

"Alpha actual to co-pilot."

"Go Alpha actual."

"Team Alpha and Team Bravo are loaded and ready. All cargo verified loaded. Ready for lift at your discretion."

"Roger Alpha actual. Prepare for lift in less than five."

"Acknowledged. Alpha actual out."

Morehouse lifted his right hand and spread his fingers. "Five minutes or less. Get comfy. We have a bit of a ride ahead of us."

He noticed that Riley was asleep before the big rotors even began turning.

Vernam Air Force Base (Closed), Clarendon, Jamaica
18 November 1986
1733 EST / 2233 Zulu
Derelict Hangar

"Well, I have to admit this is one of the more, ah," Corporal Riley cleared his throat a bit noisily, "quaint locations we have been sent to recently."

The storm-damaged ruin of a World War II–era hangar was the largest remaining structure for several football fields. As briefed, a pair of M1025 HMMWVs sat inside the hangar's dilapidated interior, covered with tarps. A young black man in a white suit leaned against an aging faded yellow VW Vanagon. The van appeared to have been on the island slightly less time than the hangar had, though not by much. Morehouse found it telling that the driver had stayed outside of the questionable structure.

Sergeant Morehouse glared at Riley, and then turned towards the gentleman. "Sergeant Morehouse and squad," he reported.

"Ah jolly good," the man said as he approached, his British accent as crisp as the starched lines of his tropical suit. "The lads have arrived. Reginald Winforth-Taylor, U.S. State Department." He held out his hand to the sergeant.

Morehouse gripped the man's hand quickly and released it. "Sounds more like you're from around here." Morehouse waved his arm about indicating the entire island.

"Well, the accent is pure Queen's English. Parents were from Leicester and moved to the colonies when I was eight. Spent the rest of my time learning that middle Iowa is no place for a man who either looks or sounds like me to grow up." He laughed, ivory teeth flashing in the sun. "Enough about me though. You chaps are here for the issue on the coast." His grin faded.

"That is correct."

Reginald grimaced. "Distasteful business. The ARG continues to investigate the cause. Here," he said and passed a thin folder to the team lead. "Final information as of three hours ago. The lorries' NAVSTAR units are pre-programmed with the routes. Follow the guidance system and it will take you to the Milk River entrance. There is very little for several miles nearby, so local interference is unlikely. The local coast guard, as well as our own, have been warned of possible drug interdiction activity in the area. They'll keep small vessels from approaching. The agreement with Kingsport is for this to be completed by the morning. After that, local support will not be available for some time."

"Nothing like a deadline to make one focus."

"Truly." Reginald laughed quickly again. He pointed to the tarp-covered vehicles. "The lorries are full of petrol and ready for your men to load the gear. Scuba gear, including additional full tanks, are in each lorry. Once you have verified your additional equipment, you are cleared to proceed. Extraction for you and the equipment will be here in eighteen hours. Good luck." The diplomat smiled once more and stuck out his hand. Morehouse shook it again and watched as Reginald climbed into the VW bus. The ancient Vanagon started with a cough and puff of white-gray smoke. Then Reginald drove onto the taxiway towards an overgrown road heading out from the base, the microbus's carriage swaying as the wheels dipped in and out of the multitude of potholes sown across the ancient airstrip.

Morehouse turned back to the men. "Strip and stow the canopies. Then each team loads one vehicle. Identical load-out for each. Ensure that an equal number of batteries are stowed on each Hummer. I do not want to get there and find out that Alpha got all the cattle prods and Bravo got all the batteries. Hanzo and Hubbard, you have lookout."

A squat lance corporal disengaged from Bravo Team and walked to the perimeter. On the way, he checked his M16 and verified the weapon was ready. He began pacing the line, keeping his eyes scanning between the vegetation along the airstrip's edge and the sky. Hubbard split off from Alpha Team, following a similar procedure but working his way along the opposite side of the strip.

The other marines unhooked the weatherproof tarps from the HUMVEEs and rolled them up, tying the straps to the outside for easy stowage. Once the tarps were stowed, the teams manhandled the weapons crates into the back of the Hummers. Finally, Riley verified that the cattle prods and batteries were split evenly and loaded.

"That checks out. Lookouts, mount with your teams. Weapons are safe. Reminder…No one outside of a few members of the State Department, JTF 13 Command, and probably no more than three members of the Jamaican government are aware we are here. Keep your heads down and respect the area. The only hostiles we're here for are the devil rays. Is that clear?" Sergeant Morehouse looked at each of the men.

"Clear, Sergeant," replied Sergeant Wade for Bravo team.

"Alpha understands," replied Corporal Riley.

"Plan on driving together to the entrance of the Milk River. From there we will split up and patrol. Questions?" Morehouse waited for any. "Mount up and start the engines. Alpha has point." Thirty seconds later the two HUMVEEs were quietly rolling out of the abandoned airfield.

The dense Caribbean jungle crunched under the HUMVEE's wheels, a fragrant mixture of greenery and loam. *This is the easy part*, thought John Morehouse. *Next comes the screams and the firefight. I know all of us have seen it at least once, but it still scares me. Knowing that there are things under the beds and in the closets. How do we convince our kids it's safe out there when the monsters really do exist? Or explain to them that there*

are people who will fight to stop those same creatures? How do I make it safe for my son?

A sudden flash of sunlight interrupted his musings as the lead Hummer broke out of the underbrush and onto the edge of a river. The Milk River was eighty to a hundred feet across, a sluggish, green-brown ribbon of water, similar to most of the rivers around Columbus where Morehouse had grown up. On the other hand, that meant it was wide and deep enough for the devil rays to hide in.

Morehouse stepped out of the idling truck and carefully walked to the edge of the river. The jungle loam sloped down in a muddy belt to the water's edge. To his right, he could just make out the first bend. There were several more before the river broke out onto the beach to meet the unimaginatively named Milk River Bay. He pulled out his walkie-talkie and clicked it on. "Secure the hummers. Alpha and Bravo teams dismount. Assignments to follow." He released the switch and waited.

Within moments, the vehicles were quiet, and the two teams assembled. Morehouse laid out one of the maps and pointed to the opposite side of the river. "Bravo team. Go ahead and ford the river with your hummer. Track back to about here. I think you can cross there. Don't go all the way to the resort if you can help it. Again, we don't want to be seen or if we are, stopped for questions. Once you return, each team will continue to this point." He marked a spot about half a mile from the river's mouth.

"Leave the Hummers, and march on foot. Patrol to the beach and then three miles away from the river with the river to your back. Members will all carry at least four fully loaded magazines besides the one in your rifle, two frag grenades, a cattle prod, and at least one additional battery, and one member to carry the 590A1. Use solid slug. I don't want someone catching a stray or just pissing these things off. Remember, the more firepower we put into these bastards the more likely we are to go home unhurt. Leave the scuba gear in the trucks. Once we find the pack, we can kill it. Then we can search for the nest. Based on the reports, the supernaturals will most likely hit us while we're on land. It's the nest that will be underwater. No sense in burdening ourselves with gear that won't help in the main fight." The marines nodded. Extra weight made for harder fights and faster exhaustion.

"Also remember, fade if you see civilians. Use the radios if you need, but minimize how long you are on. Safety and silence. Go weapons hot."

The silent marines all nodded. A series of thunks and clicks followed the order. Every one of them had at least one supernatural kill under their belt. They had also all seen other unfortunate men die at the hands of creatures from the beyond. A weapon on safe was a poor club rather than a ranged asset.

"No one gets it on my watch. Oorah?"

"Oorah!"

"Bravo, we will wait for your return."

Forty minutes later Alpha team waited at the deployment spot. The second hummer pulled through the screen of bushes across the river and Bravo team fell out. Everyone performed final weapons checks. The sun was an hour or so from the horizon.

Hunting time, Morehouse thought as he gave hand signals for Bravo and Alpha to start their respective patrols. The loudest sounds were the insects buzzing in the late afternoon light. The scent of rotting vegetation clung to their noses. Alpha team ranged out, Riley taking point with his rifle at the ready and Hubbard covering the rear with the shotgun. Morehouse and Johansson were in the middle. Each man scanned his sector, paying particular attention to the water. The angle of the sun prevented being able to see into the water, just a shimmer of light. How that light moved was very important. No telltale V-shaped wakes. Yet.

The team broke out of the jungle and onto the khaki-white sands of the Jamaican shoreline. Small waves broke in hushed tones against the fine sand. Then the same water whispered its way back to the ocean, leaving a smoothed surface of wet sand in its wake. The only motion was a few tiny crabs playing in the surf and a lonely gull calling above them. Bravo team turned southeast as Alpha followed the tree line to the northwest.

An hour passed, the sun leisurely sinking into the ocean to the west. The sky changed from the bright blue of afternoon into the mauves and pale oranges of early evening. Morehouse checked his map. The team was coming up on the turn-around point.

"Alpha, Bravo actual. We have encountered a trio of SNs. Engaging, over." The sound of controlled gunfire crackled over the channel while the team lead was reporting.

Morehouse keyed his mic. "Roger. Inform at end of engagement. Alpha actual, out." He hand-signaled a halt, and the team stopped. Everyone scanned their sector, rifles pointed towards the waves and keeping a close eye on the water for any warning of attack. Nothing changed except the shape of each wave as it crashed quietly on the beach.

Off in the distance Alpha team could hear the *pop pop pop* of Bravo engaging with their rifles. A moment later came the deeper boom of the 590A1 shotgun. The rifle fire stopped, and then started up again. Everyone continued to watch the water but kept an ear open for the gunfire and radio.

Another pause in the rifle fire. Seconds later the radio crackled to life. "Alpha, Bravo Actual."

"Alpha Actual…Go. Over"

"Three SNs KIA. No wounded. All friendlies accounted for and safe. Request to continue patrol. Over."

"Roger on three KIAs, no WIAs, no friendlies hurt. Continue patrol and keep your eyes open. There are still several more SNs unaccounted for. Alpha over."

"Continue patrol and keep eyes open. Roger. Bravo out."

Morehouse replaced the radio on his hip and waved for the team to resume their patrol. "As I told Bravo, keep your eyes peeled. We're now in the normal hunting time for these things."

Alpha team arrived at the end of the patrol range and turned around. The team paused and drank from their canteens before starting the slow hike back. The three miles were not arduous, but they had been maddeningly boring. The constant watching of the waves had threatened to lull the team to complacency, so Morehouse had taken to swapping zones of concern around the team every fifteen minutes. This prevented any single marine from staring at the same sector and becoming so comfortable with it that they failed to notice any changes.

The current assignment for Corporal Johansson was the oceanward rear sector. He called out, "Motion in the water behind."

Morehouse immediately stopped the team. They crouched, rifles aimed towards the water, and backs to each other.

Morehouse keyed his radio. "Bravo, Alpha actual. Possible movement in water…"

An explosion of water behind the team cut off the remainder of his report. Johansson's controlled firing in semi-automatic gave a steady *pop pop* pause *pop pop*. A quick glance over his shoulder showed Morehouse that eight rays had taken flight to attack the team.

"Eight targets rear. All engage."

As one, the other members of Alpha team spun and took bead on the flying monstrosities. Riley covered the mid-level flyers while Morehouse and Hubbard engaged two higher-flying creatures. The eight were swarming towards Johansson.

One of Morehouse's rounds caught a ray through the left wing, causing it to cry out and spiral down into the wet sand. It began a humping motion to move towards the prey. Morehouse fired three more rounds into the creature and waited to see if it was still moving. After four or five seconds of no motion, he returned his attention to the rest of the firefight.

Riley shifted to full auto for a magazine and shot all thirty rounds into a tight cluster of five devil rays that were flocking just past the edge of the waves. Several rounds impacted bodies and three of the five creatures flopped into the ocean's edge, apparently dead or wounded past the capability of flight. The corporal ejected the spent magazine, allowing it to drop to the sand near his feet, and slammed a full magazine into the well. He shifted back to semi-automatic to engage the remaining two rays.

One of the rays wheeled past Johansson's rifle and slammed into the corporal's head, biting at his helmet with its huge mouth. The sudden weight caused Johansson to lose his balance and he fell to the ground, rolling to keep his rifle barrel from plugging with sand. The creature continued biting the helmet, tearing the fabric cover, and gouging the ballistic plastic beneath. One lucky bite sliced through the material of the chinstrap, and the creature ripped the helmet from covering his head. Johansson screamed in agony as the devil ray's teeth plunged into the back of his scalp and began peeling the skin from his cranium.

"Shit…Riley, cover me!" Morehouse dropped his rifle, letting the friction strap hold it to his body, and grabbed for the cattle prod in its loops on his back. The bright yellow and orange length of plastic and metal slid free, and Morehouse thumbed the power switch. The twin prongs emitted a faint hum, and he could feel the trembling vibration of the powered tool. He lunged forward and jabbed the twin prongs between the wide-spaced eyes of the monster. Holding down the switch, he pushed the prod downward. Bright blue arcs of plasma spread out from the contact points. The creature's eyes widened in pain or surprise as its body attempted to contract in on itself. The scent of ozone was strong in the air.

The ray flopped bonelessly off Johansson's head and slithered onto the wet sand.

"Hubbard, shotgun!" Morehouse said as he dropped the stun weapon and pulled his rifle back into position. He could see a lone ray wheeling near Riley and a pair that had gained altitude. Aiming carefully, he fired three rounds into the ray nearest the team. It screamed once and plunged into the ocean, the impact raising a gout of blue-white water. The creature floated to the surface, a purple stain expanding from it in the water.

Hubbard fired one more time at one of the remaining rays that was flying around, searching for a good opening.

It flopped to the ground. He then released his rifle and unslung the shotgun in a fluid motion. He stepped forward three paces, placed the barrel against the upper section of the ray, and pulled the trigger. The wet sand absorbed most of the blast, but the sound was a palpable impact to everyone. The ray twitched once, then stilled. Blue-purple blood leaked from the hole the shell had blown in the creature and sluggishly soaked into the sand. Johansson lay on his side, one hand pushing against the flap of scalp the ray had torn free. Blood oozed around his fingers and dripped to the ground.

"Hang on…You got this man," Hubbard said calmly as he cycled the pump and dropped to a knee next to his squad mate. He scanned the darkening sky and fired a slug toward a ray as it passed overhead. The shot missed. He cycled the pump action again.

Morehouse slammed a third magazine into his rifle and took aim at the ray now skimming in ground effect just above the darkening ocean. The white stripes seemed to merge with the ocean foam in the twilight, making accurate tracking of the creature difficult. His first few rounds were off, but they caused the ray to jockey, making the stripes run perpendicular to the waves and thus easier to see. Morehouse's next two rounds found their target and the ray pinwheeled across the water, a wingtip catching a wave as it dipped from blood loss.

Having reloaded, Riley brought his rifle back into action. He took his time and breathed, tracking the final ray as it wheeled around and headed back to the safety of the ocean. Once it had finished its ground loop, Riley fired four times. All four rounds struck the creature. The two wings folded towards its belly and the devil ray dropped like a stone from the heavens.

Silence descended suddenly. The only sounds were the faint noise of contracting metal from the cooling casings, a mild breeze in the trees, and the shushing of waves. The three marines looked at each other and then around at the carnage. The rays lay crumpled where they fell, blue-purple blood staining the sands and water around them. Shell casings were scattered across the fight zone, gleaming red-gold in the dying light of the sunset. A hidden bird cautiously called, then burst into song.

Morehouse checked his watch. The entire firefight had taken less than five minutes. "Riley, help Johansson. Hubbard, you have watch. I'll make the report." He keyed his radio. "Bravo, Alpha actual."

"Go Alpha Actual. Over."

"Eight rays KIA, no WIA. One marine WIA. Corporal Johansson injured and in possible need of medivac. No other injuries. Over"

"Roger Alpha. We are about halfway back to our vehicle. Once we arrive, we will head your way for pickup. Over."

"Roger Bravo. Alpha out."

Morehouse put the radio away and kneeled next to Riley. Riley had wrapped Johansson's head in a gauze bandage, but the bright white cloth was quickly staining red. "His pupils are pretty dilated. I think that he got dosed with the poison. Well, he's also in shock. Additionally, he isn't bleeding as fast as I might fear for this kind of scalp wound. The rays may have a blood coagulator in their saliva as well as venom. I can't tell here. Medical could probably tell us." Riley had dragged the semi-conscious marine to the jungle's edge and carefully propped him against a tree. He also wrapped a belt around Johansson and the tree, ensuring the wounded man could not fall over.

John nodded. "Bravo is going to drive here once they get back to the vehicles. While we're waiting, we need to police this area. Can't have some local stumbling across one of the rays and sending it to the local fish scientists." Morehouse waved Hubbard back over. "Usual cleanup pattern. Brass and magazines in one sack, the biologicals sealed in plastic and then put into another sack."

The three men first scoured the beach for all the expended shells and magazines, throwing them all into a small canvas bag that Morehouse had been carrying. Next, they unfolded and laid out two large industrial-grade sheets of plastic. They carefully manhandled each of the six dead rays onto plastic. Riley remained ashore with Johansson while Morehouse and Hubbard waded into the surf. Minutes later, they struggled ashore, dragging the two remaining carcasses. The pair of marines laid the bodies next to the other six and wrapped the plastic over them, taping the seams and folds with silver duct tape.

"Use number two hundred and fifteen. Sealing dead supernatural creatures in sandwich bags." Riley made a hobby of notating all the ways that the Marines could and had used duct tape. He actually pulled out a small green notepad and jotted the use down. Hubbard just shook his head and continued taping the plastic shut. Already the dead creatures had begun giving off a pungent, rotten fish smell. They doubled up on the material to prevent any leakage of smell or fluids.

Riley stepped over to Johansson and checked his vitals. Johansson moaned a bit but other than that remained comatose. "Breathing is good but a little shallow. His heart rate is still elevated, could be the venom or toxin from the bite, could be shock. Pupils remain dilated." He stuck a thermometer under Johansson's tongue, maintaining a grip on it to prevent the man from accidentally swallowing it. "Temp is just over ninety-nine degrees. That also could be from the creature's bite or simply increased temp due to the damage. I can't tell for certain since I'm not a doc, just our partially trained emergency medic. I'd say he's stable enough for us to move."

Morehouse thought it over for a minute. He shook his head negatively. "We'll wait for Bravo to get here in the HUMVEE. I don't want us encumbered by him and the rays if we get attacked again. Plus, we can sit him fully upright and strap him in to keep the bleeding down to a minimum. We still have the nest or nests to find."

The radio crackled. "Alpha, Bravo. Over"

"Alpha actual. Over"

"We are at the vehicle and heading your way. ETA is approximately ten minutes. Over."

"Roger Bravo. See you then. Over and out."

Chapter Four

Milk River Bay, Clarendon, Jamaica
18 November 1986
1913 EST / 0013 Zulu
Milk River Bay Beach

Morehouse heard the rumble of the HUMVEE before he spotted it coming around the bend. Bravo was keeping close to the water line to minimize leaving tracks that the tide would not destroy. He maintained a guard posture as the vehicle drew up alongside Alpha team.

Without looking away from his perimeter sweep, he said, "Get Johansson loaded. We want to keep him upright to minimize bleeding so make sure you strap him in well. I'll maintain the perimeter while you guys get him loaded. Afterward, we reconfigure the teams for searching out these damn nests."

A chorus of ayes rumbled from the truck and the marines dismounted, already scrambling to set up a place to strap the wounded man in. It took a few minutes to move Johansson from the tree to inside the HUMVEE and get him strapped upright. Riley was next to him, making sure that the bandages were still in place and that Johansson did not pass out. Corporal Grizzle pulled a saline bag out of the emergency kit and got it strung up. Riley ran the line and set the IV in Johansson's left arm. He had no idea of the extent of possible damage that the ray had done and was unwilling to take any chances with his patient. Fluids would help a bit with blood loss.

Sergeant Wade, Bravo team lead, waved Corporal Hanzo to cover the area and walked over to Morehouse. "Johansson is in the truck and Riley has him ready. I went ahead and cross-loaded your dive gear into our HUMVEE, so we can gear up and go after the nest as soon as you are ready."

"So, keep Riley and Johansson here while we go swimming for funsies?"

Wade grinned. "Something like that. I figure that after we destroy the nest, none of us are going to feel like hiking several miles through the dark, mosquito-infested jungle when we could ride."

"I can agree with that point," Morehouse said, returning the grin. He pointed at the scrapes in the sand where they had wrapped up the dead creatures. "I think we will head out to sea from here. Swim past the breakwater and then start searching. Tanks will be good for just over an hour of searching and one, maybe two, deep dives to check things out. We can only cover so much ground with the six of us, so two of us, a sergeant and a corporal, will start here. The other four take the HUMVEE down about a mile towards the river, split into two groups, and head into the water to start there. We are all going to be sweeping towards the river. I am hoping the nest is on this side of the river since we saw a higher concentration of rays here. That's just a guess on my part though."

"I can't really see any major holes in your logic though," Sergeant Wade said. "I'll take Hanzo and head down the beach. I'll leave you Clink since he has more time in the water than the rest of us. That puts Hubbard and Bear together. If all else fails, I figure Bear can haul all of us out."

"Sounds good. Let's unload the tanks and fins and get ready to splash about."

Ten minutes later, Morehouse and Corporal "Clink" Gustav had stripped down to simple swim gear, hitched a double scuba tank with regulator onto their backs, side pouches carrying explosives and detonators, and were waddling around in large black rubber fins. They could feel the day's heat leeching out of the sand into their feet. The sun was well below the horizon now, the sky a pale mauve that darkened to deep purple in the west. The men kept the regulators out of their mouths and their masks on their foreheads.

"Wade, Clink, and I are ready. We will meet the truck in an hour or so about a mile and a half up the coast. Be careful out there. This is prime time for sharks to be hunting. Also, just set the explosives. We will detonate from land. I do not want any of us in the water when they go off. Any questions?"

The five conscious men in the HUMVEE shook their heads. Morehouse gave them a thumbs-up sign and turned to Clink.

"Let's do this." He began walking into the sun-warmed waters of the Caribbean and through the waves. Once the waves were high enough that they were striking his chest, he motioned for the two of them to lower their facemasks and start using the regulators. Morehouse verified that Clink was ready with hand signals. The two dove through the next incoming wave and began stroking for the breakwater, a swim of about two hundred and fifty feet.

Clink, longer in the arms than Morehouse, slowly passed him and then maintained a pace to keep the two swimmers in close proximity. Breakers batted floating debris around in the water, keeping it trapped in the wave zone. Once the pair cleared the point where the breakers hit, the water cleared up. The sand was a pale blue beneath them, rapidly darkening as the light from above faded away. Each man checked his depth gauge and chronometer. They were currently averaging thirty feet underwater and were fifteen minutes into the dive.

Morehouse kept a careful watch for the telltale glow of the nest as well as any predators. The devil rays would have killed any of the large predators like sharks or barracuda, but they could not be certain that the teams had killed all the devil rays. Moonglow began filtering down through the water once the sun had fully set. The colors disappeared into a monochromatic palate of blues. Nocturnal fish, having stayed hidden in the soft sand and rock crevices, began flitting around the two men, nibbling at hands and fins.

Clink tapped Morehouse on the shoulder. Morehouse paused in his swim, treading water to maintain location. The corporal pointed out towards the deeper water and downward. A faint glow emanated from a patch of seagrass about forty feet down. Morehouse nodded as he caught sight of the glow. The two marines rotated in the water and swam towards the light. The color shifted from blue to blue-green the closer they got.

The seagrass, thirteen to fifteen inches in height, waved in the current and obscured any good view of the light emitter. Gustav pulled his dive knife and cut away the upper sections of the waving grasses, leaving the cut stems to float away in the mild current. In a depression the size of a loaf of bread were several black leather-clad egg cases, each emitting a soft blue-green glow.

Morehouse signaled for Gustav to turn around. The corporal gently spun in place, presenting his carry pack to

Morehouse. He reached inside and withdrew four M112 blocks of C4 plastic explosives and then packed the grey clay-like explosive over the top of the nest. Morehouse held out his hand and waited for Gustav to pass him the detonators. Gustav pulled a set of detonation cords and blasting caps out of Morehouse's pack and passed them to him. Morehouse carefully grasped each of the bricks as he pressed a blasting cap into it. He then carefully unwound the connector ends of the forty-foot detcord and ensured that they were firmly and properly attached to the blasting caps. Morehouse hooked the free ends into a board, feeling the click as each wire locked into place. The board connected to a small self-inflating rubber bladder by a thick plastic loop. Morehouse nodded to Gustav and the corporal pulled the pin on the inflator. With a rush of bubbles, the white float inflated and pulled towards the surface. A red light began blinking inside the semi-transparent float, indicating that the radio receiver was now active. Gustav released the floatation device and receiver and Morehouse played out the wires, making sure that they were not tangled or pulled free.

Moments later the receiver was floating neutrally about ten feet below the surface. The wires were taut, but not pulling. Morehouse and Gustav back finned slowly from the nest. Once they were far enough away to prevent jarring anything, the pair flipped over and swam for shore.

Gulls cried overhead in the warm evening air as the two marines emerged from the waves. Morehouse lifted his mask and scanned the water. The red blinking signal was invisible, the light fully swallowed by dark waters. He drew his radio out from its waterproof pouch.

"Bravo, Alpha actual."

"Go Alpha."

"We found the nest and are hot. Are you safe?"

"We are parked at the mile-and-a-half marker. How far down coast are you?"

"I don't think we swam more than a half mile at most. I am going to set this off. When you hear the explosion, head in our direction. Alpha out."

"Roger. We will be listening."

Corporal Gustav had stripped out of his tank and assisted Morehouse out of his. The two men walked back to the tree line. Morehouse pulled a small radio transmitter/receiver with a safety switch from his side pack. The telltale on the receiver glowed a solid green.

"Fire in the hole," Morehouse stated as he unpinned the safety switch and depressed it. The telltale blinked in rapid time.

There was a muted thump and a geyser of white-green water out past the breaker line. The water splashed back down in a micro rainstorm around the blast area. The telltale on the detonator was now dark.

"That should have taken care of the nest." Gustav commented as he watched the ripples from the explosion spread.

"Five pounds of C4. I would think so. That much explosive would rupture a whale, let alone a couple of leather-clad egg cases. I think we can safely state in the after-action report that the nest was destroyed. However, Bravo team will need to perform an independent verification before we can call it a night."

Twenty-two miles east-northeast of Norfolk Naval Base
19 November 1986
1117 EST/1617 Zulu
USS *Sea Devil* (SSN 664)

The submarine broke through the class three seas at thirty degrees against the waves. Bright white water shattered against the bow, foam boiling across the exposed black hull and racing aft to split at the intersection of the sail and the ship. Frigid spray reached higher than the top of the sail, causing the fine cold mist to drizzle down in the late morning sun. Commander William Owens could feel the 3,800-ton vessel shudder each time it plowed into one of the waves. He wiped a hand across his eyes to clear them and twisted, looking over his shoulder to the men down on the deck aft of the sail. The COB had previously assured him that only the most capable and experienced sailors were topside to handle this transfer. Each of the men wore a bright orange Mae West life vest and had a safety line clipped into the rail groove running the length of the submarine. They waited patiently for the tugboat carrying the SEALs to arrive, rocking with the motion of the ship under their feet. Two of the men were smoking cigarettes, their exhaled white puffs of smoke fading quickly in the cold November wind. The topside group was obviously ready.

Reflexively brushing a few stubborn drops from the visor of his baseball cap, Owens returned his gaze to the men with him in the sail. A fine layer of water droplets coated each sailor, gleaming with a diamond-like sheen, as they stood their watches, shivering slightly in the cold. The top of the *Sea Devil*'s sail was a claustrophobe's horror room, three feet across with walls barely reaching mid-chest, leading to an acrophobic nightmare of a three-story drop with no safety rails. He and three other sailors shoehorned themselves into the tiny space. A fourth sailor, the lead phonetalker, was not even inside the sail. His position was sitting on top of the sail, nestled between the number one and number two periscopes while the lookout, the Main Propulsion Assistant, stood behind him. The two of them were wearing safety harnesses that clipped to the ship.

"Tugboat at eight o'clock," stated the lookout, scanning the horizon with a pair of binoculars. He did not stop his sweep as he called out to contact.

The CO lifted his binoculars and adjusted the focus. He could just barely make out the top of the tug's smokestack. "I make it right at six and a half miles. Good eyes Lieutenant."

The Lieutenant grinned and thanked the CO, never breaking his scan of the horizon.

"Phonetalker, request bearing to tug from sonar."

The petty officer acknowledged and passed the request below. Moments later he stated, "The approaching tug, Sierra Victor one-six-two bears two-four-six relative."

"Inform Control that we have the tug visual topside," stated the CO.

"Aye sir," replied the phonetalker and passed on the information.

Owens keyed his radio. "COB, the tug is approaching from the east, on our starboard side. Let's get ready to receive. They should be ready to tie up in about ten minutes."

"Aye aye, sir," came the reply, the COB's Maine accent coming through clearly on the radio.

William watched as the men on deck smartly wheeled around and moved into position to catch and tie off ropes from the tug. Both smokers tossed their cigarettes to the sea, the butts disappearing instantly in the roiling wake. The wind gusted suddenly, and all the men in the sail hunched down a bit and tried to tighten their coats more. The mid-November winds cut through the fabric as if it were not there. The men on deck continued to stoically rock with the ship's motion.

These kinds of unpredictable winds and heavy seas made an at-sea transfer dangerous. Everyone was aware of it and the briefings had focused heavily on what might go wrong. The safety came second only to the need to perform the actions. As much as possible had been done to make things safe, but the entire situation was inherently unsafe. Two vessels, one round-bottomed without a keel and a second designed primarily for towing were attempting to meet broadside in the winds of November in a sea state that kept most small craft in homeport. His men were trained for this work, and they would perform the job.

The tug approached, swinging about to parallel the course of the *Sea Devil*. The ship-to-ship channel crackled.

"Yankee tango bravo seven-seven-one to Efficiency, requesting permission to come alongside."

William lifted the mic and replied. "Seven-seven-one, you are cleared to come alongside. Once alongside you may tie up for transfer of goods. Efficiency on standby." He grinned as he unkeyed the microphone. He was not sure who had developed the names for the operation, but giving any Navy ship the moniker 'efficiency' was humorous. However, the orders in his stateroom were quite clear. Any unencrypted radio signals originating from the ship would only use the name Efficiency. At no time were the words submarine, naval vessel, hull number, name of ship, or any variation of those to be used in any communications.

The tug's crew all wore heavy winter coats to fight the chill, with their bright orange life jackets on the outside. They moved with purpose, checking and rechecking the positions of the grey rubber bumpers on the side of the ship. The bumpers were precautions against contacting the hull of the submarine. The tug's captain adjusted the throttles on the heavy diesel engines, surging the ship ahead and then retarding it back to zigzag nearer and nearer to the best position alongside. Five minutes of maneuvering and the ships were riding along at four knots with less than ten feet separation.

With keen interest, William watched one of his sailors' topside coil and toss yellow rope with an orange rubber ball attached across the gap. The man had judged the wind perfectly, and what had appeared to be a throw out past the tug instead landed elegantly into the gloved hands of another sailor waiting on the tug. The catcher pulled more of the rope across and then tied the ball end around the pillar of a transfer gantry.

Two other sailors on the submarine's hull unrolled an orange and black ladder, sending it over the side. Nicknamed a Jacob's ladder after the item in the Bible, the flexible rope ladder would provide firm purchase for the men transferring from the tug.

Onboard the tug *Keokuk*, a chief petty officer turned on the crane and verified everything green. He contacted the tug's captain and got permission to begin swinging the gantry into position. The gantry connected directly to the tug with a pillar and a set of steps. There was a guide rail along one side of the gantry. The gantry itself was made of steel mesh over a pair of girders to allow for drainage. The steel walkway pivoted on the pillar and the crane operator slacked up, allowing the gantry to swing out and approach the ninety-degree position.

Two sailors on the submarine guided the ten-foot construction until it was perpendicular to the hull. They held it in position as a sailor on the tug inserted the holding pins to lock the gantry in place. As soon as the last pin slipped into place, he flashed a thumbs-up sign. The tug's captain radioed that the gantry was locked and ready to transfer personnel and goods.

"Roger YTB, commence transfer of personnel and cargo. All personnel have permission to come aboard."

Five SEALs, dressed in the same jungle-style camouflage that the ground forces wore, came onto the tug's deck, each helping to carry one of the large bundles of gear that needed transferred. First one, then a second SEAL carefully made their way across the metal gantry, gracefully accepting the hand of the submarine sailor at the other end. The submarine was riding the waves sideways to minimize spray, though this ended up causing significant motion between the two vessels. Sailors on both decks braced as one vessel rose and the other vessel dropped. Once aboard the sub, both SEALs hooked in lifelines that were already locked onto the deck safety track.

"Efficiency, YTB. Significant motion between the vessels. It is outside of the allowable usage parameters for the deck crane. Recommend we shift to passing cargo by hand and rope."

Captain Owens thought a moment, his brain ticking through the possible outcomes. "YTB, Efficiency. Agreed. Your crew has lead for transfer." He clicked off the radio and turned to the phonetalker. "Inform COB that plans have changed. The cargo transfer will be by man and rope. Seas are too heavy to trust the crane."

The phonetalker repeated the command and then passed it to the topside phonetalker.

"COB acknowledges and agrees, Captain."

William nodded in quick reply and focused on the aft of the submarine as the men prepared to move the white cargo bags across.

The SEALs remaining on the tug carefully tied the handles of large white canvas bags together and then ran a pulley line around a metal station on the tug. They then tossed the free end across the gantry, allowing the two SEALs on the sub to gather up the remaining rope.

"On three. One, two, three." As the last word rang out, the two groups of SEALs lifted their ropes simultaneously, drawing the first white bag into the air. They carefully pulled the ropes, sliding the heavy bag across the gantry without it touching the metal floor. Once it arrived, the submarine crew took control of the bag, untied it from the transfer rope, and maneuvered it to the forward personnel hatch. More crewmembers stood by on the ladder inside the submarine ready to carefully move the unwieldy container into the hull.

The tug team drug the transfer rope back and the entire procedure repeated with the second and third bags. The SEAL commander was next, carefully crossing the gantry, one hand on the rail the whole time. His lead NCO followed next.

The seas were beginning to worsen, the wind and waves both rising. The two vessels were struggling to maintain a safe distance between themselves in the heavy seas. The gantry slammed into the topside of the submarine, bouncing hard against the anti-sonar rubberized coating, and gouging black paint away.

The junior SEAL carefully began his crossing. A wave caught the submarine, the trough lowering the boat unexpectedly nearly fifteen feet. Two of the sailors lost their hold on the gantry ropes. The ropes flapped freely in the wind, just out of reach above the hands of the struggling sailors. As the wave passed, the submarine rose suddenly and slammed into the bottom of the gantry. The impact knocked the crossing SEAL off his feet. He grabbed onto the handrail, holding hard as his feet flew out from under him. He hit the gantry deck with his hip, bouncing on the grated metal, but held onto the rail, preventing a plunge into the ocean.

No one noticed the vibrations causing one of the locking pins to back out. The continued back-and-forth movement of the gantry sheared the pin's head off. Only a single thin piece of metal held the gantry in place.

There was a short lull between waves. The junior SEAL pulled himself to his feet and continued his crossing. Metal swayed unpredictably beneath his feet, forcing him to grip the safety rail as moved. Sailors topside on the sub continued trying to gain control of the safety ropes and bring the gantry back to the submarine's deck with little effect. The crossing SEAL felt the gantry stop moving. He took a quick look around. The tug had moved away from the submarine, leaving the gantry gapped halfway between the two vessels, pointing into the open water.

There's no way I can make that jump. I'll have to wait until the gantry swings back toward the ship. He gathered himself together, bunched up and ready to perform a running jump as soon as the end of the gantry pointed towards the submarine.

The tug side slipped in the water, moving back towards the submarine. Using the boat hook, one of the sailors on the *Sea Devil*'s deck snagged a guide rope while another grabbed the free end. All the sailors, SEALs, and crew alike, raced forward to assist. They strained, dragging the end of the gantry back towards themselves. Explosive grunts and wheezes cut through the wave noise as they pulled the gantry, inch by inch, back into place.

As soon as the junior SEAL saw the deck of the submarine crossing the end of the gantry, he exploded into action. His legs pistoned, driving him toward the open end of the metal.

One of the SEALs topside called out, "Come on Hughes, you can make it."

Hughes leaped, arms outstretched, and slammed into the curved side of the submarine. He felt his leg and foot twist under himself as he scrambled to pull himself up. Cold black water slapped his ankles and lower legs. Hughes struggled, his flailing right arm connecting with the orange steps of the Jacob's Ladder. He wrapped his arm around the rung, halting his slip back into the ocean. Hands reached down and pulled him up. With half-focused eyes he saw the tug pulling away, the gantry twisting with its free end dragging in the heavy seas. The crew helped him down the personnel ladder gently, attempting to keep both his foot and arm from banging into the valve-studded walls.

William keyed the mic as soon as he saw the SEAL land and the tug peel away. "YTB, Efficiency. Any casualties or further damage?"

"Efficiency, YTB. No casualties. Damage to the transfer gantry and some scraped paint. How is the last man across?"

William turned to his phonetalker. "Status of the last SEAL?"

The phonetalker passed the request, holding his left headphone against his ear to catch the reply. "COB says that he twisted his ankle. Doesn't look like a break but the Doc is standing by to check once they get him belowdecks."

"Roger," stated the CO, then keyed the mic. "YTB, Efficiency. No major injuries. Possible twisted ankle is all."

William could hear the relief in the tug captain's voice. "That's great. Hate that anyone got hurt. We're lucky that things weren't any worse with this weather."

"Agreed YTB. Safe voyage. Efficiency out."

The captain looked around. The COB had cleared the deck, and the forward escape trunk hatch was closing, only a thin line showing light from below. As he watched, the hatch came flush with the deck. "Crew's mess reports that all topside personnel and transferees safely below. The upper and lower hatches are dogged," stated the phonetalker. He was completely hunched into his jacket, only the tops of his headset sitting above the lifted collar.

"Acknowledged," said William. He waved to the men in the sail with him. "Topside team, break down the sail. Everyone else head below. Phonetalker, inform control that OOD has the con."

"OOD has the con, aye."

The CO grabbed the rungs and climbed back into the interior of the submarine. At the bottom of the interior ladder, he stepped into the cramped control room. "OOD, have the SEAL commander meet me in my stateroom in five minutes. Also, have the mess decks send up a pot of coffee and two mugs."

"Aye, aye sir."

Submarines are, by design, space-limited ships of war. There are no large spaces on a submarine for people, and the CO's stateroom was no exception. It constituted the largest living space on board, nearly ten feet wide and eleven feet long, with a low ceiling and two walls that leaned inward. The bed folded into the wall and a small table folded out of the bed's bottom. There were two chairs built into the wall that both supported the bed and performed duties as head and footboard when it folded out. On the aft wall was a tiny closet, barely large enough for five or six uniforms, a fold-down desk with a typewriter, and three locking drawers. A chair, which currently was locked into the deck, stood in front of the desk. Finally, a washbasin and faucet flanked the door to the head the CO shared with the XO.

William shrugged out of his coat and hung it up on a hook mounted on the back of his door. The jacket was soaked from the sea spray. It would have to fully dry before he put it away in his uniform locker. He unlocked the small safe above his desk and removed the special orders that Admiral Reager had sent.

There was a knock on the door. "Come."

A sailor in fatigues opened the door, ducking his head slightly as he stepped through. He was not much taller than five eleven, but the doorframe was shorter than he was used to. The officer drew himself to attention and stated, "Lieutenant Commander Harris reporting as requested sir."

"Glad to have you and your team aboard, Commander. Please sit down." William waved to the three other seats in the room. Harris chose the one that put his back to the only corner in the room where he could see both doors.

William chuckled inwardly. *They never change. Always on alert, even when things are completely safe for them.*

"Coffee will be here in a moment. Then we can discuss the orders. Currently, only your team and I are aware of the mission. I'll need to inform a few members of the crew when we get closer to the. . ." He broke off as another person knocked on the door.

"Yes?"

"Captain sir? I have your coffee." The CO opened the door and a gangly sailor in a white apron and hat bustled in. He carried a coffee pot, two mugs, and a plate of chocolate chip cookies. "Compliments of the duty cook sir." The mess specialist set the items on the fold-down table and glanced expectantly at the captain.

"Thank you, Seaman Wylie. Please pass my thanks to the duty cook as well."

The seaman beamed and backed out, closing the door behind him.

William poured a mug of coffee and passed it to Harris, then poured himself one. "Have a cookie. They are some of the best you will ever have."

Harris took one and sipped the coffee. He waited for the captain to continue.

"Our orders are to locate the asset carrying two items. One is a physical item, codename Paladin. The other is a person operating under the codename Flute." William opened the brightly labeled folder and spread the pages out. "Once we have a solid track, we are to maintain proximity to the asset. Flute will signal us during the run when he is ready to transfer. We are to, at your readiness, deploy your team via one of the escape trunks to recover Paladin and Flute. This will be an underwater recovery for the two items and your team. No one on the asset is to see anything beyond possibly Flute entering the water. Planned extraction time is afternoon. The orders have a section on timelines based on when Flute starts the transmission.

The assets we will be tracking is a Soviet AGI trawler." The CO pulled out a blurry black-and-white photo from the folder and passed it to Harris. "It is specifically built to track US submarines. My job is to make sure it never realizes there is a submarine for it to track. The remainder of the orders detail how you and your team will recover Paladin and Flute without the trawler having any proof or even suspicion that Paladin or Flute were recovered." He handed the order package to Harris, keeping the portion that pertained only to the submarine. "Can your men do that?"

Harris nodded as he took the folder, then spoke. "We will remain below water the entire time. No lights. I will brief you further once I have had a chance to review the orders. My team and I will finalize our plans for retrieval and return of both the item and person to the submarine. What is the cover story?"

Williams waved a hand. "Your team is here for workups. We will give you a chance to exit and reenter the submarine a couple of times before catching up to the asset. In a bit of *deus ex machina* you will find an imperiled sailor in distress during your final workup dive. We will then isolate the individual and make haste back to port."

Chapter Five

Atlantic Ocean, 236 miles east of Halifax, Nova Scotia
19 November 1986
2006 EST/0106 Zulu
AGI *Zhiqulesk*

Night is a horrible time to perform a transfer at sea. The waves tend to be stronger and there was little to no ambient light to see by. The trawler bobbed in the ocean, each swell tossing the vessel in a chaotic manner. Ulyana Kruglov stood with two other sailors, cold and wet, waiting to throw the fender bollards over the side of the ship. They gripped the slick metal railing and looked about blankly. Since they had the fenders at the ready, they knew they must be meeting another vessel but had no idea what vessel or when.

Ulyana glanced cautiously about, trying to keep any sense of curiosity off her face. She had been on the *Zhiqulesk* for most of a year and seemed to be trusted. The several interviews she had undergone with both the KGB and the GRU had all gone well, indicating her loyalty to the State.

If they hadn't, then I'm positive that I would no longer be aboard the god-forsaken vessel. They would have dragged me away for interrogation, followed quite likely by a massive headache about the size of a .45 caliber bullet.

She continued to keep her face neutral as she thought about what she was doing here. *Protecting the nation from all threats. Especially threats of the nature of destruction. The Soviets get their hands on this, and their weapons get better. Maybe even good enough to kill American ships. Or worse, make the Soviets think that their equipment is good enough to start a war that they cannot win.*

I hope that my information is correct, and the package really is Paladin. If it's not, then who knows where Paladin ended up, who has it, and what is going to really be done with it.

Her mind unconsciously drifted back almost two decades earlier, to the late summer of 1968. She had turned eight years old that August. She could remember the sun on her face, the tiny white and yellow flowers decorating a windowsill, and the cake her babička had baked for her birthday. It held eight candles, was a mix of chocolate and vanilla batters, and decorated with a chaotic whirl of green and blue frosting. That birthday was the last real memory she had of happiness living in Prague.

Her mother had gathered Mikoslava and her brothers, one morning in late August and raced out of the city. All their mother would tell them was they were taking a train ride south, to visit friends. The two young boys were excited. They had never ridden a train and were looking forward to the adventure. Mikoslava sensed something more beneath the surface, something that meant her mother was not telling the whole truth. She also understood, even at the age of eight, that anything she asked would lead to bigger problems. Instead, she kept those thoughts to herself and assisted as best she could with her younger siblings, making sure they were ready and focused on the upcoming ride. She had no way of knowing that her mother was getting the family out of the city, fleeing ahead of the advancing Soviet army.

Her father, her dear *otec*, had stayed behind. Her mother had said he would meet them later. He never showed up, leaving Mikoslava wondering if her father had abandoned the family. Her mother refused to speak about where her father was, just that someday he would join them. It would be years before Mikoslava discovered why he had never made it out of Prague to meet them.

Like many other refugees from the invasion, Mikoslava and her family emigrated from Czechoslovakia to the United States in February of 1969, eventually settling in the tiny town of Cameron, Texas.

Mikoslava, going by the shortened name Miko, grew up on the Texas plains and eventually attended the University of Texas Austin. She majored in foreign language studies with a focus on Eastern European dialects. During her senior year, a CIA recruiter approached her with an offer to become a translator with the agency. She graduated with honors and began working as an intercept translator two days later. The fact that she was a native Czech and Russian language speaker caught the eye of several members of the Operations Department. It was while working there that she discovered what had happened to her father.

Her father, Havil Hrabal, had been a celebrated economics teacher at Charles University, the oldest college in Prague. His classes had gained a following among the younger men who saw the directions that Czechoslovakia could economically move towards. Specifically, towards a more market-driven structure rather than a system delivered from the government down. On the morning of August 21, he had become a casualty, shot by a Soviet soldier during one of the many protests against the invasion. As a result, the entire Hrabal family had been stripped of their Czech citizenship and ejected from the country.

Two years after joining the agency, Mikoslava found herself training as a deep cover insertion agent heading back into the Soviet Union under a crafted Ukrainian background and the name Ulyana Kruglov.

A shout went up from the searching man atop the wheelhouse, snapping Ulyana's thoughts back to the present. "Fishing boat on the horizon, starboard side. Signals that they are in need of assistance, taking on water."

And we are supposed to act like this was unexpected and we hadn't been called to the deck twenty minutes before he spotted the boat. Ulyana could not hear the reply from the captain. She assumed it was a positive one since she could feel the trawler coming to starboard and speeding up. The gang leader tossed away the cheap-smelling cigarette he had been smoking in the cover of one of the cranes. It bounced once on the deck and then slid through a scupper out into the water, its tip blazing momentarily in the blackness.

"Get ready, you lazy sacks. You've had enough time to smoke and check your pants to see if you still have a cock. That fishing vessel will be meeting us shortly and I know the captain expects a good show. We'll give him a good show, no? Prepare to set the fenders and be quick about it." He gestured wildly with his hands as he spoke, "I'll personally shit down the throat of anyone who causes the captain to scrape paint from the side. Then I'll hang you by your balls from the crane so you can see where to move your brush to fix the scrapped paint. So, don't mess up the paint." He paused and shaded his eyes with his right hand as if the weak moonlight were preventing him from seeing well. "Get ready." He raised his left hand. He slashed it down. "Fenders over the side."

Ulyana and the other two deckhands heaved the orange and black rubber fenders over the side. They bounced against the hull, the *booms* loud in the black night; then they floated up on the water, bumping the hull each time a wave shifted them about. Ulyana verified that her fender was properly tied off and peered over the gunwale. She could just make out the silhouette of a large fishing boat on the starboard side of the trawler. She continued to watch as the distance fell between the vessels. Now the fishing boat slipped inside the circle of lights from the trawler. It appeared to be in good shape, sitting normally on the water. She suspected that the hail for help was part of a coded signal to the captain that this was the ship carrying Paladin.

"Ahoy…Tie up ask for while fix boat?" came a poorly worded and atrociously accented Russian request.

"Toss a line to the boat," ordered the large deck manager, waving a hand. Another deckhand grabbed a coiled line and tossed it across the shallow gap between the vessels. On the fishing vessel, a blonde man caught the line and immediately tied it to the nearest deck cleat. Now the two ships were only a few feet apart, the distance maintained by the rubber fenders between them. The deckhand and another sailor heaved and slid a piece of metal gangway between the two boats, resting the far end on the fishing trawler. The metal had hardly hit the deck when the fair-haired man began walking across the gangway. He carried a green duffle slung over his left shoulder and appeared to have no concern for the lack of safety rails on the metal plank.

He glanced up at the trawler's bridge. Cupping his hands around his mouth, he shouted in poorly accented Russian "Tools to fix, request, please. Here I leave my goods payment for time, make sure to bring tools back."

The captain scowled down at the blonde man. "Yeah, yeah. Give the bag to Michel," he said and pointed at the large deckhand. "He'll take you to the tools." Michel gave a nod to the captain and ushered the blonde man into the interior of the trawler.

Ulyana watched. If Michel was taking the man to the engine room, she could probably follow easily since that was her normal watch station. She waited a minute then ducked into the dark interior, following the two men.

They *were* heading down to the engine room. She waited another few seconds before she opened the door to the compartment and stepped in. Mechanical noises filled the room, and the scent of oils, old fuel, and dirty seawater assaulted her nose. Michel glanced at her as soon as she walked through the door.

"What are you doing here Ulyana?"

"Need to see what tools they are taking. Number three is still acting up and I need to make sure that this *durak* isn't taking something that we'll need as soon as he transfers back to the boat." She paused, hoping that Michel would not be suspicious. Number three engine had been giving them trouble recently, that part was completely true.

"Fine, you watch him get the tools. I have to stow this for the captain." Michel hefted the green seabag, careful not to swing it around. In fact, he held it quite delicately.

Bingo, thought Ulyana. *They did bring the computer. Now if I can determine where Michel stows it, I can start the tracker.*

"Of course, I can watch him. Make sure he only takes what they need, and nothing that we do. Shouldn't need much to fix that capitalist boat, eh?"

Michel grinned. "True. I'm taking this with me. I'll be back in a few moments." He hefted the bag to show what he was talking about and then left through the port hatch of the engine room, opposite from how they had entered. That corridor led towards the galley and sleeping berths.

That could make finding it a bit trickier. I'll have to be on my guard.

She turned back to the fair-haired man. "What is your name?"

He stuck out his hand, a very Western gesture. She ignored the extended hand. He pulled it back slowly and smiled. "Jim…Jim O'Neil."

"Come, Jim…We will find you some tools." Ulyana turned and led him towards the tool lockers.

JTF 13 Training Facility, Jacksonville, North Carolina
20 November 1986
0721 EST/1221 Zulu
Main Training Facility

"In conclusion, you men performed extremely well. It does appear that this type of devil ray is more territorial than other versions of the species that have been seen. Good bit of intel there. Unfortunately, that intel does not mean that we were without injuries." Captain Dupree extended a hand towards Corporal Johansson, the head wound hidden beneath a thin layer of gauze tinted near the color of his skin. Angry purple bruising ringed his head just below the edge of the gauze.

"Thankfully, the injuries were survivable. As the reward for a job well done. . ."

The team groaned, knowing how the rest of the statement went.

"Settle down," growled Gunny from the back of the room.

"Everyone except Johansson is heading out tonight for Værnes Air Station. Værnes is a base just outside of Trondheim Norway. I hope you enjoyed the heat and the sun in Jamaica, because this is about the closest to the opposite climate you can find. While we have not seen many supernaturals in the extreme north, it is important that your training includes how to deal with the environment.

"NATO is holding a joint Norwegian and American Marine training exercise called Northern Roundup III. The eight of you…and yes Gunny, you get to go to sunny Norway with them, are tasked to fly out tonight and link up with the 4th Marine Amphibious Brigade. Usual cover story, your unit sent you due to missing an exercise earlier from injuries or sickness. Master Gunnery Sergeant Peck will run the cover story, so keep your ears on him. Anyone asks too much or seems to be probing too deep, send them to Gunny and he will ensure the story is set. This exercise is primarily dealing with a Soviet Arctic invasion. No other JTF 13 units will be present, so no one talks about it while there."

A chorus of "Ayes" rattled the room.

"One other thing. Sergeant Morehouse, you will be nominally in charge of this operation. The Master Gunnery Sergeant is there to fill in the spot left vacant by Johansson, but you are running the show. Think of it as 'good training'," the captain said, throwing a set of air quotes on the last words.

Morehouse grimaced but said nothing.

Captain Dupree flipped the cover off the flight map and tapped the airfield. "Starting tonight you will fly from here to Pope Air Station via a CH-47. There you will. . ."

The team pushed through the double doors leading out of the training building and walked towards the parking lot. They were on a day pass until 19:00 when they would regroup at the airfield.

"This is great," griped Hanzo. "So much for a three-day weekend or Thanksgiving. I was at least hoping to spend some quality time with my girlfriend before we headed out again."

"Nothing stopping you from doing it now," suggested Gustav.

"She's working today. Best I might hope for is to get a quickie during her lunch break. She doesn't really go in for that though."

"Well, no one claimed that the job was fair. If you wanted a normal job, you could have become a teacher," added Morehouse.

"Or a stripper," added Riley helpfully. "You know, one of those male singing strippers. I can just see you in a thong." Riley started gyrating his hips and whistling the opening notes to the song 'The Stripper'. The rest of the group broke into peals of laughter at the look on Hanzo's face.

"Shut up," Hanzo said and took a mock swing at Riley.

Morehouse paused as they reached the parking lot. "Seriously guys…Grab some relaxation. I'm hoping that this exercise will be the last until after the holidays. We're only supposed to be there for two weeks. Then we're back here in time to spend Christmas with our loved ones." He raised his hands as the others began to grumble again. "I know we're going to miss Thanksgiving. It can't be helped. The timing sucks, I won't pretend otherwise. Plus, we'd hoped for more training time here at the base.

"The captain is right though. With the way the Soviets are pushing, we could find ourselves with an outbreak somewhere we really aren't trained for. The units out of Germany have already done this exercise twice in the last three years. They're rotating to the Middle East. Rumor is some odd goings-on that direction, especially around Riyadh and Jerusalem.

"Intel thinks the most current uptick in violence is leading to some funky doings around there. Things have been crawling out of the woodwork since those assholes hit our barracks in Beirut. While we're freezing our butts off, the Stuttgart bunch will be running around in over a hundred-degree heat with no air conditioning. Don't think they will be much happier than us."

"Sarge," asked Hubbard, "what was the last thing anyone fought that far north?"

Scratching his head, he thought for a few minutes. While thinking, Morehouse opened the door to his blue Ford pickup and threw his backpack behind the seat. He turned to face the three men with him, then snapped his fingers. "Able Archer, November 1983. The exercise that the Soviets accused us of being a cover for preparing to invade them. Hah, *like* that was going to happen.

"Apparently, the exercise was so real that a few supernaturals slipped through. The major incident of the time was a tribe of ice trolls in northern West Germany. One of the Stuttgart companies was able to take them out but there were casualties. Worse, most of the casualties were civilians. Trolls hit a small town and practically wiped it off the map before any units could even be brought in. Scary stuff.

"That's the problem. Even when things seem normal, critters and others slip in from the Never-Never or other realms. We just don't know where or when the next powder keg of violence is going to happen or what might slip in during the violence. We train for everything and hope nothing happens."

There were murmurs of agreement at that statement. One thing everyone in the group had learned was supernaturals did not care what time of year it was, the weather, or in many cases the location. Once they slipped through from the Never-Never, everything went to shit. Every man on the teams had dealt with a supernatural incursion of some kind and survived before being offered recruitment into the group.

"I'll see all of you back here at 18:45. Charlie and Delta are getting the gear set up and packed. All you clowns need to worry about is personnel gear and toothbrushes. Helo will be loaded and ready for us. Take-off time is 19:30. Have fun but be ready for tonight. Which means," Morehouse paused and looked each of his men in their eyes, "no serious drinking. Crack a cold one or two, but nothing more. Now get outta here." He watched from his truck as the guys each went in different directions. He then closed his eyes and said a little prayer before turning the engine over.

John Morehouse drove off the base and through the light traffic heading through the outskirts of the city. He always had a few moments of mental discomfort when he changed his thinking from the military last name to using first names, including his own. It felt odd after days of calling everyone by their last name and ranks to say first names, even in his own head.

This early in the day, Timothy would be in school, but Marie would probably be home. He hadn't called her after the brief. Over the years the two of them had found it better for him to just show up at the house unannounced. There had been times he had called, and then been waylaid or pulled back to base. Those had caused problems. For the sake of their marriage, surprise visits home seemed to work better.

He pulled his truck into the development. It was a newer section of the suburbs, full of modest ranch-style homes built in the last ten years. A pleasant neighborhood, full of couples like John and his wife, often with one or two children. Their blue house with cream trim appeared on his right. He slowed, tapped the turn signal, and pulled onto the driveway. After shutting off the engine, he sat listening to the ticks as the engine cooled. He was nervous about going inside. It seemed to be getting harder each time he came back from a mission. Internally, he tried to smile.

I can face down a scion of a lesser deity, devil rays, and even a giant spider. Trying to figure out how I can safely explain to my wife why I won't be home for the Thanksgiving holiday, and I get really worried. Marie is going to be furious. She married me, not the Corp. He huffed. *So much for Mister Bravery.*

John shouldered his backpack and stepped out of the truck. Fifteen steps and a short climb, he rested his hand on the doorknob. He just needed to open it and get in there. He hesitated a moment more, took a quick breath, and turned the knob. Marie looked up from folding laundry on the living room table and rushed to hug John. He dropped the backpack in time to gather the dark-haired woman into his arms. She was a tiny woman, four eleven and the perfect weight. She held tight, saying nothing, just holding onto him. After a few moments, he set her back on her feet and released her.

Marie looked up at her husband. "I'm glad you're home. As usual, the command wouldn't tell us where you were or when you'd be home." Her smile lit up her face. "You're home now though. Timothy will be super excited to see you. He was just talking about wanting to throw the football around with you yesterday."

John looked at the floor and sighed. He hated the toll the job was taking on his family time.

"You're not home long, are you?"

"Got to be back at the base by six. Wheels up at seven-thirty. Probably two weeks before I am home again. I'll be here long enough to toss the football with Timothy though."

"Thanksgiving?" Marie was now frowning and had her hands balled on her petite hips. "What about my parents?"

"No. They have us scheduled to work an exercise in Norway." John wiped his hand over his face. "We knew things were going to be tough when I accepted the assignment. On the brighter side, it looks like we will be home for the entire Christmas season this year with no other long deployments until sometime mid next year. We can see if your parents will reschedule for Christmas."

Marie turned away. "They're going to my brother's place for Christmas. Anyway, it's not the long deployments that are the issue. We get word on those in plenty of time to plan. Timothy can plan. It's these sudden 'I'll just be a few days, maybe a week' deployments that are getting to us. The missed get-togethers, school plays, report cards. I, we, don't know where you are going or what you are doing.

Sometimes guys come back injured and it's a 'training accident'." Marie walked back to the couch and sat down.

"When we were with the Fifth, there weren't these kinds of training accidents all the time. You and the guys didn't just pack up suddenly and disappear for days on end. I know you think this task force is important, but it's beginning to tear our family apart." She was holding one of Timothy's tee shirts, shaking it to emphasize her point. "I think we need to look at transferring, or I think we may need to look at a divorce. I can't keep having you put me and Timothy through this."

John slumped. He knew that things had been getting bad, but he thought that he still had some time to figure things out, maybe even get some help. Counselling wasn't something that had been big until recently. In fact, many commands had thought that it showed weakness in the marine. Now both the Marines and especially JTF 13 were coming to recognize that the mental health of the soldiers was just as important, possibly more, than their physical well-being.

Marie stood back up, turning to face John. "We can't make it as a family, not like this."

He gently grasped Marie's shoulders. "When I get back, I'll get us set up with a counselor. Sit down and work through this. Figure things out."

Marie tossed the tee shirt she was holding down on the couch and collapsed into John's arms. Her voice was muffled but John could still make out what she was saying. "I am tired of this. Of trying to explain to Tim that his dad will be home. That his dad loves him. That his dad will make up missing the school play, and Halloween, and his birthday."

She leaned back in his arms and pounded on his chest in frustration. "Dammit. I don't want to be a single mother. I want us to do this together. And we can't do this together if you are always gone."

John maneuvered the two of them to the couch and sat down, Marie half sprawled across his legs. "I know sweetie. I know." He stroked her hair. "Let's get through this one. Two weeks. Then we can sit down, all of us, and figure out the best way to be a family. If that means I need to get reposted, then I will get reposted. If things are bad enough, we can look into a hardship discharge."

"I don't want you to give up your dreams though," Marie whispered, tears streaming down her face.

"This family is my dream now. If I can keep the Marines too, then I will. But I can't let them destroy us."

They sat there, holding onto each other until Timothy's bus drove up.

Værnes Airfield, Trondheim, Norway
21 November 1986
2103 CET/2003 Zulu
In Holding Pattern

The flight from North Carolina had been simultaneously boring and rough. Sixteen and a half hours with nothing to do but read, sleep, or stare at each other. Due to the weather, the ride itself had reminded Morehouse of a carriage ride he had taken years ago over a cobblestone road. The C-141 Starlifter was full of cargo, leaving only the webbed jump seats along the side for the eight marine passengers.

There is almost nothing less comfortable than a fold-down seat for a flight, thought Morehouse as he continued reading his book.

The only things to look at were the other members of his team and the cargo. For safety reasons, and because the aircraft was designed primarily as a heavy-lift cargo plane, there were no window seats. There had been no in-flight movies or first-class meals. There had not even been good-looking flight attendants. Just some MREs, a pair of Air Force staff sergeants, and a gruff technical sergeant working the cargo bay.

Morehouse had picked up a book titled *Red Storm Rising* from the PX before heading out. He had chosen it for two reasons. One was the tank on the front and the second being it looked long enough to keep his interest throughout the flight. He was about three-quarters of the way through the novel now.

He thought the story decently passible. Not many writers tried to imagine what a completely conventional European-centric campaign might look like. Everyone figured the Soviets would use nukes or chemical weapons. Not surprisingly, none of those same authors even considered supernaturals. Therefore, there were no monsters in this book, nor any of the others that did deal with nukes or chemical warfare. Not that anyone outside of a select group would think that was the biggest problem with the book. Morehouse knew from experience there was no way a conflict of that size would be without supernaturals. He heard the click of a latch and paused in his reading, slipping a bookmark between the pages.

The hatch from the crew area opened and the loadmaster stepped through. He was an older technical sergeant, grizzled, and looked like he knew his stuff. He walked to a center point in front of the cargo pallets and faced the passengers. He spoke loudly to ensure everyone could hear him over the whine of the engines and the wind outside the airframe.

"Just got an update on the weather," stated the loadmaster, his voice muffled slightly by the safety helmet he wore. "The storm has subsided a bit. The snows that were keeping us in orbit have finally cleared up some, or at least lessened to the point where the pilots can safely put this bird on the ground. Temperature currently is a balmy twenty-nine degrees Fahrenheit and winds are gusting to thirteen knots. Cloud cover is over ninety percent at eight thousand feet. This snowstorm is expected to continue through late tomorrow evening. There is another strong front expected to arrive in about forty minutes, which means there is very little time to get the plane on the deck and clear the cargo. Once the plane is on the ground, all passengers will wait until the cargo hatch is lowered and verified before exiting your seats. Which means for those of you who have never had the pleasure of performing this task, you will wait to unbuckle until I make an announcement for you marines to exit. Until then, stay strapped into your seats and out of the way. Cargo can shift during landing, and it is my job to make sure all of the cargo, you included, make it safely to the ground." The technical sergeant grinned in grim humor.

"We will be landing in approximately twenty minutes. Everyone ensure your trays are in the upright and locked positions, that all loose gear is stowed, and that, again, all of you are strapped in." He glanced around "Any questions?"

'Clink' Gustav raised a hand.

"Yes corporal?"

"How come my pillow is always colder on the bottom than the top?"

Laughter broke out across the compartment.

The technical sergeant attempted to keep a straight face. "Any pertinent questions?" He glanced across the faces. "Eighteen minutes."

The wheels on the C-141 chirped as they spun up to speed during the landing in the frigid air of Norway. The snow and ice combination made stopping the bird a difficult proposition. Morehouse could almost feel the engines strain as the pilot applied reverse thrust to slow the aircraft. The entire plane shuddered under the action, tossing the marines side to side. As the plane slowed, the shuddering stopped. The cargo compartment leaned slightly as the pilot turned the craft off the main runway and into the tarmac staging area near the hangers. The sound of the four main engines deepened as they were idled. Morehouse leaned towards the back of the plane, watching as the clamshell doors opened into the polar night and the cargo ramp lowered to the ground.

"Welcome to the freezer," stated the senior loadmaster as he passed back to the marines. "Current local time is 21:42, but the clouds are pretty thick. The sun won't rise until 08:58 and will set again at 15:12. It's going to be dark and cold most of the time. Be careful out there. Cargo ramp access is now available, and you may disembark. Please consider the 41ˢᵗ Military Airlift Squadron for all your future transport needs. Thank you for flying the friendly skies."

The marines gathered their gear from the stowage netting and proceeded out the side, hunching against the bitter cold. There was little wind currently, though the snow heaped against the building sides showed the wind would be back. The eight men quickly tramped up to the brightly lit building and out of the weather. Hot chocolate and coffee awaited them in a small break room. A baby-faced major and a captain dressed in unfamiliar arctic camouflage waited patiently as the men grabbed drinks and sat down, dropping their rucks at their feet.

"Good evening, Marines," started the major.

"Evening sir," drifted back the automatic reply.

"I won't keep you long. My name is Major Thornberg and the man to my right is Captain Liam Olsen of the Norwegian Army. He will be your liaison for Northern Roundup III and happens to be one of the main designers of this year's exercise.

"You eight marines have been assigned to aggressor group Yankee Three. The aggressor group works directly with the captain. I'll give you a quick overview of what part you will be playing in this exercise. There will be a short question session after the briefing, so please hold any you have until the end. After that, you will be driven out to the staging area and allowed to get settled in."

"Northern Roundup III is a joint Norwegian-American NATO exercise focusing on Marine and Army integration during a potential Soviet attack from the north and east. The 4th Amphibious Brigade is broken into two groups. Most of them are working with native Norwegian marines and soldiers as defenders, learning the ins and outs of stopping a Soviet attack in winter. The other group, which you men get to be part of, will be working with Norwegians acting as aggressors. You will not only be the enemy of this simulation; you will also be learning the best ways to fight the Soviets when taking the fight to them."

"You will be working directly and indirectly with the Norwegian Army, Royal Norwegian Air Force, and the

Norwegian Home Guard. Captain Olsen will be leading Yankee Three. Do us proud."

"Oorah!" chorused the Marines.

"Very well. Let's look at the brass tacks of the situation."

Chapter Six

Outside Trondheim, Trøndelag, Norway
21 November 1986
2231 CET/2131 Zulu
On Road to Exercise Area

The drive was three more hours of smooth and rough roads, with nothing to see inside the canvas-covered back of the truck. What moonlight existed hid behind the curtain of snow drifting out of the dark sky. The canvas and a small heater did what they could to fight off the bone-chilling cold from outside. Most of the marines dozed fitfully as the truck sped toward the exercise grounds.

"Gunny, you ever been to this part of the world before?" asked Morehouse after he checked over the men. It was just the eight marines in the back of the transport. Captain Olsen was sitting in the cab with the driver.

"Nope. Spent most of my early years in the jungles of Asia. Three tours in Nam. Cold here is almost nice after the brutal heat, rain, and insects. Almost."

Morehouse grinned. "Yeah, can't say I'm sorry I missed that one. Grenada was bad enough."

"Bah…It was over and done in days. Not the slog we had."

"True enough."

"Who were you with?"

"22nd out of Lejeune."

Gunny grunted. "Good set of boys. Take it something happened to shift you over."

Morehouse nodded. "You?"

"Yep. Ever hear of the PACV?"

"Can't say I have."

Master Gunnery Sergeant Peck nodded. "Program didn't last long. Patrol Air Cushion Vehicle was the long name, we just called 'em tiger sharks. They were some bright boy's idea to use hovercraft along the Mekong Delta. I guess to go into places the Riverine swift boats couldn't get to. Navy had three of the buggers. They ran them, but Special Forces and Raiders got assigned to them occasionally. That's how I ended up working on them. We were patrolling the northern end when we got word of an attack, possibly Viet Cong.

"The Chief who ran the PACV got permission to take a group of us up the delta and hit the attack from the side. Supposed to surprise the little buggers. Turned out we were the ones getting the surprise.

"When we got there, this village, little flea-speck of a place, was overrun with these reddish monkey creatures. We saw a kid, couldn't have been more than twelve or so, get run down and torn open by one of the things.

"That was all it took. We opened fire on the things from the river, the fifties in the dome chewing away at the town. Then the damn monkeys actually jumped onto the hovercraft. I mean, we were probably eighteen or twenty feet from the shore, but these things just leapt across the distance like it was nothing.

"Turned out it was a family of Người Rừngs. You might have heard them called Batatut or Asian wild men. Tough suckers. Usually needed eight or nine rounds from the M16 to put them down. Hell, took two from the fifty. Lost three guys and a pair of Navy sailors to the damn things. They are big on eating the liver of their prey. Sharp nails and long teeth.

"When we got back, the entire crew was placed under quarantine and a few of us were read in for JTF 13. I figured I was already there fighting Charlie, fighting weirder things from somewhere else was just as good."

"Whoa. I didn't realize you'd been with the task force that long."

Gunny nodded. "Most of my career in fact. Not many others have."

Morehouse looked around and yawned. "I'll have to give you my story another time."

Smiling, the gunnery sergeant sat back and nodded approvingly. He didn't say anything else, just tipped his hat over his eyes and appeared to go to sleep. Morehouse took one more look around the truck and followed suit.

The forward operations base for the aggressors was impossible to see in the early morning. Morehouse and his men caught glimpses of camo netting and dug in tents, but little else. Captain Olsen's accent was thick but clear. "First briefing is at 09:00. It's just after 03:30, so get some rest. These men will show you where the bunk rooms are." He handed them off to a pair of enlisted soldiers who moved quickly in the starlight. They said nothing and the marines remained silent as well.

The men awoke at 08:00 and got ready. They grabbed a quick breakfast in the mess tent and then shuffled up the snow-tramped path to the main tent for the briefing.

Within an hour, the squad was split out and in their designated positions. Wind blew the dry snow about, obscuring easy sight of the road the intel team had determined the transport group would use. Morehouse and Riley dug into the snow at the tree line, only the small black circle of their muzzles detectable at any distance.

Atlantic Ocean, SOSUS Line Crossing Delta
24 November 1986
1820 AT / 2020 Zulu
USS *Sea Devil* (SSN 664)

Captain Owens stuck his head through the heavy blue curtain separating the sonar section from the rest of the control room. "Still nothing on the special frequency?"

Submarines, like most benthic predators, relied on stealth and passive senses to find their prey. Sometimes though, the prey was just as quiet and hard to find as the predator.

Sonar Technician first class (STS1) Mitchell Blevins took a quick look over the three waterfall displays in the darkened room. "'Fraid not sir. Only things we're showing right now is Sierra zero-eight-six, a freighter heading south, and Sierra zero-nine-two, a probable cargo ship headed toward Iceland based on her current track. I'll make sure that you're the second to know if we pick 'er up." STS1's southwestern accent sometimes clipped words in unexpected places, making the slightly built man sound more like John Wayne than his looks would have led one to believe.

"You do that Petty Officer Blevins." The captain grinned and stepped back into the control room. They were now two days into the search and had yet to pick up any indication of the trawler. Not that he expected the ship to be easy to find. The North Atlantic was a huge area to search, and the winter storm activity made a hash of the sonar picture. In turn, the combined noises made it harder to separate the sounds of man from the sounds of nature.

He trusted Blevins. The sonar tech had the touch. Owens had not seen many sailors who had that touch, the innate ability to perform their job to the maximum effect without any real effort. He treasured the few he had while wishing more of his crew met that lofty goal. He snorted gently to himself. *Might as well wish for an orchestra of Mozarts or a basketball team of Larry Birds and Magic Johnsons. Be happy I have a few of them. And the rest of the crew is good. Not naturals like Blevins or Pascal, but a good crew.*

In the sonar shack, Blevins ran a new trace. Nothing but surface clutter and a few brave fishing trawlers, all well south and headed away. Hate to be fishing in weather like it was topside. Here at three hundred fifty feet, he could not feel the heavy waves of the strong November storm pounding the ocean. He could hear them, but only with his special equipment. This deep everything was calm and safe. He wiped a bit of condensation from a screen and began cycling through the channels in hopes of finding his prey.

The torpedo room watch, per orders from the Weapons Officer, had cleared out everyone on crew except for himself, and he had been regulated to the torpedo control board at the forward end of the room. No one was authorized to listen in on the SEALs briefing. That was standard procedure, and no one balked when the orders came down.

Lieutenant Commander Harris ensured that his voice was pitched so that the watchstander would not hear the brief. Additionally, there was a small white noise generator running to keep anyone outside the room from overhearing anything. The team arrayed around him, and he sat in the port aft corner so he could see both entrances.

"Weathers worsened. I know that all of you are trained for cold water extractions and rough seas. This one is going to be tougher than normal. Biggest issue is that none of us can broach. Stay below the wave troughs and let the packages sink to us. Two, I have no information on Flute's training. He may panic and try and swim back to the surface. I hope not, but if he does, we're going to have to let him go. Paladin is the primary target.

"I plan on having the capture net set before we signal Flute. That way no matter where he tosses the computer, we'll be in position to catch it. The plan is for Flute to follow Paladin immediately. Unfortunately, that means there is a good chance he'll get caught up in the netting as well.

"Hughes, you're responsible for getting a regulator on him as soon as possible. Carr, you're backup." Harris passed and watched the two men nod in acknowledgment. "Lyle and Chief Elliot, you will rig and secure the net. We will be using a magnet grappling system to anchor the netting to the trawler. If Flute ends up in the net as well, we'll drag both of them back to the boat in the net and untangle them in the escape trunk. Priority in that event is still to get a regulator on Flute.

"I am responsible for the signal. Flute knows to be on deck between 1500 and 1530 local. I will start up the signal." Harris showed the group the item. It was about the size of his arm, shaped like a squid, and covered with a whitish-colored, vaguely translucent rubber. Harris pressed an indentation near the machine's tail, and it began to undulate slowly, giving off a green flash of bright light every half-second or so. "If anyone on the trawler sees this thing, they hopefully will think it's some kind of squid or cuttlefish flashing in the water." He turned off the machine and extracted the battery. He held the battery in his palm, making sure all the team members got a good look at it and where it mounted in the fake fish. "As you can see, it uses a nine-volt battery. I've got a box here that you can grab them from at the end of the brief. I want everyone to keep at least two of the batteries with you at all times. That way if this gives out in the middle of the mission, we have plenty of spares."

The entire group of SEALs chuckled grimly at that. Everyone remembered a mission not so long ago where the failure of a battery had put that entire team at risk.

"For want of a nail," intoned Carr.

Harris nodded again. "Good quote. All of us need to keep in mind that the little things are important. Myself, I would prefer to prevent losing the kingdom." Harris smiled and patted the petty officer second class on the shoulder. Then his expression sobered. "The toughest part will be the speed. The trawler is expected to be moving at between sixteen and nineteen knots. That means that we'll have to deploy well ahead of it and grapple to its hull as it passes. Which in turn means we only get how many chances?"

"One," quietly intoned the team.

"Yep. One chance. On the plus side, the mag grapples will have additional padding to minimize noise. The drawback is that might mean they don't hook on properly, or they may hook but disengage before we are ready. We've all been dragged through the water like this before. It's not fun and it's painful, but it's the job this time."

"Any questions?" Harris looked around at the team. No one spoke. "It's 2230 now. Weapons check tomorrow at

0900 Zulu. We don't know for certain when the signal will go off, so grab some chow and bunk time. Maybe you guys can get some of the left-over chili from tonight."

The Chief grimaced as he grabbed a pair of nine volts. "Or we'll be really lucky, and they are serving Dinty Moore or Chef Boyardee's pillows of death."

North Atlantic Ocean, South of Iceland
25 November 1986
0711 WAT / 0911 Zulu
AGI *Zhiqulesk*

Ulyana swayed with the ship as it rolled side to side in the heavy seas. The North Atlantic was a rough patch of ocean in the best times. During the late fall and winter months, it was a taste of hell. The storm had rolled over them last evening and continued to pound the ship today. She hardly noticed the deck's motion under her, automatically correcting her gait as she walked through the passageway. After three years aboard the trawler, it was second nature. She paused, glancing about one more time. She verified that she was alone, and no one could take notice of what she was doing.

She checked the door handle. Unlocked thankfully. Ulyana turned the handle, holding her breath and hoping that the door would not make noise as it opened. She let out the breath in a soft whoosh when no noise issued from the hinges. One more glance and she ducked into the small berthing room.

Do I need to be doing this? Should I wait longer? Ulyana had not yet started the beacon, which meant that currently, no one was trying to get to her. *The beacon is only good for three days at most. I must make sure that the computer is here before I start it or all the time I have put in will be for nothing.*

The duffle had not been in any of the last three rooms she had checked. She hoped it wasn't being kept in the captain's stateroom. It would be exceedingly difficult, if not impossible, to get it out of there.

If it was in Michel's room, it was going to be bad enough to get out. She and Michel did not get along, and since the incident with the fishing boat, she was fairly certain that he was harboring doubts about her. Doubts born from her barging in on him and the agent when the agent needed tools to 'fix the boat'. She had tried to alleviate Michel's concerns by ensuring that the number three diesel engine continued to have issues. Issues it seemed that Ulyana was the best at fixing, since undenounced to the others, most of the problems were ones she was inserting into the machine.

Focus girl. This is not the time to be off in la-la land.

She pulled open the door, sticking her head in to make sure the room was empty. It was, and the stateroom was clean, a surprise after the sties the last two had been. The downside of the cleanliness was it was more likely for Michel to notice that anyone had been in his stateroom. She slipped in and quietly shut the door behind her, then leaned against it and sighed. *Check this room, then the cook's.* If the guidance computer was not in either of those, she would have to determine the best way to get into the captain's stateroom and search.

Dim light radiated from the nightlamp above the stateroom door, providing some illumination for the room. Ulyana waited for her eyes to adjust. She looked around and groaned slightly. Michel had put a combination lock on his gear locker. It was a simple rotating job, 40 numbers spaced equally around the face, three numbers making up the combination to unlock the hasp.

Ulyana slumped. Picking a key lock, she could do. Combination locks took time to open, and not a skill she had much proficiency in. If she had plenty of time, she could figure out the combination. With Michel wandering back at any point, she just did not have the minutes to spare. She began scanning the rest of the room before working the lock.

Glancing to her right, she noticed something stuffed under the desk next to the bunk. Carefully, Ulyana moved the chair and peered underneath. There was the green seabag. She unhooked the top and rolled the canvas bag down. The metal gleam told her everything she needed.

Finally.

She rolled the canvas back up, re-hooked the bag, and slipped the chair back under the desk. The thudding of approaching footsteps caught her off guard. She scrambled to her feet and carefully cracked open the door. No one was visible yet, so she slipped out, latching the door behind her. Michel and another sailor walked around the corner talking animatedly. Their heads still turned away, Ulyana took the chance and dashed sideways. Neither of the men noticed her as she sped up the ladder leading topside from the berthing hall.

At the top of the ladder, she paused. That had been too close for her comfort. She had nearly gotten caught in Michel's berthing without any real excuse. Ulyana took a few moments to gather her thoughts. The beacon was hidden in her work area and ready. There was no reason that anyone else was going to find it now before she activated it. The next step would be to determine the best time to get the computer out of Michel's room. First, she needed to start the beacon.

Smiling, Ulyana turned to cross the mid-level corridor and headed down aft to the engine room.

North Atlantic Ocean, South of Iceland
25 November 1986
0823 WAT / 1023 Zulu
USS *Sea Devil* (SSN 664)

"Chief, I have a faint signal. It's only coming in on the hull array right now. Designating Sierra zero-four-seven." Sonar Technician Third Class Gridley made a mark with a grease pencil on the waterfall display and then punched the contact information into the BQQ-5. The new multifunction sonar system coupled directly with the fire control system. This improved the communications between Fire Control and Sonar since there was no longer a need to physically transfer the information from the sonar system to the fire control computers using written chits.

Sonar Technician Chief Elliot spoke up, not lifting his head nor changing his expression from a half-lidded state. "Come on Gridley. I need more than that. Frequency and side?"

"The frequency is 1200 MHz. Right on the edge of detection. Can't tell which side since I've only got the one beam. If we maneuver, I might be able to improve the signal."

The sonar Chief nodded. "Alright, what is your maneuvering suggestion? Think of this as good training."

The young sonar technician frowned. He glanced back over the display and rubbed his chin. Cautiously Petty Officer Gridley stated, "Request that the con come twenty degrees to starboard. That'd potentially give the hull a better look and I might be able to tease it off the array. If I can do that, I will also get which side it's on." The *Sea Devil* had only gotten the TB-16 towed array sonar with her last major upkeep six months earlier and many of the sonar techs were still coming to grips with its capabilities.

"That is a solid option. I'd add another five degrees, just to be on the safe side. Plus, even if the tail doesn't pick it up, the bearing change can be used to determine which side the signal is coming from." The Chief picked up the station microphone and depressed the switch. "Conn, sonar. Request course change of twenty-five degrees to starboard. Trying to firm up a new contact."

There was a pause, then the repeater crackled to life. "Sonar, conn. Coming to course three-five-five."

The submarine banked gently as the helmsman brought the ship to the new course. The two-hundred-foot towed array followed the ship slowly like a reluctant puppy on a leash. Five minutes later the array stabilized directly behind the ship, riding several feet deeper than the hull to clear the prop wash.

"Tail is stable. What are you seeing?" asked Chief Elliot, trying to tease information out of the inexperienced sonarman.

"Still not sure. The source is still very faint. I think that…" He trailed off as STS1 Blevins stepped into the sonar shack.

"Captain said that we might 'ave picked up the signal," Blevins stated as he wiped the last bit of sleep from his eyes.

"Maybe…Take station three. Contact is Sierra four-seven. Gridley, keep at it but slave the information to station three." The Chief pointed to the sonar display closest to the door. Blevins slid into the seat and wiped the screen with the ubiquitous roll of toilet paper that was a necessary part of any sonar shack.

"Aye Chief." The sonar technician tapped a set of buttons on his console. "Data slaved."

"Got it," Blevins said and leaned closer to the screen. The green-on-green waterfall display gave his face a sickly hue. "Good snatch, Grid. You must have caught that right as it came on. Picked a good choice for the turn too. If we'd gone port, I think that we might have lost it in the dead zone. Not seeing anything on the BQQ-5." Blevins adjusted his gains and reduced some of the lower-level frequencies from his stack. The signal brightened on the display as the number of viewed frequencies were reduced. "Nope, just on the tail. Chief, I think this guy is pretty far away and we are just lucky. I think part of the signal is trapped below the thermocline and bouncing. If I was a bettin' man—"

The Chief cut him off, "Which we all know you ain't." He waved his hand in a circular 'come on' motion.

"I'd say that he is better than sixty thousand yards away. That's part of why the bow isn't catching it. Not truly enough power in the signal. We'll need to get closer though to really dial the signal in. Not too fast. Gotta' stay quiet. Wouldn't want to spook the prey."

The *Sea Devil* was currently crawling along at just over four knots, the slowest she could do, and maintain normal steerage. Below three knots she maneuvered like a bloated whale and above ten knots her own noise would begin drowning out the passive sonar, with worse drop-off the faster she went.

"I'll see if the captain can give us seven knots. That should allow you and Gridley to work the target while giving us a decent closing speed." The Chief squeezed past Blevins and pushed open the blue curtain between the shack and Control. He disappeared as the curtain fell back into place.

Chief Elliot stepped over to the CO and whispered to him. The two conferred for several minutes and moved to the Quartermaster's plot, checking the map. Their words were quiet and calm. The CO nodded and walked back to the center of control while Chief Elliot returned to the sonar shack.

"Helm, ahead two-thirds. Make turns for seven knots," commanded Captain Owens.

"Ahead two-thirds aye. Turns for seven aye." The tousle-haired petty officer twisted the engine order telegraph to two-thirds position while the Diving Officer called Maneuvering and ordered the speed set to seven knots. Swiftly, the submarine accelerated to the new speed, slowly closing the long-range gap to its target.

"Conn, sonar. New contact, designating Sierra zero-five-three. Tentative classification submerged vessel."

The lead sonar operator ran the contact through the computer to tease out a possible classification based on the noise profile. While the computer worked through the information, Captain Owens stepped into Control.

"CO on deck," intoned the Officer of the Deck (OOD).

"As you were," Owens stated off-handedly. "OOD, I have the con. Sonar, what have you picked up?"

"Unknown submerged contact. Currently attempting to classify. Initial indications are this is not a biologic."

The OOD interjected quickly, "Sir, I ordered the ship slowed to ahead one-third, turns for five. Only other contact is the intermittent pulse from Sierra four-even. Per orders, we are maintaining the track to intercept Sierra four-even."

Owens nodded. "Sonar, conn. As soon as you have a classification, inform me."

"Conn, sonar, aye."

"Chief of the Watch. Station the fire control tracking party. Primary plot for Sierra four-seven. I want the secondary plot on Sierra five-three."

The Chief of the Watch contacted Maneuvering and within moments two watchstanders from the engineering spaces manned the plotting table. They would take information from both sonar and fire control and translate the data onto a large paper plot. This plot would form part of a permanent record that could be reviewed at leisure. The sonar operator began determining speed and distance of the contact. Four minutes later the unknown contact's track was firming up and the computer spat out the probable classification.

"Conn, sonar. Sierra five-three now classified as probable Charlie II class SSGN, range 18,000 yards. Speed of eight knots. No change in heading."

The captain turned to the diving control panel on the port side of the control room. *Just our luck that we'd stumble across a Soviet boomer,* Owens thought. "Rig ship for silent running. Helm, make turns for three knots."

The Chief of the Watch passed three clicks of the microphone across the ship's 1MC general announcing circuit. Each manned space had at least one 1MC system speaker. Three clicks informed everyone instantly that the ship was rigging for silent running. The helmsman rotated the engine order telegraph to all stop, then to one-third while the Diving Officer called the Maneuvering space and told them to make turns for three knots.

Throughout the ship, men stopped and looked around. They quietly gathered up tools from maintenance and put them away. Lockers were double-checked to verify they were properly latched shut while pumps were slowed or shut off. Deck hatches were pinned open so that access to the ladders would not generate sound. Even talking quieted. Slowly the friction of the water bled the excess speed of the *Sea Devil* off, changing her from a hard-to-detect machine to an impossible-to-detect hole in the water.

"Sierra five-three maintaining speed and course. Signal is strengthening slowly."

Owens stepped over to the Fire Control station, placed one hand on the operator's chairback, and leaned over the senior fire control technician's shoulder to peer at the screen. The man was busy taking the inputs from the sonar and feeding them into the AN/UYK-20. The 'Yuck-20', as it was fondly known, was a rugged computer that did the job of crunching the sonar data into information that fire control could use. Within moments the fire control technician developed a probable course for the target from the noise.

The petty officer placed one hand on his headset, holding it in place as he turned to speak over his shoulder. "Sierra five-three is on a course of two-two-five at 8 knots, plus or minus 3 degrees and one knot. Closest approach on current course is six thousand yards in twenty-seven minutes."

Owens nodded, stood up, and walked back to the chart table. The Quartermaster of the Watch stepped aside as the CO approached. He had already laid out a suggested course change. Owens traced the line with his finger and then checked the distance with the built-in ruler. "Looks good," he said to the quartermaster, then turned back to the fore of the submarine. "Helm come right to course zero-nine-five. Maintain turns for three and do not exceed five degrees of rudder."

"Right to course zero-nine-five, three knots, five degrees, aye," replied the seaman manning the helm. He carefully turned the aircraft-style rudder control slightly to the right, his eyes glued to the rudder angle and speed indicators. The diving petty officer pulled upward slightly on the dive planes to compensate for the turn and maintain the submarine at depth. Gently, like a huge plane, the four-thousand-ton ship banked right and drove to the new course. The rudder gradually returned to the neutral position as the ship's nose approached the new heading.

"Course zero-nine-five. Rudder amidships. Speed three knots."

Owens had returned to the fire control station during the turn. He glanced over his shoulder, "Good job helm."

The track of Sierra five-three seemed to curve away from the submarine on the screen, but Owens knew that was a trick of the computer. In reality, they had changed their base course, opening the angle to the Charlie II.

The fire control reverified the inputs as the towed array steadied once more. With the slow speed and the minimal rudder angle, it was back in position in less than a minute. "Sierra five-three maintaining course and speed. No indication of changes."

"Good," Owens turned back to the Chief of the Watch. "Maintain silent running until ten minutes after we lose Sierra five-three."

Chief Sterns, sitting at the Chief of the Watch station quirked an eyebrow. Most times when a US submarine picked up a Soviet boat, especially a missile boat, they would prosecute it and follow. The captain answered the silent question. "I would love to trail her, but our current orders preclude it. Speaking of which," he turned and pulled back the blue curtain leading to the sonar shack. He stuck his head in the opening and asked, "Status of Sierra four-seven after the turn?"

"Sir, we are maintaining track on Sierra four-seven. Slight loss of signal after the turn. I think we are getting close to pointing her. Within twenty-five to thirty degrees off starboard. Speed estimate with the turn has Sierra four-seven at nearly eighteen knots. At that speed, I expect to lose signal within the next twelve minutes."

Owens bit back a curse. He nodded his head and stepped back fully into the control room. Hopefully, the trawler would stay on course, maybe even slow to do some actual fishing. He doubted it would slow, not if Paladin was on board. They would want to get the ship back into Soviet territorial waters as soon as they could. Eighteen knots was more than likely the trawler's top speed, and the engines must be driving hard to keep that up in these seas.

"Sonar, keep working the signal as long as you can. Once we clear the Charlie II, I'll slowly ramp our speed up to full and get us caught up to the target. I intend to get ahead of her and drift into her base course." Owens turned and quietly strode to the fire control tracking party. "Maintain a dedicated track on Sierra four-seven even after we lose her. I want an estimate of where she will be when we can catch back up to her." The members of the fire control tracking party nodded and bent back to the plotting table.

The control room lapsed into silence; the whir of the ventilation fans the only noise. With the ship set to silent running, none of the roving watchstanders were moving about. It gave the submarine the feel of a mausoleum. Minutes ticked by, each one slowly dragging into the next.

The junior sonar technician stepped into control and quietly walked over to the captain. "Sir, sonar reports loss of contact with Sierra four-seven one minute ago. Attempting to regain, but it appears that the signal faded out due to distance."

Owens looked at the sonar operator. "Understood." The young man hurried back to his watch station. "Fire control, time to Sierra five-three passing 20,000 yards astern?"

"Sir, estimate eight minutes."

Eight minutes, plus another ten to ensure that the Soviet's passive sonar had no chance of picking up increased screw noise from *Sea Devil* as she accelerated to full. Eighteen long minutes in which the trawler could change course or worse, stop and run silent. Then they would scoot right past her without even knowing. Well, not quite since the transmitter would still be pulsing. That thought gave Owens a smile. It was easier to track a target when the target was kind enough to wave a red flag as it moved along.

Moments later, the sonar chief pushed aside the curtain and stated angrily, "Mechanical transient from engine room."

Damn, thought Owens, *we don't need that kind of thing right now.* Mechanical transients were non-natural sounding and they carried long distances. Plus, the only thing that created them was man.

"Dive, get Maneuvering on the 2JV, and find out what is going on. Sonar and fire control, indications if Sierra five-three heard?"

Seconds passed before anyone answered. "Sonar, Conn. Sierra five-three shows no aspect or Doppler changes."

"Fire control does not track any changes. Target is maintaining course and speed."

There was a collective sigh as the control room watchstanders let out the breath they had all been holding.

"Captain, Maneuvering reports that the aft port deck hatch latch failed, and the deck hatch slammed shut. No one was near the hatch when the incident occurred. Once the ship is secure from silent running, they'll fix the latch. Does not appear to be a personnel incident."

That was good. A personnel incident of that nature, where it could be argued that the sailor intentionally placed the ship in danger, could see a sailor demoted, confined to the ship, or even kicked out of the submarine force. Now it was instead a question of why the incident had happened and how the equipment had failed.

Sixteen long minutes later, with the Charlie II ten minutes past 20,000 yards, the *Sea Devil* began accelerating. They had a trawler to catch.

Chapter Seven

Meeting of the Norwegian Sea and Barents Sea, South of Svalbard

25 November 1986

1353 WAT / 1253 Zulu

USS *Sea Devil* (SSN 664)

"Conn, Sonar. Regained signal previously designated Sierra four-seven. Designated as new contact Sierra six-three. Signal pulse and frequency matches the original."

"Sonar, conn aye." The OOD turned to the messenger of the watch. "Wake up the CO and inform him that we have regained the target." The messenger acknowledged the order and hurried out of control.

Two minutes later Commander Owens walked into Control, looking as though he had just stepped off a recruiting poster. It was not possible to look at the man and realize that he had been asleep for less than two hours.

"Our friend is back?"

"Yes sir, and almost exactly where the geo-plotter expected her to be." The OOD waved the CO back to the plotting station. The Machinist Mate first class working the plot stepped to the side to allow the officers room. "Looks like she's taking the straight-line course to Soviet waters. We can intercept here," the OOD pointed to a spot in the ocean, "right between Bear Island and Svalbard. The area is international waters, so no problem with anybody's Coast Guard. Plus, the water is deep and there's a good thermocline at five hundred and fifty feet. We can stay below the thermocline and release the SEAL team. That way the layer should trap the sounds and keep the hatch noises from leaking up to the target. Much further east of there, we enter the Barents Sea, and the shelf starts to rise quickly. We'll lose a good deal of depth if we go that far. Estimated time of arrival is an hour and twenty minutes from now."

Owens nodded. He had given a vague brief to his senior officers a day earlier. It was necessary to bring them into some understanding of what was going on. They all had signed the security paperwork and were provisionally cleared for the information he had briefed them on.

"Looks good. I'll inform Lieutenant Commander Harris. That'll give him and his team time to prepare. Have the messenger of the watch inform the other SEALs that they are to report to the Torpedo Room as soon as possible. Also, inform the COB to have the diver recovery team standing by in the Crew's Mess in an hour." Owens checked his watch. "Make that forty-five minutes for the diver recovery team."

"Aye, sir. You to Commander Harris, messenger to SEAL team members with orders, and COB with diver recovery team to Crew's Mess in forty-five minutes."

Owens slid down the ladder from Control to the center passageway of the boat. He turned to starboard and entered the Officer passageway. At the first door, he knocked. Commander Harris opened it and then gestured to the CO inside. Owens stepped in and closed the door behind himself. There was no one else currently in the three-man stateroom.

"Sonar found the target. We'll be in the relative position you requested in about an hour and fifteen minutes. Since there's only an hour and a half until you need to send the signal, this is cutting it close. If we miss today, then we're going to trail them for another twenty-four hours without being picked up. We'll be getting closer to Soviet-patrolled waters and further into the Barents Sea. Much shallower water there. That'd be pushing our luck.

"I have the messenger informing the rest of your team to meet in the Torpedo Room. This is a tighter timing situation than I wanted or expected to put you and your men in, Commander."

"I understand," stated Harris and smiled. "This just makes it more interesting. We'll get the job done."

Owens nodded and left, with Harris stepping into the passageway right behind. Harris closed the door behind them and headed for the Torpedo Room.

Fifteen minutes later the SEALs were all in their gear, flippers in their right hands, each wearing a cold-water dry suit. These suits would minimize the heat loss to water in the frigid North Atlantic depths. Their face masks were tinted with an anti-reflective cover to prevent light from bouncing off the glass and giving away their positions. Each man also wore a belt with a set of heavy hooks that would attach to the thin-line net that Lyle carried in a pouch attached to his left side. No one was armed beyond a dive knife except for Harris, and he was only carrying a speargun on the off chance that they ran into a Greenland shark.

The Greenland shark averaged only slightly smaller than the great white shark and often followed fishing vessels in these cold waters. No one thought that the speargun would be used but small chances became bigger ones if the equipment was not available. Carr and Hughes each ran a second line from their tanks to an extra mask and regulator, independently verifying the units worked properly.

One of the biggest problems was that Flute would be going into shock as soon as he hit the water. Their task was to get one of the masks strapped over his head, a regulator into his mouth, and get him back to the sub as quickly as possible. With the water temperature of 40°F, it would take mere minutes or even seconds for Flute to go into a hypothermic condition. Death could occur in as little as thirty minutes without outside help.

All the plans focused around keeping the team in the water for less than forty minutes to ensure everyone's safety. The submarine's corpsman would be standing by with warm towels, blankets, and a set of dry warm clothes to change Flute into. The most dangerous part appeared to be getting the man back to the ship.

Paladin posed a different set of problems. The temperature would have no effect on the item, but it was a large inert chunk of heavy metal. Ensuring they caught it before it plummeted to the depths would take a set of keen eyes and quick reflexes. Once they seized Paladin, their job entailed bringing it back to the submarine and stowing it safely. The SEALs stayed silent as they walked into the Crew's Mess and sat. The next hard part would be the wait. They mentally prepared themselves for the signal from Control.

In the depths, it slumbered, slowly circling the multi-mile area where something confined it. Down where light never penetrated, where day and night were the same, it drowsily coasted mere feet above the muddied bottom of the ocean.

It did not, nor could it ever, understand why there were fixed edges to this territory it could not swim past. Only a truth remained, it had tried to cross that line and been rebuffed each time. Even its music did not penetrate outside. Not long ago it had sung to a large vessel, and nothing had happened. The vessel was within a single body length of the edge of the territory, yet no one responded to the wavesong.

Tiny fish that occasioned through its hunting grounds were hardly enough to take away the edge of its hunger. It longed for the taste of terror and hopelessness of its true prey's mind. It had been far too long a time since any true prey had entered the hunting grounds. An immeasurable time since it had last eaten its fill. Without satisfying prey, it slumbered in lazy circles.

The blood-sweet tang of iron swirled through the water, strengthening slowly. Not just iron, but copper and wood, and most importantly, the sense of life. Awareness flooded the simple brain, the surging blood flow awakening the creature fully. It paused its ceaseless circling, tasting the change in the water. The flavors and scents came from two places. There were two separate prey, one on the surface, and a larger one in the depths. Both were crossing the edge of its territory. The taste of the metals intensified in the water, the sensation of the pressure changes by the rough outer casing that contained the sweetness inside. Hunger drove the creature, the need to taste the flesh and minds within those rough casings.

The fins pushed against the water, turning in place until it faced the strongest of the scents. Massive tentacles coiled and twisted in anticipation, occasionally flicking out to grab at an imagined target. With a single movement of its massive tail, the creature began the long slow ascent from the bottom of the ocean, rising out of the dark. The tail fin stroked the water, pushing the enormous beast towards where its prey swam.

Neither of the prey noticed it. They both swam directly through the hunting ground, unaware. It would hunt them in silence. The wavesong would be used only after the prey were captured, to create even more tasty fear in them. No need to lure this prey, for they were coming to him.

The forward escape trunk was just large enough for the three smallest SEALs to fit into with their gear. Each wore a green Cyalume stick in an uncovered pocket. The stick's chemical glow provided the only light for the men. They watched as sailors shut the lower hatch, cutting them off from the influence of the submarine. In the dim green light, they listened as the seal shushed tight. Carr carefully turned the flood valve until a four-inch stream of near-freezing ocean water began flooding the trunk. It dumped into the space, swirling in chaotic vortexes around their feet. A minute later, the black water was lapping over their heads.

Below them, a combination vent and drain line allowed the extra air to escape back into the ship. When water solidly flowed out, the sailor shut the drain/vent valve and banged once with a rubber-faced mallet on the lower hatch. The hammering sound transmitted upward to the three men, and they opened the outer hatch.

Stygian blackness greeted them outside the submarine. The feeble light from their glowsticks projected less than six feet from them before the inky water swallowed the glow. The SEALs could sense more than see their flippers slowly kicking back and forth, as they hovered above the sub. Carr and Lyle pushed the upper hatch down and then used a special wrench to lock it shut. An indicator in the hull would inform the remainder of the team that they could empty the escape trunk and repeat the process.

While they waited for the others to cycle through, Lyle connected the return line to the ship. It was four hundred feet of woven nylon line with an underwater balloon and lantern assembly. The team would swim back to the line and follow it down to return to the ship. The light was designed to not be visible more than a hundred feet away. From this depth, there was no chance of the light being visible from the surface.

Ten minutes later the entire team was out of the submarine and swimming upward toward the invisible point marking the rendezvous with the trawler and its contents. Behind them, the line and balloon floated serenely in the blue-black water, glowing faintly.

Meeting of the Norwegian Sea and Barents Sea, North of Bear Island
25 November 1986
1508 WAT / 1408 Zulu
AGI *Zhiqulesk*

This afternoon, the wind clawed at her skin. She was positive it was even more biting now than last evening. Ulyana wrapped her chilled fingers around the hot cup of dark sweet tea, enjoying the sensation. She stared into the water aft of the ship and then slowly checked both sides.

If the team did not show up by tomorrow afternoon, there was little chance of rescue on this trip.

One, the transmitter will stop tomorrow, and two, we are nearing Soviet waters that the rescuers probably are not going to want to enter.

She shivered, not just from the cold but also from the entire situation.

Michel was getting suspicious. Ulyana suspected he had found something amiss with his stateroom. He was asking questions of everyone, if they had seen anyone near his stateroom or had anyone been messing with his stuff. When nobody had come forth, he had started calling out threats. Which Michel did most of the time and therefore they were useless. Ulyana suspected she was safe since Michel's questions had not focused on anyone in particular. Her main concern was that if Michel really began investigating the ship, he might discover the transmitter. Then the whole gig would go up in smoke.

She walked towards the trawler's bow. At the speed they were traveling, she expected there was no reasonable method for the rescuers to catch up to the trawler from behind. That meant they would probably approach from the front or sides. She stared forward. She believed the bow would be the easiest location to spot their signal. As an added bonus, with the wind and spray, it was unlikely anyone would come up and find her there. She began pacing just below the bridge window, checking first the port, then starboard forward waters for any indications.

The SEALs were waiting in two groups ahead of the trawler, treading water with the long dive fins trailing under them. Primary Group, consisting of Chief Elliot and Lyle, were the key. They waited in front of the rapidly approaching vessel. Floating calmly in the water, they could feel the push of the vessel from its bow wake. There would only be one chance to attach the hooks before the ship passed over them. A thick covering of barnacles coated the bottom of the trawler, white teeth ready to tear into the unwary. Both men were barely a foot below the vessel, each on the starboard side so that they could avoid the heavy propellers churning the water at the aft of the ship. They fought the disturbed water flowing over the hull to prevent cutting themselves on the thick coating of shells. They hoisted their mag grapples and on signal, both men tossed the devices upward. With a muffled *thunk* the hooks caught to the hull, dragging the net and the two SEALs along.

Secondary Group, made up of Lieutenant Harris, Petty Officer Carr, and Petty Officer Hughes, waited half a mile further along the trawler's track. As the vessel passed over them, they grabbed the net and locked their arms into the material, the eighteen-knot water turbulence battering them. Harris rolled over and struggled to reach the fake jellyfish on his chest harness. With a grunt, he pushed in the switch and the green light began to slowly strobe. He held up a hand and signaled fifteen minutes.

Ulyana caught a glimpse of green light. She stopped pacing and leaned over the side staring. The light faded and pulsed again. And a third time. The rescue team was here.

She threw the tea over the side and rushed into the port entrance of the ship. Without any conscious thought, she dropped the empty mug into one of the ubiquitous ring-style cup holders on the bulkhead. Down one flight of stairs and inboard. Michel's stateroom was just ahead. She paused. There was no light creeping under the door.

What if he is in there asleep? I don't remember what his current watch schedule is. How do I get the gear and get out without waking him? Ulyana paused and resolved her doubts. Michel had never been a favorite of hers. A good strong blow to the temple would keep him from moving after her, at least long enough to get the package out of the room.

Carefully she turned the handle. The stateroom door opened outward, the light from the hall illuminating the area. Michel lay snoring on his rack, one arm dangling over the side. Ulyana could just see the dark shape of the seabag under the desk where the chair held it in place. A chair she would need to move before pulling the bag out. Her heart pounded. Not only was there the chance of waking Michel up but stay time for the rescue team was running out.

Below the trawler's hull, Harris flashed another hand signal. Eleven minutes.

Ulyana slipped into the room and lifted the chair. She scooted backwards, careful to prevent both scrapping the chair across the floor and hitting Michel's dangling arm. Michel snorted and she froze her movement. Seconds passed. Michel rolled slightly but did not make any further noises. Quietly releasing the breath she was holding, Ulyana relaxed as she set the chair down.

Bending over, she reached under the desk, grasped the cool canvas of the seabag, and hefted. It was heavier than she expected, and she tipped forward, banging her head on the desk drawer. Michel awoke with a start, his eyes unfocused from sleep.

"What?" He blinked several times as Ulyana pulled the bag out. "What are you doing in here? Leave that!"

Michel reached out and grabbed Ulyana's leg, attempting to drag her towards him. In his semi-wakeful state, he failed to notice the chair's new location. He hit one of the legs hard with his elbow, causing his arm to go numb.

Ulyana struggled around and swung the heavy bag with all her might, catching Michel in the shoulder and head as he started to slide out of his rack. His head snapped upward from the glancing blow, and his body was pushed back into the rack. Instantly his free arm reached for the impact point on his head. Michel groaned in pain. Ulyana pushed herself to her feet and threw the heavy bag over her shoulder.

Harris flashed another sign. Nine minutes. The team held on, legs and fins trailing uncomfortably in the trawler's turbulent wake.

Michel slid partway out of the rack, reaching. He grabbed the chair and heaved it after Ulyana. Its legs banged against the doorframe, setting the chair spinning from the impact and the backrest caught her legs. She stumbled and dropped to one knee. With a roar of anger, Michel pushed himself fully out of the rack and charged her. Desperately, Ulyana reached over and slammed the stateroom door inward. The thin metal covering the door dented as it smashed into Michel's head, knocking him backward and tripping him with his own legs. He screamed in rage and pain as the door bounced back open.

She pushed past the chair and ran outboard, heading for the stairs that led upward to the main deck entrance. Fright was causing her to breathe heavily, her lungs fighting for enough oxygen. Michel stumbled out of his stateroom, blood streaming from a gash on his forehead. He grabbed the loose chair and flung it after her again. She turned into the stairwell just as the chair slammed into the bulkhead a whisker from her shoulder. Other stateroom doors were now opening. The sea bag's weight pulled her down, slowing her as she fought her way up the stairwell.

Below the SEALs rose the massive beast, its tentacles tucked close to its body as its strong tail drove it in its ascent.

Five minutes signaled Harris. He glanced over and noted that the green pulsing light of the fake jellyfish was still blinking. He hoped that Flute had seen it.

"Conn, Sonar. Receiving mechanical transients from Sierra six-three. Sounds like they are banging on the bulkheads. No change in course or speed. Transients don't match with any expected signals from the target."

Michel was on her heels. He grabbed the rough canvas of the bag and pulled, nearly yanking it from her grasp. She reversed into the ladderwell, leaning back so that the steps were supporting her weight and kicked the deck manager in the chest with all her might. Michel gasped and stumbled back, wheezing as his lungs momentarily forgot how to operate. He released his grip as the muscles spasmed, his hands opening of their own volition. Ulyana turned again and hurried up the stairs, struggling to get the bag back onto her shoulder in the process. She grabbed the railing at the upper edge and hauled herself around to the starboard side. The door to the deck was only five or six steps ahead of her. Michel's footsteps rang, echoing up the ladderwell. He was right behind her.

Under the trawler, the five SEALs clung, heads tucked into their chest to keep their masks on in the rushing water as well as keep an eye on their leader. Harris flashed his hand again. Four minutes.

"Transients have stopped. Sierra six-three maintaining course and speed."

In the blue-black water below and ahead, the creature uncoiled its tentacles. Most were sent probing towards the vessel on the surface, the last two towards the cluster of tiny prey creatures swimming just below the vessel. They would make a fine appetizer.

Ulyana snagged the door handle and spun, pushing the door outward, and sliding into the frigid air. Sometime during the fight, her coat had gotten ripped, and the wind cut to her bones. She tried slamming the door back into Michel's face, but the hydraulics prevented such a move. He glared at her, pushing past the slowly closing door. Ulyana backpedaled, trying to keep some distance between herself and the boatswain. A wave broke over the bow, drenching both Michel and Ulyana and making the deck slick with water.

"What are you doing Ulyana? What do you hope to accomplish?" The confusion in his tone was genuine. He had no idea what was really going on right now, other than the apparent loss of sanity by one of his shipmates. She could see the blood from a cut above his eye welling up, startlingly red against his pale skin. Much of the blood had washed away in their drenching. "That sea bag and its contents, they are useless to you. There is nowhere for you to run to. Nowhere for you to go." He shook his head, trying to understand. "Why are you doing this?"

Gathering herself, she stopped moving and stared directly at him. "Striking a blow against everything the State stands for." She heaved. Instantly the bag disappeared over the railing. Michel made an abortive gesture to catch it, then realized that it was gone, sinking fast in the black icy waters of the Barents Sea. He shook his head angrily this time. "That was a bad idea Ulyana. The KGB and the GRU will fight over who gets to ask you questions first. Of course, I will need to get some answers first." He cracked his knuckles and started towards her. She tucked her head down, chin against her chest.

During the talk, Ulyana had moved until she stood with her hips against the starboard gunwale. *One step closer*, she thought to herself. She raised her eyes to him without moving her chin. He took another step, fist raised to strike. "I don't think so." With a grunt, she heaved herself over the side, flashing Michel a fist with an extended middle finger.

Impact with the water drove the air from her lungs as the knife of bitter cold stabbed inward, freezing her breathing. She struggled. Something wrapped around her face, forcing its way into her mouth. She opened her mouth to scream, and fresh air blew in. She coughed and blew bubbles past the regulator. She kept her eyes shut as the cold continued hammering at her consciousness. A strong pair of arms wrapped about her, and she could feel herself being drawn deeper into the water. Her ears popped painfully as the swimmer continued further down, down towards what she hoped was a safe place. She kept her eyes screwed shut, breathing fitfully as they continued into the blackness. Neither of them felt the passage of a large body just overhead.

Paladin had landed in the center of the net, immediately drawing Elliot and Lyle towards each other. They worked in the dim water, wrapping the net around the package and tying it off. There was a second splash but that was not their concern. Elliot climbed against the current and released the first mag-grapple. He was reaching for the second when something wrapped around his leg. He reached down, concerned that the free end of the netting was trapping his leg.

Instead, he saw and felt a leather muscle-filled . . . something. Something that looked like a giant snake or tentacle. Then the pain set in as the tentacle contracted and drove knitting needle-like spines into his leg. In the turbulent water he could barely make out the thick thing wrapped about his leg. There was little to feel beyond the pain and strength as the appendage was nearly the same temperature as the surrounding waters. He pulled out his dive knife and began attacking the tentacle with his left hand, twisting his right through the netting to maintain his grip.

Lyle felt the sudden disturbance of the net and looked upward to where Elliot was working. A huge black object obscured most of his vision. Whatever it was had wrapped around Elliot's leg and was pulling at him. Dark blood began to color the water. Harris, also holding onto the net, was tossed about as the tentacle attacked Elliot. He tried to roll over, but the bouncing of the net was making it nearly impossible.

Harris' mask came loose, filling with frigid water. He could just see the bottom of the trawler from where he had twisted. He fought to keep a grip and clear the mask. The strangest thing was the feeling of bulk between him and the rest of the team. There should be nothing out here but them and the trawler.

Topside, five gray-green tentacles snaked over the top to the gunwales, slamming down on the deck. Michel looked in horror as the appendages, each at least as thick as his leg, gouged out sections of the deck, the wood and metal shrieking in protest. One tentacle wrapped around the starboard fishing boom. The long metal arm groaned under the new weight, slowly bowing in the middle. It broke with a sudden metallic rending sound, and the tie lines screamed as they snapped and whipped back towards the main hull. Michel threw his arms over his head for protection, screams of pain echoed from inside the bridge as one of the lines tore through the windows of the bridge, showering glass to the deck below.

He was thrown off his feet as the ship's bow plowed into the water, the aft end lifting out of the waves. Michel threw his arm out, grabbing a stanchion as he began sliding toward the bow. The vessel shuddered to a sudden stop as the screw spun ineffectively in the air sending white plumes of aerated water around. He fought as gravity dragged at him, until another shudder shook him loose. His scream cut off with horrible suddenness as he slammed back into the forward gunwale.

Below, the loss of forward motion allowed Harris to finally turn and see what was happening. Huge tentacles snaked out of the darkness and over the edges of the trawler. He watched in horror as the tentacle holding Elliot jerked the SEAL free of the net and into the depths below. Though he could not hear anything, the sudden straightening of Elliot's arm and then the way it fell to his side told Harris that the arm had been broken. He felt more than saw a whale-sized shadow in the poorly lit waters. His last sight of Elliot was the man furiously plunging his knife repeatedly into the thick appendage pulling him towards the dark bulk of the creature.

There was no time for mourning. Harris pulled himself to the bottom of the trawler and unhooked the second mag-grapple. He swam back with it and the trailing edge of the net to where Lyle was treading water. Lyle attempted to stay in place but twisted his head about; searching for whatever had grabbed Elliot. Harris removed his regulator and put his head next to Lyle's.

"We've got to get back to the sub. Elliot's gone. Swim!" He hooked the end of the netting into his rig and unlimbered the speargun. It was like hunting elephants with a BB rifle, but it gave him a form of offensive weaponry. He shoved his regulator back in, blew to clear the water, and swam deeper towards the waiting ship. Lyle was slightly ahead, trying to maintain a safe pace with the heavy package pulling them awkwardly deeper.

Horrible sounds followed them through the water. Sounds of metal shearing and wood snapping. A rain of debris slowly fell past them, wood, metal, and other less identifiable materials sliding in and out of the occasional light patches. The pair dodged as they could, but a large chunk of broken hull struck Lyle in the back. Sharp metal tore open both his drysuit and the deltoid muscles in his back. He spasmed in pain, instinctively curling inward.

Harris fought to keep control of the netting as Lyle twisted. He shoved forward with his fins, racing to close the distance between the two of them. The speargun dropped from his grip, the friction strap catching and the speargun tumbled in the wake, spinning and twisting. Harris grabbed Lyle with his left arm, attempting to keep his hands clear of the wound.

"Keep going man. We're almost there!" Harris shouted, his regulator popping free. The light from above was gone. They had no way to see the submarine. He scanned around. The balloon had to be nearby. Craning his neck, Harris caught sight of a faint light behind and slightly above them. That should be the balloon, and the travel line would be directly beneath it.

He pulled Lyle in the correct direction, fighting to keep the net from slipping from his grasp at the same time. There. He caught sight of the line and put Lyle's hand around it. "Swim down. I am right behind you. DOWN!"

Stars began clouding his vision as Harris fought to get the regulator back into his mouth. The cold water sapped his strength while the weight of Paladin tugged him toward the depths. He struggled, oxygen levels plummeting as he sank downward.

The hull of the submarine clanged as Paladin and Harris hit. Lyle grabbed the Commander and the regulator. He pushed it back into Harris' mouth. Harris coughed and gagged, then expelled the excess water. The two leaned against each other and lifted the net-covered unit. They slowly made their way to the hatch, then lowered the prize and themselves into the escape chamber. The outer hatch closed behind them.

Owens waited in the control room.

"Green light. Outer hatch indicates shut. All SEALs accounted for per communications."

"Roger Chief." Commander Owens turned to the Diving Officer. "Dive, ahead two-thirds. Come starboard to course two-two-seven, full right rudder. Get us out of here." Nothing had hit the submarine yet, but he was taking no chances. The command for ahead two-thirds rang out and the huge prop began spinning up to full rotations. The ship banked as the helm applied full rudder, crew leaning sideways and grabbing desk or chair edges to stay put.

"Coming starboard to two-two-seven at fifteen degrees. Maneuvering answers ahead two-thirds."

Above the submarine, the creature paused in its destruction. All the available morsels had been captured or eaten. Two still struggled in its grip, their fear and anguish sweeting the water around it. Now the other prey was beginning to move. Even more frustrating was that it was turning towards the edge of the hunt zone.

Now it called out. A strident song of peace and safety. A song of pleasure and hope. The prey would stop. The prey always came to the wavesong.

Chapter Eight

Meeting of Norwegian Sea and Barents Sea, North of Bear Island

25 November 1986

1622 CET / 1522 Zulu

USS *Sea Devil* (SSN 664)

"Conn, Sonar. We have continued indications of Sierra six-three breaking up. There are additional indications of biologic activity in the same location. Could be sharks, but the noise is not consistent with any previous biologicals I have heard. Primarily splash and surface activity. Seals?"

"Any determination of what caused the destruction?" Commander Owens asked.

"Conn, Sonar. No indications of an explosion or impact with another vessel. The ship sounds like it began tearing itself apart."

"Roger Sonar."

Owens turned around. "OOD, you have the conn. I am going see if the SEALs have any answers." He spun away and headed out of control, only unconsciously noting the OOD's reply.

The SEAL team was using the Torpedo Room to disrobe and change into dry clothing. Owens knocked on the door to make sure everyone was clear, then popped it open. He was stepping through the hatch when Lieutenant Commander Harris, clad only his undergarments, grabbed him by the uniform's shoulders. Harris pulled, dragging the submarine captain close.

"What was out there?" Harris bellowed into Owens face. "What the hell attacked my men and that trawler? What is going on?"

"Chief…" began STS3 Gridley, his voice somewhat slurred.

STSC Elliot glanced over to the second Sonar display where Gridley sat. The petty officer said nothing else, just stared ahead. Elliot tapped him on the shoulder. "What is it Grid?"

Gridley hardly moved. He made a minor adjustment to a gain feature. Then he spoke slowly in an even, flat tone. "I think we should turn back. Back to our old heading. That's where the music is coming from."

"What are you mumbling about?" Elliot sat straight and glared at the junior sonar tech.

"The music."

The STSC switched channels to listen to what Gridley was talking about. A moment later, he called the conn and requested the course change. Before he heard a reply, Elliot switched the sonar to output through the speakers in control. An unearthly song poured out, entrancing everyone who heard the song.

In the Torpedo Room, Owens and Harris tumbled to the ground as the deck tilted precariously under them. The fall broke Harris' grip on Owens shoulder and they rolled apart. Engineman second class Carr grabbed Harris.

"What the hell are you doing?" he yelled at his commanding officer, pinning Harris's arms. "You think he sent us out there to attack whatever the hell it was?"

The ship shuddered again, turning even harder.

"Keep him here," Owens said to Carr as he stood up, grabbing the bulkhead to maintain his balance. "I've got to find out what's going on with my ship." He wrenched open the door, leaning sideways and shuffling to stay upright in against the hard turn.

The roving auxiliary watch slipped noisily down the ladderwell and sprawled at the Commander's feet. Owens leaned down, getting an arm under the sailor, and hauling him back to his feet. The watch's ubiquitous mickey-mouse style ear protectors sat twisted on his head, knocked askew during the fall. "You okay?"

White wide eyes stared into the Commander's face. "They've all gone nuts!" The sailor adjusted the ear protectors, so they rested properly once more.

"Who?"

The watch pointed upwards. "Everyone in Control. There's this weird music playing over the speakers. I had just stepped in from the fan room and everyone is just sitting there. Then the helmsman turns the ship as hard to port as he can, babbling about how beautiful it is and how they've got to get back to it."

"Back to what?" Owens asked confused.

"I've got no idea. He's just babbling 'back to it, must get back to it'. Back to where we just came from, I guess. The music was just weird. So I backed out as fast as I could and headed down here."

Owens cursed under his breath. If they were taking the ship back, then whatever had attacked the trawler and the SEALs was waiting for them. "You said you could hear the music."

"Yeah. But I had these on." The rover pointed to the hearing protectors. "It made the music distorted."

Owens snapped his fingers. "Get me a set of those."

The watchstander raced into the Auxiliary Space and returned a second later with a pair of bright yellow hearing protectors.

The captain grabbed them with a quick nod of thanks. He slipped the heavy cups over his ear as he raced up the ladder towards the Control Room.

The wavesong was working. The steel-clad prey had turned. They were swimming quickly back towards the creature. It changed the tone of the song, now an even greater promise of health and satisfaction. It had no wish to frighten the prey yet. That would wait until it had wrapped its tentacles around and was squeezing. The wooden prey had yielded some food, though the beast still felt pangs of hunger. It had been so ravenous that it had not sung the death song, the song that sweetened the flesh with the taste of terror. It would not forget to sing to this prey before consuming the morsels inside.

He heard the music prior to entering the Control Room. Two petty officers stood slack-jawed at the base of the ladder. Neither of the men responded to his commands and Owens ended up forcing his way past them to get up the ladder to Control. The ship had finally completed the hard turn and the deck was settling back to the normal flat condition.

The roving watch had been correct. Though he could hear music playing over the speakers, the hearing protection muffled it and twisted the tones. It became just cacophonous noise.

Cupping his hands around his mouth he shouted, "Attention on deck, the captain has the conn!"

No one flinched. No one even glanced at him. Owens could see a line of drool from one of the fire control technicians' mouth to his screen. Everywhere he looked as he worked his way forward through the space, he saw blank faces and empty eyes. He waved his hand in front of the OOD, and the man did not even blink. A chill ran down his spine.

"Shit."

The expletive burst unbidden from Owen's mouth. He checked the ship's course, then paced back to the inert quartermaster's plot. The submarine's current course was an almost perfect reciprocal of the escape route he had ordered.

He moved to the diving officer's station, reached over the helmsman's shoulder, and attempted to turn the rudder control. The man held the airplane-style steering wheel in a steel grasp. Even with both hands pushing and pulling the wheel barely turned. As soon as Owens relinquished his grip, the helmsman made a small correction and returned the vessel to the original course.

Owens stood up. He could do nothing from here. Turning, he dropped down the ladder as the music continued to blare from the Control Room speakers behind him. He ignored it and rushed aft.

Owens finally slowed down when he reached the Maneuvering space.

The Engineering Officer of the Watch (EOOW) and the three enlisted watchstanders all turned to stare as he whipped the heavy blue curtain back and lifted the chain. Even in the concerned state he was in, the captain still followed the protocols that had been instilled in him during his time at the Naval Nuclear Power School in Mare Island California. There were certain things that Admiral

Rickover had ingrained so deeply in every nuclear officer that, even in dire circumstances, they could not ignore. Calmly, still holding the chain in his right hand, Owens announced himself. "Captain entering Maneuvering."

"Aye," stated the bemused EOOW.

"EOOW, get me the Upper Level watch and the ERS. Have them meet me at shaft alley. Then man the sound powered phones. Things are going to happen quickly." He reattached the chain and ran aft. The blue curtain fluttered down to rest after him. Owens heard the order for the Engine Room Upper Level (ERUL) and Engine Room Supervisor (ERS) to meet the CO at shaft alley over the Engine Room announcing circuit, the 2MC. By the time he arrived, the ERUL was standing by, attaching a portable sound powered headset to the 2JV circuit.

The ERS popped up behind them from lower level a moment later. "Machinist mate Wilson reporting as ordered."

Owens nodded to him. "We are taking local control of both the rudder and dive planes. Wilson, grab the SSM for the dive planes and rudder. I'll read. Petty officer Smithfield, you relay everything to Maneuvering."

"Aye sir. Should I get Control on the line as well?" asked the ERUL watch.

"Not at this time." The captain grabbed the Ship's System Manual (SSM) volume from the ERS hands and opened it, flipping pages until he found the appropriate section. He jabbed a finger at a section of one page. "Wilson, open the rudder hydraulic bypass valve HR-…"

The creature was surprised. Its prey was now turning away. This had never happened. Once the prey acknowledged the wavesong, it could not ignore the command. It must obey and must come to the beast.

Great flukes flexed and the creature surged forward. Two tentacles wrapped themselves around the flat protruding fin on the right side of the prey. It was careful to avoid the prey's gnashing teeth. It could sense them tearing at the water. However, the prey seemed unable to turn its jaw to bite, so as long as the creature attacked from one side or the other, it would be safe enough from harm.

It used a third tentacle to grab the large flat fin on the bottom of the prey. The prey shuddered at the beast's touch. The prey's skin was hard. Much harder than anything the creature had eaten before. In an attempt to slow the prey down, the creature extended its spines. Even these hardly penetrated the prey's skin.

Then the prey began to fight harder. Its fins rose and fell in great sweeps, with a strength that the creature had difficulty fighting. In addition, the prey was pulling even harder now, beginning to drag the beast behind it. The monster changed its wavesong. Now came the discordant tones of dirges and death. A terrifying melody of horror. This music would freeze the prey's blood and destroy its will to live.

A new feeling flashed across the tiny brain of the beast, surprise. Even the new wavesong was having no effect. The prey struggled just as hard as before. Another pair of tentacles lashed out, grabbing the left side fins. Perhaps if it could hold all the fins, the prey could no longer swim fast.

This did slow the fin's motion, but the speed at which the prey was moving continued to increase. Thick, air-filled water battered the main body of the beast as it continued to be drug behind the prey. First one, then another tentacle was pushed off by the increasing pressure of the water past the skin of the prey. Several spines broke free, remaining imbedded in the prey's hide.

Eventually, the battering and speed proved too much. For the first time in the creature's memory, its prey escaped.

Chapter Nine

CIA Headquarters, Langley, Virginia
26 November 1986
0052 EST / 0552 Zulu
Secure Briefing Room Echo

K eith Butler double-checked the lock on the door before he began talking. "As a reminder, everything stated in this room is classified under top secret codeword automobile." All eyes turned towards the Marine major in the room. The CIA and the military were awkward bedfellows in the best of times. "This is Major Brevard, Pentagon liaison for Joint Task Force Thirteen. He will conduct the first portion of the brief."

Major Brevard nodded curtly to Agent Butler and turned to the other four men in the room. "Less than five hours ago, during an authorized rescue mission of an intelligence asset, a submarine code named Efficiency was attacked and damaged by a previously unknown and unclassified ocean supernatural. One member of the SEAL team was killed in action during the attack and a second severely wounded. Efficiency also reported the loss of the Soviet AIG trawler to the creature and some damage to herself. Efficiency was able to break contact with the creature, though they are not sure how or for how long. No one on board is part of the Task Force nor read into the protocols. The squadron commander is read into the general protocols and routed the report to us instead of COMSUBLANT. *We* can legally only hold the information for another six hours," he emphasized.

Heads nodded around the table. The CSOP, or Creature of Supernatural Origin Protocols, allowed JTF 13 to perform initial determination of the potential danger from unknown creatures before informing the control commands, no matter which branch of service was involved. However, the information had to be released to control commands within twelve hours.

"The nearest asset would normally be a squad from Stuttgart, Germany. However, most of that unit are in the Middle East on mission. Instead of completely stripping Europe, I am recommending we use a portion of the Eastern North American response team." A map of north-eastern Europe and the North Atlantic flashed up on the screen. There was a red dot midway across Norway and silhouette of a submarine between Bear Island and Svalbard. "Two fire teams are currently in a training exercise in Norway." The Major tapped the red dot. "Our plan is to release them from the exercise and get them loaded with gear into an SH-3. The helicopter will have to perform an in-flight refueling to meet the range requirements. Difficult but there are untasked refueling assets available in area. Efficiency will position to pick the team up from a helo. This is the fastest method to get a team in place. Once onboard, the JTF personnel will determine course of action to destroy the creature before any other personnel or assets are lost." Brevard stepped back and yielded the floor to Agent Butler.

"There is good news. Both Flute and Paladin were recovered safely. The two are on board Efficiency. The bad news is the damage the submarine sustained during the attack makes it difficult to exit the area undetected. Apparently either one or both diving planes and the rudder were damaged in the attack."

One of the men at the table spoke up. "Can we recover Paladin or Flute when we drop the marines to the sub?"

The Major shook his head. "Too risky. Plans are for this to be a minimal time insertion. The JTF team will fast rope both their equipment and personnel to the deck of the submarine. The helicopter will not land or linger in area. This minimizes the chance of anyone noticing the flight as anything beyond long-range flight training. If we brought Flute back, there are likely to be questions of where the marines went and where Flute arrived from. Currently Flute will remain on Efficiency."

Another agent spoke up, "What about using other assets in Norway, or even the rest of Europe?"

Keith bit back a groan and leaned on the table. "As was stated before, the Stuttgart team is currently on assignment. We really don't want to call on our allies for this. The fewer people that even suspect supernaturals exist, the better for everyone. We are not involving any non-American or non-JTF groups if possible. Right now, the best team within range for both time and distance are the marines in Norway."

Another hand raised. Keith glanced at the man.

"What is our backup plan if the marines cannot deal with the creature?"

Major Brevard cleared his throat. "In the event that both Efficiency and the JTF contingent are unable to successfully neutralize the supernatural threat, a request will be made to the President."

The questioning man glanced about. "What request?"

"A request to release a special weapon." The major looked over the group, realizing that the answer would need further explanation. "Specifically, a B57 ten kiloton nuclear depth charge. The weapon is air releasable and could be deployed from either a helicopter or P-3 Orion fixed wing aircraft. This of course, is not the preferred method since it would cause significant environmental issues as well as be almost impossible to cover up or explain to either our allies or our enemies." The major looked back at Agent Butler. The only sound in the room was the soft shush of the air conditioning fan.

"Decision time. Call for using the marines." Keith looked around as all four men, some slowly and others with vigor, lifted their right hands. "That's unanimous. Major, get word to your men. Project is a go."

Outside Trondheim, Trøndelag, Norway
26 November 1986
0829 CET/0729 Zulu
Northern Roundup III Command Base

Morehouse was happy to get out of the cold. The aggressors had been hounding the defenders for a couple of days, Days during which they were in the field and not in a warm bunk or room. The last evening had been one of the worst. The attack had included not only an infantry attack but armor as well. He shifted the rifle on his shoulder to a more confrontable position as he ducked under the snow flap and into the Command Tent.

He popped to attention and snapped a salute. "Sergeant Morehouse reporting as ordered sir," He waited for the Colonel behind the desk to acknowledge the salute before dropping his.

The Colonel waved Morehouse to a seat. "Sit Sergeant. My name is Colonel Burgess, S-4 for the Marine Corp Prepositioning Program here in Norway. I'll get right to the point. Both of the fire teams you arrived with are being re-assigned. I can't tell you why since *I* have not been informed of the reason." It was obvious that Burgess was not happy with the fact he was being left out of the loop. "Just that I was to get you and your men kitted up as quickly as possible. All I know is that I received an order Priority Red Metal Plutonium Copper."

Morehouse steeled his face to show no emotion.

"Based on the completely blank expression you just achieved, I assume you have an idea of what that means. I've ordered runners to either gather your men from the field or rouse them as necessary. Your Master Gunnery Sergeant is already verifying the tent I suggested for your team briefing. I am also to inform you that your teams have been authorized to draw from the Pre-Po any necessary man-portable weapons. If you determine there is a need for heavier weapons," the Colonel grimaced at that, "you will need additional authorization from your primary command. I am guessing at this point your primary command is not the 4th Amphibious or any direct part of that formation?"

"Sir, with all due respect, I am not at liberty to answer that question."

Colonel Burgess waved away the answer. "I know better than to put a man on the spot like that. I have a case of incurable curiosity, which is why these wings are as high as I will probably ever achieve." He stroked the eagle insignia on his collar tabs. "Enough about that. As soon as they come through, printed orders will be delivered to you and your men. Please inform me as soon as possible what additional materials you are going to require. Sooner is better in this case."

Burgess stood and Morehouse popped up immediately to attention. "My adjutant will show you to the briefing tent. Semper Fi, Sergeant Morehouse."

Morehouse flashed a salute, dropping it after the Colonel acknowledged it. "Oorah sir."

"…and that is the total information we have about the attack," concluded Morehouse.

The tent Gunny had chosen was a heated island in a sea of snow. The next closest building was a Quonset hut over a hundred yards away, so there was no worry of anyone eavesdropping on the briefing.

"The suggested load-out for this large a supernatural would normally be mortars or light armored vehicles. Unfortunately, there's nowhere on the submarine to effectively mount the mortars in a way where they won't get either knocked off or blow themselves off the deck during attack. And for obvious reasons the light armored vehicles are out."

The squad snorted at the weak humor.

Morehouse smiled and continued. "As such, I believe our best bet will be grenades. Specifically, the 40 mm used by the M203 and the belt fed Mark 19. Is there anyone here who has not qualified on the M203?"

No hands went up.

"Good. Gunny, Hanzo, Wade, and I are all qualified on the Mark 19. We will load out four Mark 19s, several boxes of grenade belts, and a couple of boxes of reloads for the 203s. Everyone will mount an M203 on your rifle. We need to ensure that we load out for maximum firepower given what we're going up against."

Corporal Grizzle raised a hand.

"Go Bear."

"Which type of grenade?"

"Good question. Primarily, I plan on requesting HEDPs. Supernaturals, especially larger ones, are often armored. Also, water borne supernaturals usually have some sort of resistance to fire, even against magnesium. That means that blowing holes in them is one of the most effective ways to damage them. I figure a combination a high explosive charge with armor piercing penetrators is our best bet. Use the HE to open them up and the penetrators to get in. More bleeding and bigger holes means they go down faster.

"Wade, you'll interface with the Pre-Po marines to get the equipment. The rest of us will pack out and load the helo. Once the Pre-Po guys deliver the equipment, we'll load out the bird. Plan is to get all of this done in the next three hours." Morehouse raised his hands placatingly. "I know it's not much time, but we're on the clock here. The flight alone is going to take nearly six hours with an in-flight refuel."

The Barents Sea, North Northeast of Bear Island
26 November 1986
1558 CET / 1458 Zulu
USS *Sea Devil* (SSN 664)

"Conn, ECM. New radar contact, Echo zero-zero-two. Relative bearing is south south-east. Echo two is broadcasting on a wide band. Initial classification is Big Bulge."

"ECM, Conn. Periscope detection threat?" Owens leaned on the plotting table and listened.

"Negative. Signal strength well below threshold. Big Bulge radars are carried on Ka-25 Hormone helicopters and Tu-95 Bear maritime reconnaissance aircraft. Can't determine aircraft type at this time."

"Very well ECM," the OOD replied. He turned to the captain. "Think their looking for the trawler?"

"It's a good bet," Owens stated as he stood up. "Keep the ECM mast up. Be ready to raise number two scope. If they come this way, we'll get them on video. Maybe something good will come out of this situation."

"Yes sir. Any word on when we can return to port and get the rudder and planes fixed?"

"No. Command wants us to stick around here. We are getting a group of 'experts' that deal with this kind of situation."

The Weapons Officer looked around and lowered his voice. "We have experts on *sea monsters?*" The last words were whispered so quietly that Owens had trouble hearing them. No one wanted to admit what had happened. Official word around the submarine was that the boat had struck a large biological and damaged the rudder and diving planes. Which was true on a very general level.

Most crew realized that whatever had happened was much different than striking a whale in the middle of the Norwegian Sea. Like what had really happened to the watchstanders in Control during the situation, who was the additional person that had been brought aboard, and why was the SEAL commander pissed at the CO? There were no answers available, though the rumor mill was providing a fair number of wrong suggestions.

"I don't know. All I have is the orders to remain near the sinking point but away from whatever it was that attacked us."

"How are we getting them?" The OOD looked pointedly at the chart. "I can't see them sending a tug this far out."

"Nope. They're coming via helicopter. Should be here in about another hour." Owens tapped a spot marked on the map not far from the ship's current position. "We'll be setting up to receive them in thirty minutes or so. If this other helo is still around, I am not sure what the plan is going to be. Stay flexible and be ready to adjust position if it comes to that."

STS1 Blevins adjusted the gain on his set. He still had not yet actually picked up the biological that had attacked the ship. It did not seem to make noise the way large whales or dolphin pods did. In that respect, it reminded him of a shark. Sharks were almost impossible to catch on sonar since they did not rely on an active system to find their way around. Everything was electrical and passive senses for them. If that was the case with this one, there would be almost no warning that it was present unless it sang the weird song again.

He did pick up a faint thumping on the tail as he was scanning channels. He dialed in and cross-checked the sound. Then he hit the microphone switch.

"Conn, Sonar. New contact, Sierra zero-one-four bearing one-five-three or two-zero-six. Faint rotor sounds. Initial classification is helicopter. One of the bearings on the tail matches the bearing for echo two. Recommend coming port thirty degrees to reconcile bearing discrepancy."

"Roger Sonar. Coming starboard to course one-nine-five. Time to stabilize?"

"Tail will be stable in six minutes."

"Raising scope number two." The Weapons Officer twisted the orange ring and flipped the training handles down as the number two scope rose. A fire control petty officer flipped on the small twelve-inch black and white repeater monitor and pressed record on the VCR. The Junior OOD and the Captain watched the repeater as the scope broke through the waves. The OOD turned a full three-sixty quickly, verifying there were no close contacts prior to settling on a visual search. Thirty seconds later he lowered the scope.

"Can't see him yet. Sonar, range to Sierra one-four?"

"Still waiting for the tail to stabilize."

"Roger."

Captain Owens checked his watch. "OOD, I have the deck. You maintain the conn."

The Weapons Officer acknowledged the command.

"Tail stable. Range to Sierra one-four is twelve thousand yards. Contact is sweeping starboard to port in a wide S pattern. I'd say he is in search mode for a surface contact."

"Conn, ECM. Concur with Sonar. No indication of sonar or dipping radar. Only receiving surface search band from the Big Bulge."

Every thirty seconds, Owens raised the periscope and performed a five-second search. Finally, on his eighth cycle, he spotted the distinctive twin rotor design of the Soviet helicopter. "New visual contact, victor zero-zero-two bearing one four eight, moving northward. Correlate victor two with echo two and Sierra one-four. Victor two classified as a Kilo Alpha Two Five Hormone-B. I can see the Big Bulge radar. It is now in hover. Looks like they might have spotted some of the wreckage.

"Quartermaster, how far from sinking point are we currently?"

Owens heard the Quartermaster moving about and measuring on the map. "Approximately three nautical miles. Point eight nautical miles from no-go approach line."

"Very well. OOD, suggest a new course to parallel the line. Do not get any closer than one thousand yards max."

The OOD replied and Owens performed another clearance sweep before returning to focus on the hovering aircraft.

"Looks like they are lowering someone into the…Holy shit!"

Eight tentacles exploded out of the water. One wrapped around the individual on the winch. Three penetrated the body of the helicopter; two through the windscreen and the third through the open side door. The other four wrapped around the fuselage. Blood and flesh tore and splattered as the twin blades sliced into the flesh of the gargantuan appendages. White and grey smoke billowed out of the engines and one set of the rotors disintegrated, tossing metal pieces in all directions.

Muscles contracted, and the entire body of the helicopter crushed inward. Various fluids sprayed out of the mass of tentacles as the helicopter collapsed and was drug underwater. Seconds later, there was nothing to mark its existence beyond a faint ring of flotsam and oil dispersing quickly in the waves.

"Lowering scope." Commander Owens stepped back and turned the orange ring in the lower direction without thought. "Did we get that all on video?" He glanced down at his shaking hands, closing them into fists to stop the trembles.

A horror-stricken fire control technician nodded silently.

"Eject the tape." The sailor did so and handed the cassette to the CO. "Everything that you just saw is classified top secret with a code word. You are not to speak of it to anyone without my express permission. Mark down in the log that Sierra one-four/echo two/victor two was a lost contact. Do not, I repeat, do not mark it as a sunken vessel or downed aircraft. Anything else comes up, I will be in my quarters. OOD, you have the deck and the conn. Keep us away from that line."

The OOD nodded mutely as Commander Owens ducked into the sonar space, the toxic tape tucked under his arm.

Blevins looked over as the CO pushed past the blue curtain. "You heard what I said out there. I need a copy of everything from the last half hour, then scrub all the data from the system. Do not keep any additional backups."

The lead sonarman just nodded and ejected the data tape from the data computer. "I figured that was what you were going to want. Already backed it up to the tape." He entered a set of commands and pressed a blinking button on the computer. "Last hour of data is destroyed except for this version." He handed the small data tape to Commander Owens. "I can't seem to pick this thing up on passive. Once it broke the water, I could hear the splashes. Until then, the only thing I had was the helo. This thing is invisible on passive. If we need to find it, I think active 's the only way we're going to."

Commander Owens nodded. "Keep working on it. The more we can figure out from here, the less likely we get attacked without warning again."

Chapter Ten

The Barents Sea, North Northeast of Bear Island
26 November 1986
1645 CET / 1545 Zulu
SH-3 Sea King approaching USS *Sea Devil* (SSN 664)

The pounding of the rotors now matched the pounding of the headache Sergeant Morehouse was nursing. The flight had taken almost seven hours with the winds against them. They had refueled in-flight about two hours ago, which had been the most interesting thing to happen since the helicopter had taken off.

The eight marines were spaced haphazardly around the two weapon and ammo pallets they had loaded up back in Norway. Once the gear had been loaded, space was at a premium. Everybody strapped in as best they could and hoped the spot they chose would be comfortable for the duration. In the end none of them had spots that were particularly comfortable.

Morehouse's headset crackled to life. "We're about ten minutes out from the rendezvous. Go ahead and set up your lines. As discussed earlier, you'll send two of your marines down first. They will rig the safety line to the submarine. Next, you'll connect the pallets and lower them. Marines subside will guide the pallets to a safe landing. Finally, after the pallets are down, you six will fast rope down.

"My flight engineer will get the ropes up. We'll be returning to base once you guys are onboard. The evolution is scheduled for no more than seven minutes. I have fifteen minutes of reserve to hover. That's it. Once that's gone, so are we. I can't linger since there is nothing between this patch of ocean and the Norwegian shoreline that I can land on. Questions?"

"No sir. Briefing understood. We are connecting the lines now." With a quick set of commands, Corporals Riley and Gustav scrambled out of the straps holding them in place and began attaching the heavy ropes to tie downs on the starboard side of the helicopter at the door.

The helicopter swung wide to port and changed course.

"What's going on sir?" Morehouse asked over the headset.

"Just got word from the submarine. Looks like they are in a slightly different spot than we planned. They also gave us warning to avoid grid sectors twelve, thirteen, fourteen, and twenty-two. That means we have to adjust the flight path to keep clear and still catch up with them."

"Is that going to effect the hover time?"

The pilot's voice was calm and steady. "Nope. This is a minor change in course. We'll still have the same amount of time to disembark you and your gear, Sergeant."

"Roger."

A sailor, looking a bit like an insect in the bulbous helmet and tinted visor, climbed out of the flight deck and positioned himself by the door.

"Petty officer second class Turner. I'm the flight engineer. I'll be assisting you marines in the off-load." He reached up and pressed his right hand against the side of the helmet. "Yes sir. Three minutes aye." He glanced over at the two marines with the ropes. "I need you gentlemen to back over to port. I'll be opening the door in about two minutes. Once we're over the sub, I'll kick the lines out and give you two thumbs up for the fast rope."

Gustav and Riley grabbed the bundles and climbed over one of the pallets. The flight engineer gave each knot a solid tug and nodded. Then he hooked a safety line from himself to an attachment point just aft of the door. Another set of tugs ensured the line was properly connected.

"Pilot, engineer. Opening door." He waited a moment for the unheard reply and then rotated the door's latch. The sliding door popped open around the edges. With a grunt, the flight engineer pushed the door forward. It slid easily along the railings on the outside of the helicopter and hooked into the open position. Cold wind blew through the opening and the sound of the engines and rotors intensified.

PO2 Turner rotated a latch and mechanically locked the door open. He grabbed the side safety rail and leaned out. "Alright. I can see the submarine." He pointed out the door and down. From his position, all Morehouse could see was the dark ocean and clouds. The bulk of the helicopter hid the submarine from his view.

"Aye aye pilot." Turner looked back at the marines. "We're starting the hover. Get ready." He paused and looked down again. "Ropes!" he shouted and held out a hand to assist.

Riley tossed his rope cleanly out. Gustav's rope took a bit of assistance from the flight engineer to completely clear the hatch.

"Hook up, then you are clear to descend." He waved the two marines down.

Before they stepped out, Morehouse tapped each of the men on their shoulders. "Once you're down, hook in safety lines. I'll get the pallets to you as quickly as we can."

Gustav and Riley nodded and stepped out of the hovering vehicle, quickly sliding down the ropes to the waiting deck below. Several sailors stood topside in bright orange life preservers ready to assist as necessary.

Turner watched until the men had successfully landed. Then he hit a set of switches to release the clutch system on the winch. He carefully reached out and up, pulling the hook and a section of wire cable into the cabin. The cargo pallets had been set up for lowering when they were initially loaded onto the helicopter. Now it was a matter of attaching the winch hook and maneuvering the ungainly load out the door. He verified one last time the load straps, then clipped the hook through the lifting lug.

"I'll lift it slightly," Turner told the six remaining men. "When I give the sign…and not before…I need you guys to push the load out the door. Be careful. This thing is going to swing a bit once it is off the deck. Make sure it's straight and clears the sides. Once the cargo is suspended outside, I'll winch it down and the guys on deck can unhook it." The flight engineer grabbed the safety bar as the helicopter slid sideways in a gust of wind. "And make sure all of you are connected with a safety harness. I don't need any of you sliding out the bird without a chute or rope. It'll look bad on my record. Oh, and you probably won't enjoy the experience either."

Everyone gave a dry chuckle at Turner's words. Then they made a serious check of their safety harnesses. Six hands flashed thumbs up signs.

"Here we go."

Master Gunnery Sergeant Peck and Sergeant Morehouse looked around the deck while the ship's sailors carefully lowered the last of the marine's gear into the submarine. The helicopter that had deposited them was no longer in view having disappeared into the gray sky some fifteen minutes earlier.

"I think you were completely correct Gunny. There's no way mortars would have been effective here. The Mark 19s should do okay. Just wish these things still had deck guns." Morehouse waved across the expanse of black deck as he spoke. "Not much cover here. I'm not big on needing to get so close to a huge supernatural as we're going to need to for this."

"Yep." Master Gunnery Sergeant Peck smiled and spat over the side of the submarine. "I'd feel better using a TOW or even a 50 mm chain gun. Problem is, size and weight. We might have brought a couple of TOW missiles, but overall, we got more bang for the buck from the grenades. We're just going to need to get a little closer than any of us is comfortable with."

A sailor walked up and waited patiently for the master gunnery sergeant to finish speaking. "Gentlemen, if you'll follow me down. All the gear is below, and the captain would like to clear the decks."

"I don't suspect he likes being on the surface in this situation." Peck stated.

"Doesn't like to be on the surface in any situation," stated the sailor. "Submarines belong underwater, not on top."

The two marines grunted at the statement. They followed the sailor to the escape trunk and climbed down the steel ladder into the bowels of the ship.

Morehouse was struck by how cramped the submarine was. He had served on several navy ships, primarily carriers, during his time in. This was his first experience with a submarine. The overhead was about a foot lower than he expected, and the passageways were significantly narrower. He watched sailors walking along them and seemingly without thought or notice turn sideways to allow each other to pass. He might have been able to slip four sheets of paper between the two when they passed each other. Certainly, no more than that. Their escort stayed quiet until they reached a faux wood door with a small porthole in it.

The sailor knocked once, then opened the door after a moment of silence. He ushered the pair of marines into the room. It was the largest space they had seen so far. Faux wood paneling covered most of the walls, though a few locker handles of shining aluminum were visible. The floor boasted a deep blue carpet rather than the beige tiles the rest of the floors sported. A large table dominated the room, covered with fitted maroon Naugahyde. An embroidered version of the *Sea Devil*'s emblem had been sown into the center of the cover. Five padded metal chairs were arrayed on each side of the table, with a larger chair at the aft end. The forward end of the table boasted a bench seat built into the forward bulkhead.

"This is the Officer's Wardroom. The CO will be down in a few moments. Have a seat…except the big chair. That's the CO's and no one sits in it but him. Tradition. You guys need coffee or something to drink. Besides the coffee we've got water, sweet tea, or bug juice."

Gunny glanced at Morehouse. The sailor, whose nametag read Ramone, spoke so quickly it appeared his mouth was nearly tripping over the words. Surprisingly, he had managed to get all of the statement out in a single breath.

"Which colors of bug juice you got?" Morehouse asked off-handedly.

"Purple and orange. I think."

"Orange if you've got it, water if not. Thanks."

"I'll take a sweet tea," Peck added.

The sailor nodded his head in return and stepped out of the wardroom, carefully closing the door behind him. Peck and Morehouse sat down at the table, near the head and across from one another.

"I want you to give the brief Morehouse," Peck began. "You've heard the spiel enough times before that you should have it down. If you stumble, I'll back you up. Just focus on the usual setup. This guy is not previously read in and it's his first encounter with a supernatural."

The two men looked over as the door opened again. A larger man with silver maple leaves on his coverall's collar strode in, followed by a brown-haired officer with bronze maple leaves. The brown-haired officer wore khakis with the gold eagle and trident badge of a SEAL. The larger man sat down in the CO's chair and the brown-haired SEAL sat one chair down from Peck. Petty Officer Ramone hurried in through the aft wardroom door. He set drinks in front of the four men, ensuring that each man got the correct glass. Then he silently placed a Naugahyde cover over the small window on the aft door and scurried out, closing the door behind himself.

"I am Commander Owens, captain of the *Sea Devil*. Welcome aboard." The commanding officer took a small sip of the coffee in front of him, then leaned forward to look the two marines in the eyes. "I was informed that you would have a briefing to explain what is going on. I am glad someone can. I suspect that Lieutenant Commander Harris feels the same way." Harris gave a quick, sharp nod of agreement.

"Yes sirs," began Morehouse. He stood up so that he could face everyone in the room. It also gave him the ability to pace a bit.

"What I am about to brief you on is classified to the highest levels. Consider it above Top Secret code word. There really isn't a true classification for it. And once you are read in, there is no way to back out. Commander Owens, you unfortunately do not have a choice in this briefing."

Morehouse turned and looked directly at the SEAL leader. "Lieutenant Commander Harris, you do have a choice. If you leave right now, we can debrief you and your team prior to arriving in port, but you won't be considered as read in." He paused and waited.

Harris waved a hand. "I've seen stuff on this mission that I need explained. I've already got things that I've done I won't even be allowed to confess to Saint Peter at the gates. This will just be one more thing. I lost men, and *someone*," he emphasized, "is going to tell me the truth about why. I'm staying."

Morehouse glanced at Peck, who gave him a slight nod to continue. Morehouse retrieved a folder from inside his pockets and set it on the table. He opened it and extracted some papers.

"Very well." He passed both the officers a sheet of paper. "I need you to sign the memorandum of acknowledgement prior to the brief. Everything else will be covered under the classification described on the sheet." Once the two men read over and signed the sheets, Morehouse began speaking again.

"This part is always a bit difficult to explain clearly." He took a deep breath and continued. "Almost every creature from fairy tale, legend, myth, or fantasy story has some basis in truth. Not just the truth of some early person seeing a more advanced person in a horse and thinking *Oh, a half-man half-horse.* No, rather the fact that some person or persons *actually* encountered centaurs. This set of facts has been deliberately kept from the population at large for centuries. To our knowledge, none of these creatures evolved on this Earth, or more aptly, this particular plane of existence or dimension. The experts aren't even sure what the right name is for it. They currently call it the Never-Never.

"For the purposes of this brief, I'm only going back as far as the beginning of the United States as a nation. During the Revolutionary War, a regiment of Colonial Marines and British Royal Marines ran into a group of supernaturals, specifically a pack of werewolves. The same group dealt with several other supernatural threats during the war. Afterward, things became more formalized. The Brits developed the 13th Marine Commando. Here in America, we started off as the Special Unit.

"This unit's charter is designed around dealing with anything that is of supernatural origins. Through the years, the task force has slowly changed, gaining members from all branches of the military as well as support inside the government. Eventually, the Special Unit evolved into Joint Task Force 13. Thirteen was chosen as the unit identifier since the number itself has both positive and negative beliefs tied to it." Morehouse paused and took a drink from his glass, then continued.

"The Marines maintain overall command of Joint Task Force 13, but there are members serving in all branches currently. Some units, like mine, are formed and trained specifically to act as primary aggressors against supernaturals. Others remain imbedded in other units to act as guidance in case an event occurs."

Harris ignored the glass of water in front of him. He leaned against the table and interrupted the briefing. "I get the overall idea of what that means. Now tell me what the *hell* you guys thought sending *my team* up against one of these supernaturals *without warning us!*" His voice rose in anger as he finished, nearly growling out the last words.

"Sir, with all due respect, no one even suspected there was a supernatural here." Morehouse remained calm as he spoke. "Your team's mission, whatever it might be, has nothing to do with supernaturals. The government and, more importantly, JTF 13 do not intentionally send untrained teams against supernatural occurrences. The discovery of this creature was unexpected and every bit as surprising to the rest of us as it was to your team and yourself. You have my condolences on the loss of your men.

"My squad," Morehouse emphasized, "is trained and will work with both you, Commander Owens, your crew and interface with the SEAL team to destroy this supernatural."

Owens shifted in his seat and Morehouse glanced at him. "You have a question sir?"

"You keep calling this thing a supernatural. Do you have any idea of what it really is?"

"Sorry. Habit showing there. We label everything a supernatural as a general label." Morehouse flipped through a couple of pages in his folder and drew out a sheet with a copy of a woodcutting. The black and white picture depicted a huge squid-like creature wrapping its tentacles around a sailing vessel. The creature was nearly the size of the ship and had two huge eyes. "Investigation suggests that the creature you encountered is a kraken. Most of the information about krakens comes from various Scandinavian stories. According to the stories, they are very similar to giant squid. They have eight primary arms and two feeding tentacles. The mouth is a large beak-like structure, though some stories have a larger maw filled with inward-facing teeth like a lamprey. The body is a large tapering cone with a pair of strong swimming fins parallel to the body.

"JTF 13 has never dealt with a kraken in this region, nor have they ever heard of a kraken having the sonic ability you described in your report, Captain. Sonic influence is very unusual in supernaturals. A few examples are banshee screams and the nue's hunting cry. The researchers feel the closest approximation to the mind-altering ability you described is the mermaid and siren songs.

"Mers, sirens, and other such supernaturals don't tend to show up in Scandinavian myths and never in the same stories that include the kraken. The two creatures, especially the mermaids, are extremely common in the myth and story cycles found from peoples bordering the Mediterranean Sea, both southern European and northern African. Frankly, the name kraken is more of a placeholder than a definitive classification of what you got attacked by here." Morehouse pointed once more to the photo and glanced at the SEAL. "What do you think Mr. Harris?"

Harris pulled the picture closer and took a sip of water. "I only saw the, well arms I guess, of the creature. They were very thick and muscular. When one grabbed a team member, he could not fight his way out of its grasp. I never saw the body, nor any feeding tentacles. The arms also had retractable claws or hooks in the center of the suckers." He laid one of the things that his team had removed from the port diving plane. It was yellow-white in color and nearly seven inches in length. It was half an inch across at the base and tapered to a sharp point. "When we assessed the damage to the submarine, we found several of these imbedded into the diving planes and a few in the rudder. There were also score lines in the metal where it looks like an arm lost grip and scratched the paint as it slid off."

"Those arms are very strong. Once it grabbed the ship, we had to get past ahead two-thirds before we broke free of its grip," interjected Owens. "Plus, its hold ended up damaging the rudder hydraulics. We are currently limited to shallow turns since we can't get full motion back until we replace certain parts."

Harris glanced over at Peck, who continue to sit and listen as Morehouse briefed them. The master gunnery sergeant gave the SEAL a bland look, then returned to watching the interplay between Morehouse and the officers. "How do you intend to deal with this kraken then?" Harris asked.

"Our plan is to lure the creature to the surface and engage with grenades. Based on the size and strength descriptions, anything less powerful than grenades won't be effective. I wish your ship still had a deck gun. Artillery, mortar fire, or surface-to-surface missiles are the preferred method of dealing with large supernaturals. The key concept has always been indirect fire and distance.

Anything to keep us as far from it as possible. Because close and casualty start with the same letter and are often hand-in-hand for these battles.

"Unfortunately, there was no effective way we could come up with of mounting mortars on the deck of a submarine. Everything else that could provide sufficient indirect fire was too heavy to lift in the time we had."

Commander Owens steepled his fingers and rested his chin on the point. "Would torpedoes work? I only have three on-board. I would suggest SUBROCs against this target, but we aren't carrying any at this time."

Sergeant Morehouse frowned in thought. "I don't see any reason the torpedoes wouldn't work. They're designed specifically for attacking seagoing targets. As a bonus, they allow the ship to stay far away from the kraken. Gunny?"

"I can't think of any reason it wouldn't be effective," Peck stated in a mild voice.

"Good." Owens laid his hands flat on the table. "I'll get with the Weapons Officer and load three tubes. Then, if for some reason this thing survives the attack, we'll close and in the words of the diesel boats of old, 'prepare for surface action'. We may not have a deck gun, Sergeant, but I think I can get close enough for your squad to perform the final kill using grenades."

"I concur," Morehouse began. "I'm sure…"

"My team wants in on this," broke in Lieutenant Commander Harris. "We've already been blooded by this damned thing. There's no way in hell me or my team are going to stand by and let someone, anyone, else take it out."

Before Morehouse could speak, Gunny motioned for him to wait. "We'd be glad to have you and your men, sir. Are all of your men familiarized with the Mark 19?"

"If any are not, we'll get familiar before we kill this…kraken."

Owens stood up, effectively ending the brief. "Gentlemen, I believe we have a course of action. We'll reconvene right after dinner and finalize the plan."

"…will be the biggest problem. We'll launch as soon as we have a good solution. Then, if necessary, we will surface the ship and the assault teams will attack using grenades. Any questions?" Owens looked over the assembly of officers and enlisted men. No one raised a hand or spoke. He waited a moment more before proceeding. "I know it will be difficult but keep all of this to yourselves. No talking to any else about this or what we are going to do. Treat it like a live fire exercise if any of the crew get too nosy. Then, if they continue to push, send them to me. *I'll* answer their questions."

Four men worked to load the first torpedo. It was the solid green of a live warhead, no orange striping on any part of the 19-foot weapon. The youngest torpedoman's mate whistled in awe as they removed the fitted rubber safety cover from the torpedo's sonar dome. He'd never expected to actually launch a live torp.

Three men, each with specific jobs, listened carefully as a fourth read out instructions. The torpedo loading procedure ensure the weapons could be readied with maximum efficiency and minimum danger. The junior torpedoman's mate listened carefully to the procedure and acknowledged his part. Then he turned and checked the drain valve open. He shone a flashlight at the drainage funnel and drainpipe, verifying there was no water.

"Number one tube is fully drained," he reported.

"Fully drained aye. Open tube one hatch."

"Open tube one hatch aye." He operated a set of hydraulic valves and the watertight door unlocked and cycled open. The long empty pipe sat waiting for the weapon, the light from the torpedo room reaching barely a third of the way down the dark maw. He shone a flashlight down the tube, verifying there was no pooled water in the tube. "Tube one dry."

The instructions continued. Two of the torpedomen used special wrenches to cycle the transfer gears. This system lifted the torpedo out of its storage cradle and moved it gently to the loading ram. Once the weapon was verified stable on the transfer ram's rails, the taller of the two torpedomen unscrewed a cover plate over a test port. He connected a set of wires and ran a short diagnostic test, verifying the motor and fuel were ready. When the test was completed satisfactorily, he removed the diagnostic wires and screwed the cover plate back in place. A quick check with his finger around the edges verified the watertight seal was still intact. Satisfied, he flashed a thumbs-up sign.

A shorter, well-muscled torpedoman's mate lifted a heavy round can out of a storage locker. He hefted it up and slipped the can onto the torpedo just aft of the propulsor unit. The can contained the guidance wire, the only way the ship could direct the torpedo once it launched. The lead torpedoman's mate verified all hands were clear and pressed a button. Hydraulics hissed and the first torpedo slid slowly into the number one tube.

The gleaming chrome can nearly touched the sides of the tube, blocking any view further down. The lead torpedoman's mate verified the guidance wire connected properly to the port inside the tube. He stepped back and to port, returning to the Weapons Control Panel. He ordered the junior torpedoman's mate to continue. The junior sailor lifted a valve handle and hydraulics swung the heavy brass and steel door shut. The sailor then cycled another valve and the outer latching ring rotated to the LOCK position with a soft clang, ensuring a watertight seal for the door.

At the Weapons Control Panel, the lead torpedoman's mate ran another test, this time verifying the guidance wire, torpedo guidance computer, and the Fire Control System properly communicated with each other. The test indicates green for all messages sent. The first torpedo was ready.

"Conn, Torpedo Room. Torpedo tube one is loaded with a Mark 48. Guidance communication test satisfactory. Arming circuit is in standby."

The other sailors ignored the communication. As soon as the door to tube one shut and the ring lock cycled, they turned and headed to the port side of the room to start the process over. There were two more torpedoes to load.

The biggest concern right now was that he had a civilian on board that no one beyond the XO, the SEALs and the ship's corpsman were even aware of. He had not mentioned her to the marines when they came on board. Now he was heading into battle with a giant sea creature. She had not signed up for that.

Owens knocked on the door to the XO stateroom. "Ma'am, its Captain Owens."

A muffled "Come in" drifted through the door.

He carefully opened the door and slipped into the cabin, shutting the door behind himself. The woman the SEALs had rescued sat at the room's fold down desk. The only light came from the small lamp inside the desk. It illuminated her head while the rest of the room remained in shadow. It was obvious she had showered and slept since being brought aboard. She looked better for it. She had braided her long dark hair in a simple plait worn over her right shoulder.

"Flute, my name is Commander William Owens. I am the captain of this vessel."

"Please, call me Mikoslava." Her voice was light, with just a hint of an Eastern European accent. "The first time I heard Flute as a name was when the men brought me aboard. I had another name when I worked on the trawler." She grimaced as she mentioned the ship. "I understand it was somehow destroyed during the action."

Owens hesitated a moment. "Yes, it was. However, not by any U.S. force. That is part of what I need to talk to you about."

Mikoslava's face contorted in confusion. "Was there a bomb or something aboard? Did the Soviets themselves destroy the *Zhiqulesk*?"

"Hold on," stated Owens as he held up his hands placatingly. "No, no bomb, no Soviet attack. We know that the Soviets did send a rescue unit in an attempt to discover what had happened to your trawler. We haven't determined exactly what it was," Owens lied. "However, I have orders to go back and figure that out. Which means that this submarine is going into harm's way. I'm not even in a position to drop you off somewhere so I've got to take you with us. You are not a member of the armed forces…"

"No, but I am a member of the intelligence community, a government job. I understand orders. I recognize that this will be a dangerous situation, one you have little to no control over. That is the nature of the beast." Her Slavic accent sharpened as she spoke.

She stared unblinking directly into Owen's eyes. "What might have happened to me if I had been discovered prior to your men's rescue would have been worse. Much worse. Death is a one-time thing. The GRU has perfected ways of making you wish for death, and then keeping you right on the edge of it."

Owens took a breath and held it, then slowly released it. "Alright. I'll need you to stay in here during the rest of the cruise. I'll make sure food and drink are provided regularly, probably be the doc bringing you that so he can ensure you are still healthy." He gave a short laugh. "We also have a small library on-board. I'll get you a listing of titles, so you have something to do rather than just look at the walls."

Mikoslava nodded in understanding.

He looked down at the object he was carrying in his hands. "This is going to be even stranger request…I need you to put these on. And keep them on until I return and tell you they can be removed." He held out a pair of bright yellow ear protectors. "You are going to hear some odd music. Keep these on, don't remove them. We are pretty sure that if you wear them, no harm will come."

"You expect danger from," she gazed at him quizzically, "music?"

"Oddly enough, in this particular situation, yes I do."

She calmly slipped the protectors on and felt them, ensuring they sat properly on her head. She suddenly grinned, speaking louder than she had previously. "Do I look as silly in these as I feel?"

"No Mikoslava, you just look protected."

He turned to leave, his hand reaching for the doorknob when she spoke quietly. "Captain?"

Owens turned back. "Yes?"

"I am not sure what may occur." She waggled her right hand back and forth. "I know you have not given me all of the information, and that is acceptable. Just be aware I'm trained in emergency medicine. If things go sour, please do not hesitate to call on my assistance in any way."

"Thank you for that Mikoslava. I will think on it." He then left the room, closing the door behind him.

Chapter Eleven

The Barents Sea, East of the Kraken's Hunting Ground
27 November 1986
0824 CET / 0724 Zulu
USS *Sea Devil* (SSN 664)

"Captain, the ship is manned for battle stations. As ordered, all members are wearing full hearing protection," reported the Chief of the Watch.

"Very well, Chief. Helm, five degrees left rudder. Make your course one-two-five. Maintain speed."

"Five degrees left, new course one-two-five, aye."

"Fire control. Flood tubes one, three, and two. As soon as they indicate flooded, open outer doors on tubes one, three, and two."

"Flood tubes and then open outer doors for tubes one, three, and two aye."

Commander Owens felt like he needed to shout in order for the men to hear him through the heavy sound protectors. Everyone in Control wore either green, gray, or yellow colored hearing protection. He was taking no chances in his men falling under the song's spell as they hunted down the kraken.

A faint grinding noise filtered up from below. On the dive control board, indicators shifted from green bars to red circles as the three metal doors opened along the side of the submarine. "Torpedo tube one, three, and two flooded and outer doors indicate open. Weapons loaded and ready. Tubes one, three, and two clear and ready to shoot."

Commander Owens gathered himself. For the first time since the Vietnam war, an American naval vessel was heading into battle. All his on-board weapons were set. The SEALs and the marines were waiting inside the torpedo room with weapons. Everything was in place. Now the hunt began.

"I've not been able to find it using just the passive sonar," STS1 Blevins reported. "I've run every trace I can think of. This thing is silent in the water. Normally we could overcome the problem using a method called 'negative bio tracking'. The bigges' problem is there isn't a lot of other biologics up here, so I can't track it using the biological noise hole it makes, the way I might be able to track a shark through a school of anchovies or a manta ray through krill."

"Meaning the only way to spot it is with active sonar?" Owens asked, already fairly certain of the answer.

"I am afraid so sir. It won't require a full yankee search, mind you, just some ranging pings to get a fix on it. Might even be able to get away with the depth finding sonar system or under ice. Fire control can use the pings to determine the firing solutions and steer the warheads to their target. Then BOOM! No more mister monster."

"Not my preferred method." Submarines were assassins, and like assassins, did best when no one knew they were around. Using the active sonar system was a bit like shining a flashlight in a dark room to find your quarry. "How close will we need to be in order to spot it?"

"If it's as big as we think, twelve to fourteen thousand yards. Unfortunately, whatever is preventing it from following us is also hashing the sonar systems. Chief and I ran a couple of checks using the under ice and the depth checker. Both instances we had clear sonar signal until the signal hit the 'something'. Then the sound just stopped. Like it was absorbed or neutralized. Normal noise comes through, which is why we heard the helo and the creature's attack against the helo. On the other hand, it appears active sonar is a no-go to penetrate the, well for lack of better term, fence holding it in. We mapped it and had the Quartermaster of the Watch mark it on the navigation plot."

"I saw that. Wondered who had determined the shape."

Blevins grinned. "Wanted to know where the beef was," he stated, misquoting the popular commercial.

"This means we can't even search effectively for this beast until we cross that line?" Owens tried to hide his frustration.

"That's how it seems sir. I can go full search once inside and hope the sonar works. There's no guarantee that it will."

"Hope it really is a fence and not some area where somehow, magically the sonar system's active portion is rendered useless. Great." Owens shook his head at the look on Blevins' face. "I'm not pissed at you or the sonar team. I'm frustrated at the situation. Let's plan on sonar being effective inside the fence line.

"I'd like to use the minimum number of pings possible. Once the seeker heads go live, they will track the creature on their own. I'll give you my final decision in a few minutes."

"Officer of the Deck, Quartermaster. Two thousand yards to objective zone. Twelve minutes until crossing."

"Very well Quartermaster"

Owens stepped out of the Sonar room and over to the phonetalker. "Have Marine Sergeant Morehouse escorted to Control. He is currently in the Torpedo Room."

The phonetalker acknowledged the order and passed it on. Three minutes later, another sailor escorted Morehouse into the Control room and up to the captain.

Morehouse braced at attention and stated, "Sergeant Morehouse reporting as ordered sir."

Owens smiled. "At ease Sergeant. Please, step back to the navigation plotting table." He motioned to the flat table in the aft portion of Control, past the twin periscopes. The Quartermaster and Battle Station Plotter stepped out of earshot as the two men approached. "Do you have any knowledge of the best way to find or track the kraken?"

"I am afraid not, sir. Most of the information that Research sent to us was based on myths and stories from the age of sail. Last decent report dealing with krakens dates about eighteen years after the end of the Civil War. There was an incident during the Civil War, but the creature described there was much smaller and controlled by a witch. The sum of the information on tracking or attacking them boiled down to 'Bad idea, will eat ships and men, avoid at all costs', which does us very little good in this situation. How would you normally track an enemy?" Morehouse finished.

"Passively. Stealth above all else." Commander Owens answered. "Get the torpedo off before the enemy even realizes you are nearby."

"And right now that can't be performed?" Morehouse gave a quizzically look. "Why not?"

"Two reasons. First, the kraken is a waterborne creature and will have a much better idea of its environment than we will. Secondly, and for us more importantly, it doesn't seem to show up in any of our passive sonar tracking. The noise it made attacking the ship does, but that was things like the ship breaking up and splashes on the surface. Reviewing the tapes revealed no signature noises for the beast. My sonar team is looking into it to see if they can find any workarounds, anything that could give us an edge. I hoped that your data might have something as well. Since you don't, which I do not blame on your team or Research group, I'm back to using the active sonar."

Morehouse shook his head in commiseration. "Best of luck sir. We're continuing to stand by if you need us."

"Thanks Sergeant. Can you get back to the Torpedo Room on your own?" Owens asked.

"Yes sir. Down a couple of ladders is all." Sergeant Morehouse came back to attention.

"Dismissed."

"Aye sir." Morehouse stepped out of Control, carefully dropping down the aft ladder.

Owens walked forward to speak with the Weapons Officer. "This is going to end up being a gunfight. We're going to have to be ready to fire from the hip as soon as we spot this thing."

"Agreed sir. Fire control is running a continual update for all three torps. You give them a target; they're going to lock it up and get the weapons to it. Wait and see." The thirty-three-year-old Lieutenant said with gusto.

Owens smiled at the confidence in the Weapons Officer's voice.

"Officer of the Deck, Quartermaster. One thousand yards to objective zone. Six minutes."

Commander Owens stuck his head through the curtain dividing their space from Control. "As soon as we cross the fence, I want a wide band sonar cycle. Just give it a single cycle. Hopefully we can spot this thing as soon as we cross. It will also let us know immediately if the active system is effective in there."

Five minutes later the *Sea Devil* passed the invisible line of energy that penned the kraken in. STS1 Blevins triggered a single wide-band pulse. A sharp *BO-ONNNNG* rippled through the deep, reflecting off denser water pockets and a few deep-water fish swimming in the area. The display in Sonar lit up with the scattered returns.

"Active sonar works inside the zone. No indication of the target," Blevins told the Sonar Chief as the display began lighting up.

"Right. I'll inform the captain," STSC Elliot stated just as Commander Owens stepped into the Sonar space. He smiled.

"Inform me of what?"

"Sir, active sonar does operate on this side of the fence. Initial search was negative. Could mean that the target is outside the basket, deeper than expected, or at worst can hide from active returns. If it's guess three, we're pretty well screwed," answered the Chief.

"Can you continue to map the edges of the fence line?" Owens questioned.

"I believe so. Each time we send out an active signal, we get a little bit of information."

"Good. I want to try and stay near the fence line. That way if this damned thing comes after us, we can hopefully duck out of its path. Search plan?"

"One sweep every minute off-set by a deep-sweep on the thirty second mark. That gives pretty solid coverage and hopefully we spot him quickly."

Several fathoms below, the beast swam a slow circle. The flying prey had been vicious, a tiny morsel not really worth the damage it had inflicted on the creature's arms. There had been some edible bits, but most had been waste, inedible metal, and horrible tasting fluids. Its wounds would heal in time. A pulse of tone washed along its spine. With a lash of its fluke, the beast turned toward the sounds.

A taste of rust tinged the water. The same taste as the metal prey that had escaped earlier. Had it returned? The creature listened closely for the prey's sounds. There was the faintest pulse of the prey's jaws as it constantly tore at the water. Then a second tone rippled along the creature's spine. It could hear the weak searching song the prey sang. There was no real melody, no sense of anything beyond *I am here* in the music. All it would do is help others find it. Not that finding it would matter to anything else. This was the beast's prey. It gathered itself and began to croon the wavesong. The music that would draw the prey unerringly to it.

In the Sonar Room, Blevins reached over with his left hand and knocked Gridley's headset off while tearing his own off with his right.

"Too damn close. Grid, put on the hearing protection." Blevins did not wait to see if the STS3 followed the order. "Conn, Sonar. We've picked up the music. Trying to narrow the bearing now."

"Sonar, Conn aye. Fire control, prepare for snapshot. Tube two, on my mark and bearing," Commander Owens ordered as he checked his own hearing protection.

The senior fire control reverified all his settings. "Tube two ready. Waiting for range and bearing."

"Sonar, Conn. Single wide-band pulse."

BO-ONNNG

"Conn, Sonar. Large contact bearing zero-four-three, designated Sierra zero-one-one. Range eight thousand yards and closing. Bearing shifting to port."

"Fire control, target is Sierra one-one. On my mark…Shoot!"

The boat shuddered as the compressed air pushed the 3,400-pound weapon out of the submarine. As soon as the accelerometer reached the proper reading, the torpedo's propulsor activated. Chemically created steam spun the motor and the weapon accelerated to top speed. Tiny movements in the propulsor steered the weapon onto the programed bearing. The long thin guidance wire snaked out behind the long green underwater missile as it reached out to destroy its target.

"Torpedo tube two shot successful. Weapon is accelerating and on course. Good guidance telemetry."

"Conn, Fire control. Sierra one-one is closing faster. Speed estimated now at twenty-five knots and rising."

Owens looked at the Weapons Officer, his eyes widening at the report. Twenty-five knots and increasing? Few ocean creatures reached speeds over twenty knots, though large game fish like marlins are sailfish had been clocked at over forty-five knots.

"Conn, fire control. Loss of guidance. Looks like the wire has been cut."

"Does it appear the weapon has shifted to internal guidance?"

"Yes sir. Weapon is coming about now. Weapon has acquired. Closing…"

On the fire control plotting screen, the pulses from the torpedo suddenly shifted, racing from point to point across the relative bearing compass.

"Weapon appears to be spinning out of control. Indications weapon is sinking out of zone."

A distant noise registered on the sonar screens.

"Conn, Sonar. We have sonar indication that the weapon has imploded at crush depth. No indication of explosion. Sierra one-one has slowed but is still on approach, bearing zero-two-eight."

The wavesong was now loud enough to penetrate the hull of the *Sea Devil* unassisted. Only personnel without hearing protection, of which there were none on the ship, could be directly affected. The song, as pleasant sounding as it currently was, distorted in odd ways through the hearing protection. While the general concept of what the kraken wanted could be felt, without being able to clearly hear the wavesong there was no direct compulsion on the crew. Some crew still found themselves affected by the tenor of the wavesong. The longing and need the song suggested pulled on their psyche.

In the Torpedo Room, Corporal Hubbard recorded the wavesong on a special CD recorder developed by Phillips for the military. The machine could capture up to 80 minutes of noise on the unique one-time recordable discs using either the built-in or an externally connected microphone. Sounds were digitally recorded by etching the disc and did not degrade the way that signals on magnetic cassettes would. Nor did electrical interference or X-rays, both of which could wipe traditional magnetic media, affect the CDs. JTF had managed to get one released to the squad when it was discovered the kraken had sonic abilities. There was hope the recordings would help the Research group develop sonic countermeasures.

"That is just weird," whispered Corporal "Clink" Gustav to Lance Corporal Hanzo. "It kinda wavers left and right. I really want to remove the headset and hear it more clearly."

"Hence why we're wearing these. This thing can make you want to get close enough to it that it can grab and eat you. I mean, the death concept of a banshee's scream is bad enough. This though, making you simply walk into its mouth." Hanzo's naturally pale complexion seemed to lighten even more, and he shuddered. "So, keep the damn protectors on Clink."

Corporal Hubbard gave the two marines a strong frown.

"Sorry," Gustav said quietly and stepped further away from where Hubbard was recording. He sidled closer to where Morehouse and Peck sat. "How are we going to deal with this kraken?"

Morehouse glanced over at the junior marine. "Hopefully we won't have to. These Navy guys seem to have a good handle on using the torpedoes to take it out. We may just end up doing nothing more than taking a few photos of the sinking body."

"Or" Peck interjected, "we may end up topside trying to take it out with the grenades. Usual situation: we will apply our killing talents in the best way we can. This isn't your first rodeo Clink. What's up?"

"It's this damn music. I need to hear it better. I know on one level why I shouldn't, but on another. . . It's like having a nic' fit after quitin' smoking. Intellectually you know you shouldn't smoke anymore, but your body keeps telling you it needs it."

Master Gunnery Sergeant Peck's response was drowned out by the submarine firing a second torpedo out of the starboard tube. The entire vessel rumbled, and the noise was overpowering in the space.

"Torpedo one away. Accelerating to attack speed." The fire control technician suddenly gasped. "Loss of signal. Sir, guidance wire has broken."

The stinger from the prey sped towards the beast. The creature spun in the water, eight tentacles flaring out to knock the stinger from its course. The thin line connecting the stinger to the prey snapped as one tentacle sliced through it. Another pair of tentacles slammed down on the stinger, striking hard and crushing in a portion of its body. Steam boiled out of the rent and cold water rushed in, overbalancing the bit of metal. The stinger sank rapidly, erratically spiraling and keening a death cry. The beast ignored the cry. There was no need to follow it. The tang of poisoned fluid flooded the area where it had leaked from the broken body.

"Shoot three, same bearing."
The fire control technician pressed the LAUNCH button. A buzzer went off and the button flashed red on and off.
"Failure of torpedo three. Running checks." His hands flashed over the console keyboard, calling up the error codes. He ran a finger down the screen and pressed another button on the screen's side, bringing up another page. Reading quickly, the sailor tapped a set of commands into the keyboard. The button continued to flash.
He pressed another button and verified the readings. Once more, the fire control technician entered the commands and pressed the button. In the darkness of

Control, the button's light continued to blink on and off, the red gleam bathing his face in the color of arterial blood.

"Conn, Fire Control. Failure to launch tube three. Error code from the guidance package of torpedo three. Launch command rejected."

The submarine lurched as the kraken slammed into it. Bodies and equipment tumbled as the ship tilted hard to port, rolling along the center axis.

Owens grabbed a stanchion, struggling to maintain his balance. "Close all outer doors. Diving Officer, full left rudder! Ahead flank!"

He turned, his body swinging as the ship shuddered again. "Fire control, shut down the weapon. We can't eject it right now."

The Diving Officer dialed the order to Maneuvering while the helmsman twisted the rudder control hard to left. The rudder shifted slowly, the hydraulics backpressure fighting his movement.

"Sir, maximum rudder angle is seven degrees. I can't get it further than that."

"Depth two-eight-five feet and increasing. It's dragging us down!"

"Keep working the rudder. We've got to get to the other side of the fence!" Owens barked over the crashing sounds of books and mislaid objects falling.

Outside the ship, the kraken's tentacles had wrapped around the bow and hull up to the sail. It began probing for openings. If it could drive the prey deep enough, the skin would tear open on its own. Then it could pluck out the meat at leisure. The beast adjusted its song to the death keen.

"Holy shit!" Hubbard exclaimed as the music morphed from a pleasant melody of need into the screech of nails on a blackboard. He could feel the song pluck at his bones and his heart sped up. His body wanted to fly away, hide from the sound that reverberated through the thick hull of the ship.

One of the torpedomen tore off his headset and began screaming. He pulled and scratched at his ears as if trying to tear them off. Hughes, one of the SEALs, grabbed the sailor and pinned him down. The man continued to scream and cry out a high-pitched wail, struggling to free his hands. One of the other SEALs and the largest torpedoman's mate pulled the sailors hands away and bound them with green duct tape. Then the burley torpedoman's mate replaced the hearing protection onto the keening sailor's bleeding ears.

"Damage Control, Torpedo Room. Request medical assistance for Petty Officer Flores," stated the phonetalker as calmly as he could while holding onto the grips at the Torpedo Control Panel. The ship continued to shake and rotate from side to side.

Hanzo glanced over at Riley. "Not going to write that one down?" he asked and pointed with his chin towards the struggling sailor.

"I had that use for duct tape in the first ten I recorded."

"Twelve degrees down bubble. Depth three hundred twenty-five feet and increasing. Sir, we've got to get some up angle, or this thing will drag us to crush depth. Rate of dive is several feet per second."

"Quartermaster, how close to the line are we?" yelled the captain.

"Approximately three hundred yards. The line is currently bearing three-five-one relative."

The best idea was to make a run for the line and scrape the monster off the ship with the fence that held it in check. However, the bow currently pointed towards the ocean floor and their speed was assisting the creature in getting the *Sea Devil* to the bottom. Owens took a chance.

"Helm, zero rudder. All stop. Back emergency!"

The entire vessel shuddered as the massive propeller slowed quickly and the started spinning in the opposite direction. Water flowed backwards along the hull, pulling the kraken's body away from the ship. It struggled to maintain grips as first one, then a total of five of its tentacles tore free from the hull.

"Chief of the Watch, emergency blow. Let's see if we can shake this damn thing off the bow. We're running for the line."

The Chief of the Watch reached up and pulled the 'chicken switch' valve controls for the submarine's ballast tanks. Pressurized air rushed into the water-filled spaces, pushing tons of liquid out through thick grates on the bottom of the hull. Two more of the kraken's tentacles slid off the ship due to the pressure of the outflowing water. Seven tentacles now flailed wildly as the submarine suddenly became significantly more buoyant. A single tentacle remained wrapped around the sail.

"All stop! Ahead flank."

The ship shuddered again as the stress of sudden changes in propeller direction rippled through the submarine's hull. Water, both from the ship rising and the speed it was accelerating to, washed past the kraken as it struggled to regain balance in the water. The beast sensed the approaching fence, the feel of density and released the prey before it found itself crushed against the barrier. Once more, the prey had escaped, chattering nonsensically at the beast as it fled. If the prey returned, there would not be a third reprieve for it.

As if a power switch had been thrown, the creature's wavesong cut off. The only sounds that could be heard were the men in the compartment, some retching, the environmental sounds of the boat, and a single man screaming in pain. Morehouse pressed STOP on the CD player and glanced about.

People filled every seat in the Wardroom, with some members of the meeting leaning against the bulkheads. Everyone from the initial in-brief were there, as well as the XO, Weapons Officer, the submarine's Independent Duty Corpsman (IDC), Sergeant Wade from Bravo Team, STSC Elliot, STS1 Blevins, and three sailors from the Engineering Division who had been invited due to their significant knowledge of fantasy literature and myths. The Engineering Department could have offered more geeks, but these three seemed to be the best choices.

"That was the moment the ship crossed the fence line containing the kraken. It may have continued to call, but none of the sound reached through the barrier. Also, most of whatever causes reactions in humans is lost in the recording. You notice that no one in this compartment was affected by what you just heard." Morehouse looked around at the four wood-boxed speakers mounted in the corners. "As far as I can tell, the speakers don't seem to matter. Something essential is not captured by the CD. Might be psychic in nature. There is evidence that some supernaturals have direct mind influence."

"Vampires?" asked one of the 'nukes' unexpectedly.

"Yeah, some. Kitsune are even worse. Same with any form of succubi. They don't need to look you in the eyes. Those supernaturals can straight up take you over, leaving your rational mind trapped. In the case of the kraken, the ability appears to be directly tied to its sonic abilities. The nature of the effect is tied to which 'song' it sings."

"How do we prevent people from being affected? Even with the hearing protection, seventeen men, including two officers, ended up injuring themselves. Several more sailors experienced extreme nausea. Petty officer Wilson may end up losing an ear. Doc was able to patch him up and stitch his cheek back together. All of the men are currently sedated and regulated to bedrest." Commander Owens stared hard at Sergeant Morehouse.

Master Gunnery Sergeant Peck spoke up. "Sir, more than likely those will be the only men affected. Prior to crossing the barrier on our return, my suggestion is to give them hearing protection and physically restrain them. They'll still be affected but should remain safe. I don't know if you have men who can watch over them, but that is another option."

Owens looked to his right. "XO?"

"I think we're just going to have to brace them in racks. Lock the bedpans upright and tie the bunks upward. It won't be comfortable but, as the master gunnery sergeant states, they'll be safe. I can't think of a better idea to keep them out of the way."

One of the nukes, a sandy-haired man with a thin mustache raised a hand.

"Go ahead Jordan."

"Sir, the marines are more than likely correct. Anyone who has been exposed and didn't freak, more than likely won't again. Basically, they made a successful SANS check." Machinist mate second class (MM2) Jordan began.

"A successful what?" asked the Weapons Officer.

"SANS check. Means sanity check. In the role-playing game *Call of. . .*"

The Weapons Officer grunted and rolled his eyes. "Forget I asked."

Jordan frowned and closed his mouth.

"MM2 Jordan makes a good point," stated Commander Owens. "I had not thought of it that way. Exposure and resilience. Very well. When we return to the inside of the barrier, all previously affected personnel are to be restrained and locked in their bunks. Doc, I need you to oversee that and ensure none of them can further harm themselves."

"Yes sir," replied the corpsman.

"Next item, weapons status? I'll start with the SEALs, then Marines, and finally on-board."

Lieutenant Commander Harris stood up. "We currently have five M9 9mm pistols, one gas-operated speargun, and five Mk 3 dive knives. Additionally, each gun has three fully loaded magazines and I have an additional gas canister reload for the speargun." He sat down as soon as he completed his report.

Morehouse followed suit, standing to report. "Sir, we have eight M16s with M203 grenade launchers, three Mark 19 belt fed 40 mm automatic grenade launchers, six cases of 48 round belts, and four reloads for each rifle. The plan is to use the Mark 19s from the deck or sail of the ship as ranged explosive and armor piercing capability for a surface engagement. We also have eight M9 bayonet knives." Morehouse waited a moment for questions, and then sat down, shifting his chair a bit closer to the table.

The Weapons Officer remained seated as he gave his report. "Our small arms haven't changed since we left. Currently our only tactical weapon is the remaining Mark 48. The guidance computer has a failed chipset. It appears an electrical surge during the engagement damaged the computer. Problem is, we don't carry spares for that section of the torpedo. I already discussed that with the Chop."

Owens frowned. "And we're not carrying any practice torps either, which means no cannibalizing them for parts. Have the Supply Officer run a cross-check and see if the chipset is used by anything else on the boat. Also, have the TMs pull the tech manuals for the weapon's computers." The CO looked down the table. "ET1 Bishop, I want you to take charge of determining what we have on-board that might be . . . ah . . ."

"Jury-rigged?" asked the tall electronics technician.

". . . developed into a workable solution. Get with Chief Lancomb and anyone else in the division who might be of assistance."

"What about Paladin?" the XO chimed in.

One of the nukes snorted.

Owens chose not to notice the sound. "That's a good possibility. Brief Bishop and Lancomb after this. I hadn't even thought of using that." He nodded appreciatively at the XO.

"Next issue. Sonar, have you been able to develop any additional methods of tracking this creature?"

STSC Elliot answered immediately. "No sir. Worse, the music might be interfering with the torpedo's active sonar.

I think that might have been why the first torpedo didn't acquire correctly. I'm not certain if it's an active interference with the sounds or if the creature is partially sonar-absorbent. Blevins re-ran the tapes from when we initially spotted it with the active sonar. Even then, the signal strength of the return was significantly degraded compared to the expected value. Could be either or both. Just not sure."

Harris perked up. "What if we tagged it?"

"Tagged it how, Mr. Harris?"

"The team still has two of the tracking beacons we used during the mission." Harris was not sure who in the meeting was cleared for information about the rescue. "They can be set for pulsing a specific frequency. Could a torpedo home in on that?"

The Weapons Officer nodded. "Yes. In fact, they can be specifically preset for frequency control."

"How do you plan on tagging the beast?"

"That's the rub sir," Harris answered, looking a bit sheepish. "I'd need to attach the beacon to a spear and then shoot the spear into the creature. The speargun has a range of almost twenty feet. Twelve to fifteen for decent accuracy." He shrugged.

Owens coughed and took a drink of water to clear his throat. "Fifteen feet. And you have a plan for how to do this without endangering the ship?"

"Not a plan. More of an idea." He went on to explain. The CO blanched three sentences in.

Chapter Twelve

The Norwegian Sea, West of Kraken's Hunting Ground
27 November 1986
1136 CET / 1236 Zulu
USS *Sea Devil* (SSN 664)

Only two men remained in the Wardroom. Everyone else had scattered to prepare for the upcoming evolution.

"You'll have to wait until I fire the flare. That way you'll know for certain that I've got the transmitter set. Don't move till then."

Commander Owens gave the SEAL a hard look. "I *will* need some time to get the ship moving," he emphasized. "The *Sea Devil* isn't a racecar. I can't just shove down the accelerator and race off. Once I have stopped the engines, it takes nearly a minute to get enough thrust to actually begin moving. Plus, I may need to lower the outboard in order to maintain position. If I do that, it's another forty to fifty seconds until we start moving since I have to raise the motor. Shouldn't we start as soon as the kraken attacks in any manner?"

"No." Harris shook his head. "I can't be certain how long it will take me to get the shot off. Until then, I *have* to stay in the fenced area. If I leave, there is no guarantee I can get the transmitter attached. That is the most important part of this isn't it?"

"Killing this thing is the most important part right now. Keeping you and everyone else alive is second."

"And the transmitter is our best plan for killing it, since it will allow the torpedo a better chance of tracking it. That's why you have to wait for the red flare."

Owens huffed and sighed. "Seems like there is a lot that can go wrong with this. Starting with the fact we aren't certain that the kraken will come after you."

"If this doesn't work, we can try something else. This has the smallest risk to both equipment and personnel. Any other plan risks the lives of more people. Which is what we may have to do if this plan fails." Harris waved his hand about, encompassing the entirety of the room. "I've already lost one team member to this bastard. Another is going to be in the hospital for a good while, possibly losing partial use of an arm. I need to make sure that no one else gets injured or killed on my watch if I can prevent it. No matter the personnel risk."

Commander Owens reluctantly nodded. "I get it. I don't like it, but I understand."

"We're not torpedoman's mates. We really don't have the equipment for this," mentioned ET1 Bishop for the fourth time. "Not that they do either, but the point is—"

"Again, the point is it doesn't matter," ETC Bishop interrupted. He glanced over at a hastily typed paper on the deck next to him, then grunted in satisfaction. "We have one chance to make this work. We use what we have, what we know, and what we can cobble together."

Nuclear-trained submarine NCOs were an odd bunch. They tended to view any technical problem as something that not only could be solved but would be solved. By them. Whether or not they actually had the tools. Or proper parts. Or technical manuals. Or training. They just simply *believed* so hard that they could do it, that things happened. A kind of technological faith and miracle-working brotherhood. A faith, which, strangely enough, created miracles more often than it should have.

After twenty-two years as an electronics technician in the nuclear submarine navy, ETC Lancomb was viewed by some as a high priest of the technological faith. A trouble-shooting shaman as it were. Something as complex as trying to integrate a stolen, then recovered, then immersed in sea water, experimental torpedo guidance computer with a non-operational torpedo guidance computer of a different design in order to create a working torpedo guidance system that would home in on a makeshift transmitter attached by a fishing spear to a supernatural sea monster, was not as much of challenge to him as it would have been to other non-nuclear sailors. They more than likely would have thrown their hands up in disgust, claiming the entire operation was crazy. In fact, ETC Lancomb thought the challenge was interesting. A word he used only when describing electronic issues he felt were worth his time.

"Besides, it's interesting." Chief Lancomb stated stoically.

"I really get scared when you use that word," Bishop said as he tested another chip on the original guidance package. "Getting a one point two five millihertz throughput."

Lancomb looked hard at the wiring diagram taped to the 5SB switchboard in Auxiliary Machinery Room Two (AMR2) Upper Level. "That's the one-one-nine-three series?"

Bishop verified the board connection. "Yep."

The chief found the number on the diagram and crosschecked it with voltage values. "Good. We can leave that one in place. Check the one-eight-seven-seven tack alpha to one-eight-seven-six tack bravo crossover. If the connector is good, remove the chips. We will substitute this one from the other package." He held up the green-striped sixteen-connector pin chip that he had just verified operational. "If not, we'll need to determine how to bypass the track or lay down a new circuit."

"Roger. Checking the one-eight-seven-seven tack alpha to one-eight-seven-six tack bravo crossover." Bishop bent down and touched the probes of the Fluke multimeter to the circuit board.

The entire aft portion of the Torpedo Room was covered in opened cases and transport wrap. Alpha and Bravo squads were pulling out components and sorting them according to maintenance guides.

"Break them all down and verify everything. Start in two-man teams with the nineteens. Then we'll do the two-oh-threes and rifles. We can't afford for any of the weapons to foul." Sergeant Morehouse stepped over one of the cases holding the belted grenades. He handed a screwdriver to Hanzo, who grunted thanks. "Hanzo and myself, Riley and Clink, Bear and Wade. Gunny will act as oversight and extra hands. Questions?"

"How come I gotta work with the guy with a funny name?" asked Riley, already beginning the maintenance teardown on the belt-fed grenade launcher.

"'Cause I trus' him to keep yoo-ew in line," retorted Sergeant Wade in a faked hillbilly accent. "Hell, you'd probably figur' out how ta mount the barrel so it'd point toward ya,"

The entire compartment, marines and sailors, got a laugh at that one.

"Any pertinent questions then?" asked Morehouse grinning. No one answered. "Alright. We've only got a short time to get everything ready. If the Navy can't kill this thing, we're going to be up next. That means heavy fire and things trying to kill us. So what will we do?"

"KILL THEM FIRST!" shouted the entire group.

"Oorah!"

The men got down to the serious business of preparing for war. Each weapon was stripped to its individual bare components. Each item got a thorough cleaning with solvent and brush, followed by a wipe down with a lint-free cloth. Then the piece was oiled and laid on a clean absorbent cloth. Once all the parts were ready, the men began putting the weapons back together. Reassembly was slower than usual. There would be no second chances. Every weapon had to be in perfect working order.

The Mark 19s were completed and set aside in boxes to prevent them from shifting around during maneuvers. Next, each man broke down his M203 and verified it was clean and ready. The single-round launchers were cycled and dry-fired to verify the correct movement of the parts. They too were placed in storage boxes when the work was complete. Finally, each marine's rifle was stripped, cleaned, verified, and reassembled.

"Gather in," Morehouse directed as Bear finished assembling his rifle. The seven marines huddled near to Morehouse.

"I'm sticking with the earlier assignments. Wade and Hanzo, you two will man the nineteens on the deck behind the conning tower."

"Sail," interrupted Gunny.

"Sail. Behind the sail. Riley and Hubbard, the two of you will act as ammo bunnies and guards. Clink, I need you as a rover back there. Bear and I will mount in the top of the, ah, sail. Gunny, I figure that you can act as primary spotter for this as well as mounting the M249. You've been in more of these fights than any of us. I'd really appreciate your insight. And you get the chance to point and shoot."

"Yep," Gunny said quietly.

"Mount you in the sail as well?" Morehouse glanced over at the senior non-com.

"No. Great sight line, and it would give me the best view of the fight. However, there is very little space. I'll stay on the deck and backstop from there."

"Very well. Marines, we have a sea monster to kill." Morehouse stated seriously as he seated the magazine into his rifle.

"Oorah," the remaining marines chorused. Their rifle magazines seated as a single sound.

Meeting of Norwegian Sea and Barents Sea, Kraken's Hunting Ground
27 November 1986
1418 CET / 1318 Zulu
USS *Sea Devil* (SSN 664)

Thick, gray clouds overhead merged invisibly at the horizon with the sea, making it impossible to tell naturally where one ended and the other began. The emergency inflatable rescue raft, a bright international orange bit of rubber, was the single speck of color in the monochromatic ocean.

On the surface the *Sea Devil* towed the raft behind them on a 200-yard line. One long enough to allow Lieutenant Commander Harris and his teammate to get close enough to the kraken to tag the monster without placing the submarine fully in harm's way. The Marine fire teams had each set up a Mark 19 on the long flat area of the hull aft of the sail. They scanned the water continuously for some sign of the kraken.

"Bait, Sea Devil actual. We are getting close to the fence. Hard turn to port coming up in three minutes. As soon as we complete the turn, I'll order the engines stopped. That should give you enough motion to drift past the fence. Sonar is keeping a watch for indications of the kraken, and we'll inform you the moment we have anything. Over"

"Roger, Sea Devil actual. EN2 Carr and I are ready for the turn. Bait out."

Harris picked up the spear and verified the zip ties holding the false jellyfish to it were pulled tight with no slippage. He flicked the switch, and the motor began to undulate the fake critter and flash a pale green light. The movement would potentially alter the flight path of the spear when he shot it at the kraken. Harris held onto the spear trying to gauge how much motion the machine imparted. As he contemplated the situation, the robot's motion slowed, stopped, then sluggishly began again. The light pulsed, barely visible this time.

"Damn it. No, no, no." Harris toggled the switch off and on. On the third cycle of the switch the machine would not even move. It gave off only a single brief flash of extremely dim light, then nothing. He opened the latch port on the underside section of the machine. Pale white acid crystals foamed around the seam line on the battery. He pulled the failed battery out and tossed it over the side of the raft.

"Bait, Sea Devil. Beginning turn. Over."

Carr picked up the radio. "Roger beginning turn. Over." He released the transmit switch and looked over at Lieutenant Commander Harris. Carr watched in confusion as Harris frantically checked pouches on his drysuit. "What's wrong?"

"Battery failed. I thought I had extras with me but can't find them."

Immediately, Carr patted the pouch on his lower right leg. He could feel two small rectangular shapes. He unzipped the pouch and felt inside. Carefully, he pulled one of the spare batteries out and zipped the pouch close. "Here. I've still got extras from earlier. They'll be good."

Harris grabbed the battery and hastily inserted it into the mass of metal and rubber that sprawled inert on the spear shaft. He relatched the door and flicked the switch to restore power. The machine flashed a firm green light and the entire body slowly rolled back and forth. Unconsciously Harris released a slow breath, calming down now that the tracker was operational again. He carefully placed the spear on the thick rubber that made up the deck of the raft. The spear rolled left and right with the motion of the jellyfish. While the motion was obvious, he was certain that he could overcome it in the spear's short flight.

The raft drifted sideways through the waves, continuing to follow the arc of the submarine's turn. Carr held the speargun upright, resting the butt in the bottom of the raft. Harris carefully pushed the spear into the gas barrel until he felt the *click* of the spear locking in place. He took the weapon from Carr's hands and began sighting down the barrel, searching the dark water for the kraken. Wave-tossed mist stung his chapped lips, and he could taste the salt in each droplet. As the submarine slowed, even the faint noise of its engines faded until the only sounds were the slap of the waves and the howl of the gale winds.

Carr leaned over the side; knees firmly tucked under the inflated edge of the raft. He scanned the waters, trying to discern anything in the constantly moving medium. "I've got nothing here. I'm going to try another spot." He stayed on hands and knees and shuffled along the port side to a new place, watching the waves the entire time. Harris continued watching the starboard section, leaning the speargun on the raft's edge to steady his aim.

One of the biggest concerns for this plan was whether the kraken would come after a small craft. Would it even notice when they entered the hunting grounds? All the other attacks had been against larger, noisy vessels. It had not attacked the helicopter until the winch had touched the water. Half an hour went by without any indications.

Harris and Carr grew cold, shivering as the Baltic weather beat at them. A light drizzle of freezing mist descended, cutting their visibility even more and making it harder to maintain the watch. Both SEALs were continually wiping the beading moisture from their eyes.

With no warning, several tentacles exploded out of the water around the craft. The suddenness of the attack, and surge of water knocked both EN2 Carr and Lieutenant

Commander Harris into the center of the raft. The tentacles snaked overheard. Each one curled and twisted, attempting to grasp one of the men in the bottom.

"I need a junction in order to get a good shot!" Harris shouted, rolling to his left to avoid one of the grasping appendages.

Carr rolled up to his knees and slapped an incoming tentacle away from himself. "I know. I think the damn thing is directly below us." He half rolled, half crawled to the edge, and peeked overboard. "Can't see for certain, there's too many waves."

"Damn." Harris hit another tentacle with the butt of the speargun and dodged as a second slammed into the raft's side right next to him.

In a quick graceful motion, Carr bounced to his feet. "I've got an idea. Get ready to shoot."

"What?" Harris yelled, glancing over his shoulder at the petty officer.

"Be ready to—"

The center of the rescue raft bulged inward and tore. A claw, nearly the size of a young child pushed through and clamped onto the petty officer's right leg. Blood fountained from the wound as the claw's vice-like grip tightened.

Carr screamed in shock and pain, his arms going wide and the radio arcing into the ocean. He joined his fists together and slammed them down at the joint of the two pincers. Three quick blows and the claw spasmed, the pincers opening enough for Carr to pull his leg free. He grabbed the bleeding wound with both hands to staunch the flow.

Harris had been nearly knocked into the water by the impact of the claw. He clung to the rope around the raft, his head nearly in the water. Only the friction strap on the speargun prevented it from falling off into the roiling waters. He pulled himself up and backwards, sliding sideways into the raft. From the outboard side, another claw grabbed Carr in the rib cage. The drysuit tore and Harris could clearly hear the celery snap of Carr's rib bones. The EN2 screamed again, grabbing one of the side ropes to prevent the beast from pulling him into the ocean.

It's got to be right below us. Harris realized. He ignored Carr's cries and dropped to the raft's floor. The vessel was taking on water through the center tear. He shoved the speargun and his head through the rip. Salt stung his eyes as he tried to see. Directly below him was the blurry mass of the creature. He would need to rely on luck here. Sighting the speargun as best he could, he pulled the trigger. Air bubbles obscured his vision as the gas canister fired. His arm jerked with the recoil. The bubbles cleared almost instantly. Pulsing green light revealed the spear imbedded in the flesh of the kraken.

Harris pushed himself out of the hole and gasped for air. Carr was still fighting the claw, but the tentacles were now attacking the rest of the raft. Air gushed from rents in the bright orange rubber. Staggering through the seawater rapidly filling the raft, Harris swung the now useless speargun at the claw. He aimed for the junction of the pincers and was rewarded with a sharp cracking sound when he hit. The claw opened and he pulled his injured team member free. Carr, half-conscious and moaning in pain lifted the flare pistol and fired. The bright red flare shot across the raft and ricocheted off two tentacles before skipping across the waves.

Both men fell into the rubber tangle as the raft jerked under them. The flare had been the signal for the *Sea Devil* to pull them out of the area. Tentacles tore pieces of rubber from the disintegrating craft as it pulled away. Harris grabbed Carr and wrapped an arm through the tow rope.

"Hold on," he told the injured man. He felt Carr's arms tighten around him. Harris freed his left hand and sliced the rope free of the raft. The pair shot out of the remains of the rapidly sinking inflatable. A popping sensation and brutal pain in his right shoulder accompanied the sudden tug from the rope. He was certain his right arm and shoulder were now dislocated out of socket. The pain continued as they rocketed across the waves, bouncing, twisting, and submerging at random times. Moments later, the submarine had slowed, and additional divers assisted the two SEALs back onto the deck.

It took a rope and life ring to get Carr out of the ocean and on deck. The sailors laid him down and strapped him firmly into the rescue litter. Another group assisted Harris out from the water. His suit was intact, but water had forced its way past the neck ring when the submarine drug him out of the kraken's hunting ground. He stood up carefully, shivering, and his right arm hung limply at his side. Water pooled around his feet as it sluiced from the drain valves on his suit. He watched in horrid fascination as the crew wrapped gauze around the massive wounds Carr had sustained during the attack. The white cloth turned a mottled dark crimson almost immediately.

"Get him below now!" screamed the lead topside petty officer. "Doc set up in the wardroom." The man turned to Harris. "Sir, we'll get you down next. Probably need to lower you as well. It looks like you dislocated your arm on that little jaunt."

Holding the litter firmly between them, the group assisting Carr scurried to the aft escape trunk. They connected safety straps from the hand winch to the litter. Carefully, the petty officer cranked the handle, lowering the litter with its precious cargo into the ship. Another sailor in a heavy coat pulled the remains of the bright yellow nylon tow rope out of the water and coiled it.

"Does it work?" Harris asked, still watching where Carr had been lowered into the boat.

"The winch?" asked the sailor who had assisted him up.

"No, is the transmitter working?" Harris waved his good arm back towards where the attack had occurred.

"No one has told me. Now we need to get you below sir. Please come this way."

Bright surgical lamps now hung from the Wardroom's overhead, fully illuminating the table. The original red table cover had been replaced with a special surgical pad. An emergency surgical kit was mounted to the far wall along with several bags of saline and a hanger. A tray of instruments clamped on a swivel arm that hooked into the overhead. Doc and Ulyana checked that everything was prepared as they calmly waited for their patient to arrive. A nervous unrated seaman, Welch, stood in the corner waiting to assist and stood ready to act as their gopher during the surgery.

Two sailors, their rank invisible under the heavy coats they wore, carefully maneuvered EN2 Carr's litter through the aft wardroom door and placed it on the table. The dry suit was destroyed. Black rubber and fabric had been torn open, pieces missing, displaying swaths of pale skin and damaged flesh. The tissues of Carr's left leg and right torso had been savagely mangled by the serrated edges of the pincers. Blood stained the hastily applied gauze.

Doc unbuckled the straps. He and Ulyana gripped the cloth their patient laid on. "On three." Doc stated. "One, two, three."

The sailors slipped the litter from the table as Doc ensured Carr slid safely out and onto the table with minimal jarring. Carr, half-conscious and slipping into shock, moaned in pain. Their current orders completed, the pair of sailors departed the Wardroom, closing the door behind them.

"We're going to need blood," Doc stated formally, as he applied a tourniquet to the leg. "Heavy venous bleeding. Looks like the femoral vein got sliced. Not as bad as an arterial cut, but still tough." He quickly injected three pre-measured syringes of anesthetic near the injury. Next, he began cutting the dry suit remains away from the wound.

Ulyana nodded as she stretched out Carr's right arm and carefully inserted the IV needle. "Do you have any onboard?" she asked. She verified the plastic tube completely filled and unclamped it. Saline began flowing through the IV tube. She checked the fluid dripped at the proper rate. Next came the sphygmomanometer cuff to the undamaged arm. Verifying the band was tight, Ulyana pressed a button and inflated it. The machine hummed as it checked both blood pressure and pulse.

Doc peeled the fabric and rubber away from the limb. "No, I'm going to need to do a transfusion. This is a bit beyond the level they expect us to perform underway." He glanced at Welch. "Find me at least two crew members who have O negative blood. I can't be certain of this gentleman's type, but O negative is our best bet."

Lieutenant Commander Harris and Commander Owens arrived at the Wardroom simultaneously.

"You need to get that arm looked at," Owens began.

With a dismissive wave, Harris deflected the comment. "Gotta check on Carr. See how he's doing. Did it work?"

Doc looked up from stitching the vein together as the two officers walked into the Wardroom. Ulyana, currently holding two clamps to maintain the wound open so that the Independent Duty Corpsman could see the work area, ignored them.

Owens blinked before he fully processed the question. "We don't know yet. Sonar is confident since it was able to pick up the test signal before we deployed the transmitter. Unfortunately, the fence is still blocking active signals of that type. However it goes, this kraken is going to die. The torpedo is loaded and checks out. How will it perform when we shoot?" He shrugged. "That's another question. ETC Lancomb is confident. The Weapons Officer less so.

"This is now my concern . . . and my responsibility," Owens stated firmly when he noticed Harris was prepared to argue. "You stay here until the Doc can check you out. We'll carry the flag the rest of the way. I've got to get back to Control. We're preparing to dive."

"I know this has been an odd voyage, and that everyone has seen and heard some odd things. This is the submarine force. What happens underway stays underway. Like our fathers before us, we are about to go into harm's way. Do your jobs as you've been trained.

"Keep the earplugs in and hearing protection on. I can't answer your questions about what is really happening. Wish I could. What I can tell you is that we are going to do everything we can to make things safe in this area for anyone else. To quote the bard 'Once more unto the breech, dear friends, once more'." Owens released the button for the 1MC.

"Conn, Sonar. We are about to enter the fence. I need bearings as soon as you have a whiff."

"Sonar, conn. You'll have it as soon as we do. Let's kill this bastard."

A small cheer went up from the sailors in Control. Owens crossed his arms and smiled. No matter what else happened, his crew was ready and confident. The deck under his feet thrummed with the power of the engines.

The kraken circled as soon as it sensed the creature. It began turning toward the problematic prey who would soon cross the edge that prevented the beast from leaving these hunting grounds. It shrieked in rage. This prey knew what was happening. There was no reason to calm the intruder and draw it placidly towards its demise. Deep within the kraken, alien parts; biological bits that had never evolved on this plane of existence, flexed. Water vibrated outward, carrying the death dirge, the tenor of terror, a melody of madness towards the prey that mocked it so. The prey came, chattering incessantly as it surged into the kraken's own territory.

"Crossing fence," shouted the Quartermaster. The sounds of the kraken erupted throughout the ship as it passed the invisible barrier.

Those who had been most affected before tossed about in their makeshift prisons, terror striking them even through the double hearing protection. They thrashed about, attempting to tear their ears off to block out the sounds. Only the fact that they were bound and unable to do more than struggle helplessly prevented them from harming themselves.

Men who had been less affected previously found themselves nauseous and dizzy. They shook their heads, attempting to restore a sense of normalcy to themselves. Everyone was careful to keep the hearing protection in place.

"Conn, Sonar. Transmitter acquired," cried STS1 Blevins in excitement. "Designate Sierra zero-zero-two. Bearing zero-three-one with a starboard drift. Up doppler. Target's circling towards us."

The Weapons Officer leaned over the fire control console as the fire control technician second class (FT2) prepared the firing solution.

"Solution set. Ready to shoot."

Owens uncrossed his arms and acknowledged. "Shoot on bearing."

The FT2's finger jabbed down, depressing the lit LAUNCH button. The bow shuddered as the Mark 48 torpedo jetted out of the submarine on a column of compressed air. Programmed to find the tonality of the transmitter, the torpedo's sonar system searched the proper band first. As soon as it picked up the signal, the weapon's propulsor sped up, accelerating the torpedo to its maximum speed.

The kraken shifted sideways, its powerful fluke propelling it down and away from the stinger. It had avoided the last two. This one was no different.

"Conn, fire control. Torpedo has acquired target. Weapon homing passive."

The sonar in the weapon's nose registered the shift in frequency from the transmitter. The program recognized that the source was now moving down and away relative to the sensor. The guidance package sent a command to rotate the torpedo to follow the transmission. The self-guided vehicle began to turn. As it did so, one of the multitudes of remade connections broke, causing the wire control to fail.

"Sir, torpedo is spinning. Loss of wire. Torpedo on internal guidance only. No indication of what happened."

With the loss of external guidance, the program energized the torpedo's powerful active sonar.

The kraken flinched as the stinger shrieked at it. For the first time in its lengthy life, its prey sang a death song of its own. A song that challenged the kraken to run from it. The stinger, or perhaps this was a youngster, newly born, streaked towards the kraken. Its song wavered as it fought to close the distance between them. It was faster than any fish the kraken had encountered before. Tentacles snapped outward, trying to capture or destroy this menace.

Due to intermittent commands from the guidance computer, the torpedo's propulsor was surging. These surges produced an asymmetric flow that induced a spin around the torpedo's central axis. It also caused the weapon to randomly corkscrew depending on where the seeker head pointed when the propulsor changed pitch or speed. The resulting path was chaotic and unpredictable. Several tentacles slashed past it as it started and slowed. None did anything more than push the weapon slightly off-course. The pings were closer now. The warhead armed.

"Conn, fire control. Weapon on terminal. Stand by for—
"

The stinger struck and blossomed into an invisible flower of pressure.

Agony.

Immense compression waves washed over and through the kraken, causing it to tumble.

Anguish.

One claw shattered from the blow and two tentacles tore off.

Pain.

Blood, pale and thin, leaked from rents across its hide and mixed with the cold waters.

Distress.

It was having trouble swimming as well, sinking unexpectedly between strokes. Something inside was damaged. To the surface, it needed to rise. Once there, it could float safely.

Weakness.

Using most of its energy, the kraken fled the area, striving both for the surface and to put distance between itself and the first prey to ever seriously injure it.

Chapter Thirteen

Meeting of Norwegian Sea and Barents Sea, Kraken's Hunting Ground

27 November 1986

1558 CET / 1458 Zulu

USS *Sea Devil* (SSN 664)

"**Y**es sir, we are going to have to continue following it. On the bright side, it seems as if it's stopped caterwauling at us." Morehouse discussed with Commander Owen. The men were standing in Control, leaned over the Quartermaster's table reviewing the local area chart. There had barely been room to fit Morehouse in since the ship was once again at battlestations, and Control was crowded with people.

Morehouse pointed to the estimated position of the kraken. "According to this, you've tracked it to approximately the center of the hunting area."

"Both visually and on sonar. We're staying far enough away that if it turns on us, we will have enough time to exit the fence."

"Has it even attempted to attack us since the explosion?"

Owens shook his head. "No, nor has it tried to dive again. I'd say the torpedo damaged it pretty heavily. Do you think we could just wait for it to die?"

Now it was Morehouse's turn to shake his head. "Sea monsters, hell, most supernaturals, are tougher than you can imagine. If this were a whale, I'd think it was done for. Sea monster though, I can't guarantee that the wounds are mortal. And for something like this, all of us must be certain. That means hitting until we are sure it's dead.

"Our biggest problem now is you're out of guided weapons. That means the grenade launchers, which in turn means we've got to get close on the surface. The Mark 19 is nominally accurate to about 1600 yards. That's with a stable platform and a stationary target. This situation is neither. We're going to need to be closer, what with the waves as strong as they are, and the kraken can still swim about." The ship was rolling ten to twelve degrees in the waves even at periscope depth.

"Scope operator judges a solid sea state four. Can I assume that your marines are trained for attacking in rough seas?" asked the captain.

"Unfortunately, no. Which is why we will need you to get closer than 1600 yards. Possibly as close as 750 to 800 yards."

"You're talking knife fighting range against this monster."

"Yes sir," Morehouse grinned weakly and shrugged. "Not my idea of fun either, but I cannot emphasize this strongly enough. We do not matter. I want to survive, get home, and see my wife and son. However, this creature cannot be left alone.

"Hell, we can't even be sure that the fence that is holding it in will continue to work. What happens if it gets free and can hunt anywhere it likes? The kraken cannot, *must not* survive. If it does, anything that travels near here is at risk. Our sole job is to destroy it."

"I understand Sergeant. Like you, I raised my right hand and swore to defend the Republic against all enemies. This one is just a bit different than I expected." Owens turned and faced the OOD. "Prepare to surface the ship."

"Prepare to surface, aye."

Orders rang out and the crew in a calm and purposeful manner went about making the submarine ready. Valves were verified and the topside crew prepared to get men and equipment up into place.

"SURFACE! SURFACE! SURFACE!" The 1MC announcement preceded the tilting of the deck as the ship rose to break through the waves. With no deep keel, the round vessel's rolls became more pronounced as it settled on the surface. Attack submarines are benthic hunters, uncomfortable and unwieldy on the oceans top.

Two seamen scuttled up the ladder inside the sail, draining the upper section and undogging the hatch. A short cascade of icy water dropped out of the opening, splashing into the grated drain below. A third sailor followed with the tiny safety railing to be set up around three sides of the opening. The fourth side remained empty in order to allow the periscopes operational room. The sailors clambered back down, freeing room for Morehouse and Corporal Grizzle to begin moving the Mark 19 and ammo boxes into position.

Several feet aft of the *Sea Devil*'s sail, the forward deck hatch opened, disgorging sailors and marines onto the submarine's deck. The sailors worked quickly, rigging up safety lines for the marines and cleats to latch the grenade launchers on. The late afternoon sun hung low in the sky, a reminder that there was little time to dally. The marines formed a human conveyor belt, and weapons and ammunition boxes flowed along it.

Just aft of the sail, Sergeant Wade and Corporal Hubbard spread the tripod for the Mark 19 and locked the forward leg into one of the cleats. The leg fit snuggly and would minimize the problem of the weapon walking backwards during the fight. The other two legs spread to the sides, stabilizing the grenade launcher side to side. Wade assembled the grips and butterfly trigger, verifying they would latch firmly and allow for full movement of the trigger. The barrel pointed off the starboard beam. Final fire plan was to keep the beast to starboard for two reasons. First and most important, it was the direction the ship could turn easiest with the damaged hydraulics. The second is that it ensured everyone knew which side would contain the threat and therefore maximum firepower would be able to be used against the monster.

Meanwhile, Corporal Hubbard opened the first box of ammunition and fed the belt into the weapon's receiver, then shut the top cover once the rounds were properly positioned. Wade verified the gun's safety was set to 'S', then cycled the charging handle with his right hand. He signaled Hubbard.

"Forward emplacement ready," Hubbard announced into the tac radio.

"Forward emplacement ready, aye." Gunny answered immediately. "Status on sail and aft?"

"Aft almost complete. Belt kinked. Fixing it now."

"Roger aft."

"Gunny, sail. Ready to rock and roll. Sail position is locked in and sighted. Well, sighted-ish."

"What's the problem?"

"I'm going to need to be very careful about aim points. These shots are probably going to be singles rather than bursts. This rocking is a bitch to compensate for. Is there any way the CO can position the submarine to minimize the movement?" Morehouse questioned.

"I'll check. Hold on."

A short conversation between the Master Gunnery Sergeant and the CO via phonetalkers commenced. The submarine altered course, shifting so the waves broke nearly directly over the bow. The side-to-side motion of the ship lessened as the waves struck the bow rather than broadside.

"The CO will try and maintain the ship into the sea rather than broad," Gunny stated, then took a quick walk to check everyone else.

ET1 Bishop peeked over the edge of the ladder well. No one in Control was looking down the corridor. He had a short window to get in unseen. Keeping a close eye on the Control Room door, he quietly snuck the remaining twelve feet. Cautiously he eased the door on the starboard side open, slipped inside, and shut it behind him. So far so good. No one had raised any alarms.

The Sonar Space was just aft of where he was standing. The door was closed, preventing anyone inside from seeing what he was about to do. He silently moved forward, squeezing past and around the cooling pipes and computers, carefully searching for a specific machine. Once he found it, he checked again to verify he was alone. He pulled the boxy contraption out of his coveralls and set it on the deck, checking to ensure that none of the wire leads had jostled out of place. He wiped his sweating hands on his blue coveralls and then deftly unscrewed a cover panel to one of the ship's active sonar processor units. Finally, after finding the right circuit, he connected a set of alligator clips, wiring the multi-million-dollar computer to the small electronic item. The wiring complete, Bishop sat back, resting his head against the coolant piping. The sound of gurgling water through the pipes was calming, and he half-closed his eyes in relaxation. It would not be that much longer. Everything was ready.

The *Sea Devil* spiraled in towards the kraken, who now floated placidly on the surface. The periscopes and observer's binoculars sought the creature.

This was the first clear look anyone had gotten of the beast. It was approximately a hundred and thirty feet long and a mottled gray-blue color that camouflaged it well underwater. Its overall shape was that of a huge fish. Bony plating covering much of its head and back, giving it a prehistoric look like an oversized Dunkleosteus. The tentacles, each about four-fifths the length of the body, protruded from the body just behind the gill slits, while the claws tucked under the jaw, near where a ventral fin might have developed. Its hide was torn and bleeding in several spots, and it moved somewhat spastically as if it could not quite get its muscles under its full control. The stumps of two tentacles were visible on the kraken's left side. Observers assumed they had been destroyed or torn off by the torpedo's explosion. The kraken seemed to be ignoring the submarine, content to swim around in the center of its hunting zone.

The ship slowly approached to just over 1000 yards from the monster. Morehouse checked the range against the ladder sight. He clicked the tac radio. "Weapons hot."

Gunny listened carefully to the metallic clicks as weapons safeties were shifted from SAFE to FIRE. All weapons reported ready on the tac radio.

"On my mark, commence firing on the kraken. Three, two, one, MARK!"

Three Mark 19 grenade launchers and the M249 light machine gun began firing almost simultaneously.

As soon as Bishop heard the count beginning, he reached for the small contraption. He stabbed a button, and the small motor began spinning. Before the first grenade could drop into the ocean, a head-banging drum and cymbal combination pounded through the water, followed moments later by Dee Snider's throat tearing battle cry.

'We're not gonna take it?" Owens mumbled, repeating the words of the song.

The submarine's own wavesong poured out of both the onboard speakers and the sonar system, flooding the water with the sounds of determination, backed up by the metallic reverb wail of dueling guitar riffs.

"What in the hell?" bellowed Commander Owen. "Who authorized this?"

The initial volley was slightly off, bracketing the monster both near and far. Geysers of white frothed water plumed into the air as the grenades detonated on impact with the water. Every fifth round from the M249 was a red tracer, which gave the impression that Gunny was firing a laser across the ocean. While most missed, a few of the rounds struck the kraken without visible effect.

Gunny snorted. Perhaps the gun would be more effective once they closed. He set it carefully on the deck and jogged over to the aft Mark 19 position. "Settle down. Feel the wave and fire during the trough. That'll give you the flattest trajectory against it. Which hopefully will improve the number of hits you get."

Riley flashed Gunny a thumbs-up and prepared to swap out the first ammunition box. The music of Twisted Sister's rebellion anthem washed over them as they continued the fight.

Twisting and turning, the kraken attempted to avoid as many of the stinging attacks and explosions as it could. Each grouping of rounds constricted its movement, herding it for the kill. In its simple mind, it recognized the actions. It also had herded prey before.

Between one set of grenade impacts and another, the kraken dove, disappearing from view in the misty haze the explosions had thrown into the air.

"Cease fire!" snapped Morehouse over the tac radio. The guns fell silent. Everyone watched, twisting to check behind to see if the kraken would appear on the opposite side of the ship. The song played out while they waited, the silence stranger than the music had been.

Unexpectedly, the entire submarine slid sideways as the kraken slammed into it from underneath. Six tentacles lashed over the side, whipping at chest height. Two sailors were knocked down but managed to avoid the tentacle's grasp. All the marines dropped into crouches. Gunny swung the M249 and fired into the nearest tentacle. Pale blood spurted from the pot mark wounds the light machine gun stitched across the mass of muscle.

In Control, everyone not directly driving the submarine watched the battle on the monitors. An awestruck voice quietly said, "It's like that old Disney movie, but with less rain and no harpoon." Commander Owens ignored the comment, especially since similar thoughts had been going through his head since the beginning of the fight. There was nothing they could do now except keep the ship as steady as possible and pray for the men topside.

"Dammit. I can't swivel far enough to hit anything," Morehouse yelled as the krakens attack intensified. Hubbard had already begun engaging the monster with his

M16, though the small caliber rounds seemed to be doing no harm.

The submarine shivered again as the kraken struck from underneath. One sailor slid toward the water at the aftmost section of the deck. He flailed his arms, attempting to grab anything before he slipped into the waves. Another sailor dropped to his belly, grabbed one of the outstretched arms, and hauled the man back aboard before more than half of his body entered the water.

"You men," Gunny yelled as he shifted his aim to the tentacle rising to attack the rescuer, "get below. It's getting damn dangerous up here and you can't help."

The senior sailor nodded. He yelled an order to the others. They all got on their hands and knees to crawl towards the hatch, attempting to stay below both the grasping tentacles and the gunfire. One by one the men slipped into the open entry and down to the safety below decks.

"Ahead two thirds. We're going to get a bit away. The marines don't seem to be able to do any damage with this thing under the boat." Commander Owens ordered.

"Ahead two thirds aye."

"Alpha, Control. We are accelerating away from the area to clear the creature. We will be circling around to maintain the creature to our starboard side. Over," the Weapons Officer reported on the radio in Control.

"Roger Control. Thanks for the assist. Once it's clear we'll light it up. Alpha, over and out."

Hubbard leaned over and informed Morehouse of the call.

"Pass it on to the remainder of the team."

The kraken slid aside as the boat accelerated. In its exhausted state there was no way it could keep up. It snapped its remaining claw at the prey on the deck as the ship slipped past.

Corporal Gustav scanned to both sides, engaging the tentacles overhead. None had come close to him, instead concentrating their attacks on either the sailors when they had been topside or the gunners. His M16 had been minimally useful but had caused the muscled appendages to jerk away when hit. The kraken was now moving aft as the ship outran it. Gustav missed seeing the huge claw burst out of the water behind him. All he knew was shock and pain as the twin pincers crushed his spine and ribcage in a vice-like grip. Blood spurted from his mouth and nose as internal organs burst from the pressure.

"Gustav!" screamed Riley.

Hanzo slewed his barrel as far aft as possible and triggered a burst of four grenades. All four hit near the kraken. It jerked in the water but maintained its grip on Gustav. The marines watched in horror as their teammate was torn apart in the beaked visage of the kraken. Crimson blood mixed with white foam as the sea monster consumed its prey.

Morehouse pounded on his knee. He knew there was a chance of losing men during a battle, but that did not make Gustav's loss any easier.

"Keep your eyes open. This bitch is fast and hits hard." He released the tac radio and took a deep breath, then keyed the mic again. "Control, Alpha actual. We can't let the kraken get that close again. Request you maintain at least 500 yards separation. Over"

Commander Owens took the tac radio from the Weapons Officer. "Alpha actual, Commander Owens. I understand, 500 yards. We'll do all we can. Over."

"Thanks. Alpha actual over and out."

"Gunny, any ideas?"

Gunny grunted before keying his radio. "Nothing beyond what you're already doing. We'll come back around and pound the shit out of the beast. Keeping range open maximizes our advantages, which is really the only thing I could have suggested in this case. Gunny out."

The kraken submerged after the ship pulled away. Riley, Hubbard, and Grizzle scanned the water, looking for any sign of the kraken's return. The sky continued to darken as clouds rolled in, covering the brighter light of the setting sun.

"I do not want to fight this thing in the dark," Bear remarked quietly to Morehouse.

"I agree. I figure if we can't take it down before we start to really lose the light, we're going to have to back off and try again in the morning."

Bear looked up at the sky. "If it's light in the morning. Those look suspiciously like storm clouds."

"Bite your tongue," Morehouse said just as the first fat cold drops fell from the heavens.

Swimming was hard. The water kept trying to drag it down. Floating on the surface had required less effort. However, the surface contained danger now. A danger that could and had injured it.

It could feel the new wounds torn into its flesh and the places where its armor was cracked or missing. This prey had become something more, something the beast had never encountered nor had the concepts to describe. In some way, the prey was like it, though it was the only one of it. How could there be another so similar yet different? The beast shook off the odd thought.

What the prey might be did not matter. It was prey, and prey existed to be eaten. It had gotten a taste of the prey's flesh during the last attack. Only a taste though, no matter how invigorating that had been. Now between the damage, exhaustion, and hunger, it must eat. There would be no backing off again. With a flick of its tail, the kraken turned its bulk towards the vessel.

The ship had followed a lazy turn in an attempt to both open range and keep its starboard side toward the last known position of the monster. Sonar listened carefully, but the creature had disappeared from the sensors shortly after the firefight ended. STS1 Blevins cycled through all bands.

"Nothing. We're going to need to hit it with active to find it," he said while continuing to search the passive waterfall for the elusive creature.

"Conn, Sonar. Request permission to active search," STSC Elliot asked. "The, uh . . . target . . . uh . . . Sierra zero-zero-two, has disappeared from the sonar."

"Sonar, Control. Permission granted for use of active sonar during this engagement." The Weapons Officer gave a surprised look to the CO. Commander Owens shrugged. "If we can't find it, we can't fight it. And we know it can find us whether we use the sonar or not."

A high-energy pulse of noise lanced out from the bow, widening in a semi-circle as it traveled away from the source. And returned nearly as quickly.

"Conn, Sonar. Regain of Sierra zero-zero-two. Six hundred yards and closing. Bearing zero-six-two relative."

The kraken stroked harder as soon as it heard the prey's cry. It had to close before the prey had a chance to escape.

It could feel the pulse of the water as the prey began swimming harder to speed up. The prey was too late in its reaction though. The kraken pushed one more time and wrapped four of its remaining tentacles about the prey's body, hugging close to the underside where the small prey could not get to it.

"Shit!" The word came out suddenly as Riley danced aside, barely avoiding being knocked off the craft by the appearance of the tentacle. It slid along the hull, past where he had been standing a moment earlier. Two more wrapped around from the opposite side. A fourth slapped the deck and tightened between the two grenade gunners. As he watched, the muscles contracted and squeezed. There was no way to get even a piece of paper between the hull and the snake-like appendage.

"Clear!" Gunny waited until Wade and Hubbard had shifted away to open fire on the tentacle wrapped between the two groups. The light machine gun's bullets did not affect the tentacle much more than the M16s had, but there were more of them and in higher concentrations. The muscles twitched under the steady stream of lead.

Morehouse cried out as a fifth tentacle emerged from the water and wrapped itself around Corporal Hubbard. The short marine barely had time to scream before he was plucked off the deck and drawn below the waves.

"Take over," Morehouse stated as he slid over the side of the sail. A set of metal rungs provided handholds down to the fairwater plane on the starboard side. He took a running leap and plunged into the Arctic waters.

The impact of a nearly forty-foot dive along with the cold drove the air from Morehouse's lungs. He gasped as he surfaced, then took a deep breath and dove again. His uniform quickly became water soaked, a leaden weight pulling at him. He could just see Hubbard in the monster's grasp. Morehouse swam, his legs kicking furiously to get him closer to the beast. He was not going to lose another marine to the monster.

With his left hand, he grabbed Hubbard's leg and pulled himself to where the tentacle wrapped about the man. Tiny bubbles of air leaked out of Hubbard's nose and his eyes were squeezed shut. Dark blood, black in the evening gloom, tainted the water. Morehouse's right hand fumbled open the strap on his knife. He freed his knife and plunged it into the muscle tissue, sawing and dragging the blade for maximum cutting. The tentacle twisted and Hubbard silently screamed, air bubbles bursting from his mouth and nose.

Pale blood leaked from the rent, and the fish-belly white and gray tissue pulsed clearly in the wound. While deep, it was apparent to Morehouse the wound was primarily superficial and would not cause the creature to loosen its grip. He slipped the knife into its sheath and drew his pistol.

He could feel his lungs beginning to burn with the lack of oxygen. He put the barrel of the gun into the wound and closed his eyes. Two pulls of the trigger and the tentacle snapped open. The motion slapped Morehouse backward in the water and knocked the pistol from his grasp. The gun tumbled and sank into the lonely depths.

Morehouse grabbed Hubbard with both arms and scissor kicked to the surface. The edges of his vision began to blur with darkness. The pair burst between the waves and Hanzo tossed a life ring to them. Morehouse looped one arm through the ring, air etching trails of fire to his lungs. He could hear Gunny yelling to get them out of the water *now*. Hands reached down and pulled them onto the deck. He lay face down, retching and coughing up water. Rain spattered fitfully about them.

The submarine's engines surged and everyone topside could feel the increased vibrations. White foam prayed around the rudder as the speed increased. Unable to maintain a hold in the water flow, the remaining tentacles pulled away noisily. None of them came close to hitting any of the remaining men. Their passage was marked with tears and rents in the black acoustic covering.

Morehouse rolled over and pushed himself to a sitting position. Riley was bent over Hubbard, cycling through chest compressions, and inflating his lungs. After a few moments, Riley leaned back and hung his head.

"Is he going to make it," croaked Morehouse. Riley met his eyes briefly and shook his head.

Lance Corporal Hanzo shouted and pointed aft. The kraken had surfaced again, lolling sideways and swimming in a jerky circle. They watched as it receded behind them.

Morehouse forced himself to stand. He grabbed Gunny's tac radio. In a hoarse voice he contacted the ship.

"Control, Alpha actual. We need to circle back. We've got to finish this before this storm really opens up. If we leave, there's no guarantee that we can find it again."

The radio crackled in silence. Then Owens' voice came on. "If we don't leave, that thing is going to sink us. It's faster than we planned on, and your weapons aren't hurting it fast enough."

"That's because we've been trying to hit it from a stationary platform. This time I want to do a set of drive-bys. We'll run past it, firing as many grenades as we can. Once we clear the area, you can circle back, and we'll do it again. Eventually we'll hit it hard enough to kill it."

Morehouse paused. "I've already lost two men and you have men injured. Let's not make their sacrifices a waste. Over."

Owens thought for a moment. The Marine sergeant had a point. Every time the kraken had gotten a hold on the ship had been when they were going slow or stationary. The creature could not hold on at speeds over two-thirds. If they maintained distance and ran past it at full, it might work. "Quartermaster, how long till sunset."

The petty officer consulted the plan of the day and checked the clock. "Forty-three minutes till sunset sir."

"Alpha actual, Conn. I can give you three, maybe four passes before you lose the light. Let's make them count. Out."

Morehouse handed the radio back to Gunny. "I need you to get into the sail. I'm not certain I can get up there in time, and we need every gun working this." Gunny did not say anything, just patted Morehouse on the shoulder, handed over the M249, and dropped down the access ladder. Three minutes later he waved from the sail.

"Alright guys. Change in plans," Morehouse stated, his command voice carrying easily to everyone topside. "The ship is going to perform fast runs past the kraken. As soon as it's in range, send everything we've got at it. Fire until you can't accurately hit it anymore. Then the ship will turn around and we'll do it again. Oorah?"

"OO-RAH!" every Marine replied.

"Let's get this done," Morehouse said and hefted the light machine gun.

The *Sea Devil* heeled over as the rudder turned her around at full bell. The marines swiveled the Mark 19s as far forward as they could. They would only have a few moments of time to fire during the pass, and the ship was still rolling through the heavy waves.

The sail Mark 19 was the first to fire, a heavy series of coughs as Gunny depressed the butterfly trigger. Waterspouts walked themselves across the mass of kraken's flesh, changing from welters of white to splashes of gore as the high explosives slammed into the beast. As soon as the kraken came into view, both of the topside Mark 19s opened up. They were closer to the waves and did not have as clear a line of sight on the monster. Their fire was less accurate than Gunny's but no less destructive when the rounds struck. Morehouse added nothing more than an aiming point with fire from the machine gun. The guns tracked as the ship sped past the kraken, firing until the creature fell out of range.

The skies continued to darken as the rain intensified. The kraken was moving fitfully now, barely able to keep itself afloat in the waves. No one knew what would happen if it dove. Would it heal itself? Some of the supernatural creatures the JTF had encountered could do that. If they could return to their lair or perform a special rite, they would return not only healed but also revitalized. Midnight, daybreak, and noon were common timeframes for such abilities. They had to get this over soon, or all their work might be for naught.

Commander Owens listened to the radio and ordered the submarine to come about once more.

Again, Gunny was the first to engage from the sail. He had the best sightline and aim points. Morehouse took over for Wade and Riley spelled Hanzo on the aft most Mark 19. Since the ammunition for the machine gun had run out during the last pass, someone had lashed it to the deck.

Each gun coughed, spewing heavy round head grenades into the beast. Explosions tore at the hide and armor shattered from the shaped charges.

"Slow the ship," requested Morehouse on the radio.

"Slowing," came the reply from the Weapons Officer.

"Ahead one-third," commanded Owens. He kept one eye on the video repeater. If the beast submerged, he would not wait for the marines to call. He would simply order the boat to full and run.

The waves broke against the bow and the rolling was minimal. The kraken writhed in a storm of shells and detonations. It attempted to call, but the wavesong only came out as a faint cry of terror for its own life. Finally, a single shell pierced an eye and detonated in its brain. The creature thrashed about, tearing mindlessly at the water as the final pulses from its scrambled cortex reached the limbs. Then, the song was silenced, and the remains slowly sank beneath the waves.

A huge ellipse of light, miles in diameter and the color of a welding arc flashed upward from the sea, shattering the clouds above. Everyone watching was momentarily blinded by the intensity. When they could see again, the ocean had calmed, and the sky was clear.

Stars shone like diamonds in the velvet blackness. Morehouse stared southward and greeted the sight of the baleful red eye of Mars gleaming down on them, just over the horizon. The god of war and patron planet of the Marines. Just above and to the right hung Jupiter, the god of thunders. Had they not just waged war with thunders here? A good sign for them, the planets smiling down.

Morehouse contemplated the situation. They had lost men, but in what battle did that not happen. Most had survived, and no others would die from this creature. They had recovered those they could and would remember those they could not. The enemy had been vanquished, and one more supernatural sent back to the Never-Never.

The tac radio crackled to life. "Is it dead or did it slip away?" asked Commander Owens.

Morehouse smiled up at the now clear heavens. "Dead. The mission is complete."

Epilogue

JTF 13 Training Facility, Jacksonville, North Carolina
06 December 1986
0917 EST/1417 Zulu
Company Commander's Office

"Between Master Gunnery Sergeant Peck retiring, the unfortunate loss of both Corporals Gustav and Hubbard, plus the recovery time that Johansson will need, the decision has been made to reorganize the entire platoon. Several new recruits are on their way here and they have to be fitted into the new squad and team setup." Lieutenant Colonel Watterson shuffled some papers around the desk as he spoke.

"Yes sir," responded Sergeant Morehouse, unsure of where the conversation was going. He had been the man solely responsible for the squad and that meant he was also responsible for the deaths of his men.

"I've read the entirety of the AAR and agree with the determination. You could not have done anything to save your men or prevent their deaths. The fact that you were able to recover Corporal Hubbard's body is a testament to just how dedicated you are to your men. You risked your own life to get him back."

There was nothing else to say beyond "Yes sir."

"I also spoke with the grief counselor. She suggests that you are no longer focused entirely on the job at hand. Which," and Watterson held up a hand to forestall any protest, "is in no way evident from the last several missions you have been on.

"However, it has become apparent to the entirety of the JTF that we need to start taking a closer look at everybody's mental health with the same focus we have on physical capability. You've been attached here for almost three years. You have a wife and son?"

"Yes sir. Married nine years. Timothy turns seven in January."

"And I will bet you, based on interviews with other marines in similar situations, that the home life is getting rougher, and you are looking at leaving the Corp at the end of this enlistment cycle. In about eight months in your case."

Morehouse was startled. He and Marie had discussed the possibility of him getting out, especially with the stresses they both were dealing with. He wondered if the Colonel had a mind reader on staff. He grimaced and answered the question. "My wife and I have discussed the option. I have not made a firm decision which way to go as of yet though."

"Let me offer you another option. You've proved you have a good head on your shoulders. You also received a glowing report on your command abilities from Master Gunnery Sergeant Peck. I trust his judgement. He led a rather green first lieutenant, myself, to make the right calls during my first serious encounter with supernaturals. If he thinks you're a good choice, I won't second guess him."

"Good choice for what sir?" Morehouse was completely confused at this point. He had no idea where the conversation was going.

"Research Arm is in need of a seasoned platoon sergeant. They are specifically looking for one with a solid record of dealing with unusual and unique supernatural creatures and a good combat record. You fit the bill in both cases. The only thing missing is they are looking for a Staff Sergeant and you are an E-5.

"That can possibly be worked around though. It's a shore position. No sudden calls in at all hours to head out for who knows how long to fight things that go bump in the night. Minimum tour is four years, so plenty of time to get the family back together."

Colonel Watterson stood up and Morehouse followed suit. The Colonel opened the door and stepped into the hall. Morehouse trailed, unsure where the Colonel was taking them.

"The Research Arm is based out of Pope Field here in North Carolina, working directly with the Joint Special Operations Command group. Won't even be a long move if you decide to take the option." The Colonel pushed open a small door, ushering Morehouse ahead of him. A set of stairs led upward, and Morehouse found himself on a stage with a small podium. Past the edge of the stage, he could see the room was filled with the platoon and support staff. From the *Sea Devil*, Commander Owens, STS1 Blevins, ET1 Bishop, and the Doc were present as well as Lieutenant Commander Harris. Marie and Timothy sat in the front row, next to Captain Dupree.

"Attention to orders."

Morehouse stopped and immediately came to full attention, facing forward on stage, his eyes resting on the room's rear wall.

"The Bronze Star is awarded to Sergeant John K. Morehouse, United States Marine Corp, for heroism in combat action against hostile enemy forces while serving at an undisclosed location with the 7th Battalion, 2nd Company, 1st Platoon. The "V" device for valor is authorized. On or about November 27th, 1986, Sergeant

Morehouse did, at risk of his own life, engage the enemy closely with knife and pistol to rescue a fellow marine from death. Disarmed during the fight, Sergeant Morehouse continued to fight until he freed and recovered the fellow marine, and both returned to safety. Given in the city of Jacksonville, North Carolina on this sixth day of December 1986. Signed John Lehman, Secretary of the Navy. Additionally, Lieutenant General Otsuka has promoted Sergeant Morehouse to Staff Sergeant through combat meritorious promotion. This promotion is based on Sergeant Morehouse's proven command ability, unwavering commitment to his team, and his ability to uphold the finest traditions of the United States Marine Corp."

Applause broke out as Marie stood and pinned the medal on her husband's chest. Master Gunnery Sergeant Peck attached the Staff Sergeant stripes over Morehouse's Sergeant stripes with a bit of duct tape holding them in place.

Grinning, Corporal Riley pulled out a small green notebook and made a notation. "Use number two hundred and sixteen. Holding on stripes in a pinch." That got a laugh from the crowd.

Lieutenant Colonel Watterson stood back, clapping until Gunny and Marie stepped back. "Congratulations Staff Sergeant." He clasped hands with Morehouse and gave a solid shake. In a *de soto* voice he continued, "and think about taking the job. You're too good a marine to lose."

"I will sir," Morehouse replied, then drew his wife into a hug. "But not until I talk it over with my family."

West Berlin, German Democratic Republic
04 December 1986
1351 EDT/0951 Zulu
Neutral Meeting House

Neither of the men were remarkable looking. They could and had passed unnoticed in most places in Europe, Australia, North America, and the Soviet Union. If asked to describe either of the men, most observers would reply that they were men with darkish hair, of usual height and weight, no memorable features, and wore clothing of muted colors consistent with what most people were wearing. Average would be the most common description given of the men. A description available only if anyone had even noticed them in more than passing. Which no one had. That was the men's greatest strength. They were invisible in plain sight.

Much like the building they now met in. It too was unremarkable in any way. A building much like the ones lining the rest of the street in this section of West Berlin. A brick façade devoid of any signs indicating who lived there or what businesses might be inside. Far enough from the Berlin Wall that even adventure-seeking tourists would not accidentally run across it during an ill-conceived excursion.

Even the room looked average. Non-descript art hung on beige walls sparsely decorated with average furniture of average make maintained with average cleanliness.

The men sat down at a small table. The table and chairs were average and protested slightly as the men settled themselves. The man on the left side of the table pulled a VHS tape out of his coat. The tape had no markings or label and the cardboard sleeve surrounding it only had the manufacturer's colors and logo. He held it up for the second man to see.

In Berliner-accented German he said, "This contains film of the attacks that occurred in late November in the Barents Sea. I am informed that this evidence proves that NATO forces were not responsible for the destruction of either vessel, nor were there any survivors to rescue. I am also to inform you that no one outside of the *Otdel Bezopasnosti Issledovaniya Paranormal'nykh Yavleniy* are to be given access to this film or even informed of its existence. This order comes directly from the head of the Arcane Research Group."

The second man nodded solemnly, replying in Berliner-accented German as well. "An agreement is already in place. I will place this tape directly in the hands of those researchers and scientists."

The first man carefully placed the tape and sleeve on the tabletop and pushed it to the other side. The second man picked it up and slipped it into his overcoat. Simultaneously the men gave each other a sharp nod of acknowledgement. They stood without a word, turned away, and disappeared out opposite doors, leaving average impressions in the seat cushions.

We hope that you enjoyed this title and look forward to many more to come. Please, leave us a review! Reviews matter to all of our authors.

Take a look at some of our other award-winning series at https://threeravenspublishing.com/series-universes/

Visit us at https://www.threeravenspublishing.com and sign up for our newsletter for the latest and greatest news on upcoming titles and events.

Other series and titles you might enjoy.

DECLAN FINN
DECLAN FINN
DECLAN FINN
DECLAN FINN
Demons Are Forever
Honor At Stake
Live And Let Bite
Good To The Last Drop
The Dragon Award Nominated Series
FREE on Kindle Unlimited!

AVAILABLE ON
AMAZON
JOINT TASK FORCE
13
HOLDING THE LINE
BETWEEN HEAVEN AND HELL
13

MYSTERY,
MAGIC &
MAYHEM
WITH A TWIST
OF ROMANCE
J.F. POSTHUMUS
ON AMAZON
FIND ME
B.E.N.T.
BIOLOGIC   ENHANCED   NASCENT   TALENT

THE RAVEN
AND
THE CROW
MICHAEL K. FALCIANI
FIND ME
ON AMAZON

STARFLIGHT
IT CAME FROM THE
TRAILER PARK

3R
Three Ravens Publishing
Are you looking for fun, new fiction?
The Written Word Will Never Be The Same…
https://www.threeravenspublishing.com
Veteran Owned and Operated

And don't forget to check out the latest edition of *Car Wars*

http://www.sjgames.com/car-wars/

Or the other amazing titles from Steve Jackson Games

http://www.sjgames.com

…or the latest in the Car Warriors: Autoduel Chronicle fiction series.

https://threeravenspublishing.com/car-warriors-autoduel-chronicles/

You can also keep up to date with our latest release announcements on <u>Scifi.radio</u> and get some of the best fandom programing on the planet.

Scifi for your Wifi

And don't forget to check out our other Sponsors and Affiliates

A southern Appalachian jewel for craft beer lovers, Buck Bald Brewing offers something for everyone. With delicious, locally brewed beverages from across the spectrum, Buck Bald Brewing offers craft brews that are consistently amazing.

From the dark and smooth Shesquatch Scottish ale, to the intense hops of Hippibilly IPA, to the puckering sour of the blackberry and cinnamon in Berry My Heart at the Trailer Park, and more than 60+ rotating brews, you'll find what you're looking for and more.

With smiling faces behind the bar ready to help you find your next favorite brew, a constantly rotating selection of delicious craft beverages, toe-tapping tunes always playing, and the biggest games on TV, you can kick your feet up in either Copperhill, Tennessee or Murphy, North Carolina and immerse yourself in the Buck Bald Brewing experience. So, come out, fill a pint, fill a growler, and fill your mind at your new favorite family-owned craft brewery.

To discover more visit us at buckbaldbrewing.com or follow us on Facebook @buckbaldbrewing and @buckbaldbrewingmurphy.

Vesper Wren's
TRAILER PARK
PIXIE
PUNCH
· A PEACH STRAWBERRY SELTZER ·
BUCK BALD BREWING